MOONS OF THE DIVINE

HEART OF THE MARKED

LYRA ASHER

Formatting, Cover Design and Page Design by Books and Moods
Editing by Emily Ribeiro
Map Design by Lyra Asher on Inkarnate

Dedicated to the reader:
May you be your own knight in shining armor.

TRIGGER/CONTENT WARNING

Violence (Graphic), Death, Mature Content, Mature Language, Sexual Content, Racism/Classism, Mental Abuse, Physical Abuse, Misogyny, Sexual Assault, Death of a Parent, Child Abuse, Torture and Confinement.

PRONUNCIATION GUIDE

CHARACTERS

Aither: Eh-th-ee-r

Arron Lennox: Ar-run Len-uhks

Bomris: Bawm-ruhs

Brodyn Choryrth: Bro-din Cho-reer-th

Cassandra: Kuh-san-druh

Caden Amour: K-aid-uhn Ah-moor

Cal Aeson: K-aa-l Aye-sahn

Carina Harrington: Kah-rye-nah Hair-ing-tuhn

Choryrth: Cho-reer-th

Dalina Choryrth: D-uh-l-ee-n-ah Cho-reer-th

Durreos Seraphim: Dur-e-os Serr-uh-fim

Edward Norbury: Ed-werd Nor·burh·ree

Eirwen: Ire-wen

Emrys: Emm-riss

Evander: Eve-vand-er

A-Evia Cerys: Eh-vi-yah Kehr-iss

Falkur Donelle: Fal-kor Don-nel-l

Gus: Guh-s

Haco: Ha-ko

Igor: Ee-g-oh-r

Kano:Kah-noh

Keva Harrington: Kay-va Hair-ing-tuhn

Minka: Mean-kuh

Radha Lennox: Raa-duh Len-uhks

Ragnar: Raag-naar

Renfred:Re-nfr-ed
Reombarth: Ri-om-barth
Roderick Harrington: Rod-er-rick Hair-ing-tuhn
Samael: Saem-ehl
Selene Kaida Choryrth: Suh-leen Kay-duh Cho-reer-th
Ulric Daivat: Uul-rihk Dey-vaet
Wesley Harrington: Wez-lee Hair-ing-tuhn
Willa: Wil-luh

TERRITORIES

Aestas: Ehs-tahs
Alryne: Al-rine
Argyll: Aar-guy-uhl
Atrium: A-tree-um
Cadere: Ka-de-re
Fons: F-oh-nz
Gambriel: Gam-bri-uhl
Hiems: Hi-e-hms
Inverness: In-vr-nes
Jindera: Jin-dare-uh
Lacus: Lack-us
Ladon: Lay-don
Lochlan: Lok-lun
Menodore: Men-oh-door
Rimont: Ri-mont
Taernsby: Tar-ness-bee
Umbra: Um-bra

CREATUREDEX

High Fae: Humanoid fae with elongated lifespans and are more powerful than the average faerie. Can possess one or more magical elements.

Lower Fae: All other species of non-High Fae. Nymphs, goblins, pixies, banshees, devas, kelpies, ogres, etc.

Demi-Fae: Half human/half fae. Powers and lifespan depend on lineage.

Human: Mortals who possess no magic within their blood.

Siren: Human turned half sea creature by magic.

Dragon: Descendents of the Gods who possess magical elements and elongated life spans.

Witch/Mage: Mortals who possess no magic in their blood but can call upon the elements to aid their spells and potions.

Sibyl: Seer of all things past, present and future. Once a witch or mage who practiced magic, turned into an omniscient creature through blood magic.

Raken: Human or fae cursed by *Medies* magic to become the living undead. They answer only to their creator.

Sea Serpent: Sea monster resembling a large snake that possesses no magic.

Galdur: Descendent of the Pegasus. Pure white, large horses known for their endurance, speed and size. Blessed by the Gods with elongated lifespans.

Medies: Dark magic that requires sacrifice to use and sucks from the life essence of the user.

The Fates: Higher entities that assign individual destinies to all beings of the realm.

SOME WOMEN FEAR THE FIRE.
SOME WOMEN SIMPLY BECOME IT.
-R.H. SIN

Circadian Sea
Hiems
Cadere
Umbra
Argyll
Fons
Sonus
Nox
Aestas
ATRIUM

LADON
N
W
E
S
Ignis
Gambriel
Dark Forest
Cursed wastes
Jindera
Rimont
Alryne
Venemos

PROLOGUE

The Moons of the Divine, which only came every ten thousand years, illuminated the battlefield drenched in the blood of our fallen. The screams and shouts of battle filled the air along with the clashing of steel against steel. The metallic tang of blood and filth lingered in the air, burning my nose with its stench. It was the fourth day of battle, with no reprieve. We had numbers on our side in the beginning, but not anymore. Almost all of our strongest soldiers were dead on the most powerful and compelling magical night in existence.

My High Fae ears ached from the sounds of them taking their last dying breaths. I didn't know how we could come back from this, didn't know how we could end this war. Running my bloody hands up and down my face in frustration, I clenched my teeth until pain bloomed in my jaw. No matter how hard we fought, our enemy just wouldn't die.

I felt a presence coming up on my side and with phantom hands, harnessed by my magic, I snapped the soldier's neck before he got within a few feet. Rolling my shoulders, I looked down at the dead soldier—no, not a soldier but a creature. His rotted spine protruded from the flesh of his neck from the snap I made. His hands still twitched and before he could reach up to twist his head back into place, I sliced his arms off up to his shoulders. The creature kept twitching and moving no matter what parts I sliced off, no matter how much damage I did physically and magically.

The limbs I amputated started to grow back and regenerate themselves at an exceedingly alarming rate. The skin stitched itself back together instantaneously. I was used to our fae healing but never like this. We could be killed with a sword to the head or heart, just like a mortal. But these things, these *creatures* could not die.

Fuck.

I had to do something else. My soldiers were dying, with no way to kill their opponents. This was a slaughter of my people, not a battle.

Quickly sheathing my sword, I ran towards the temple of Haco, our King of Gods of the Divine. A hand shot out and grabbed my forearm, and before I could realize who it was, I gripped the hand right back and snapped the arm in half as the assailant wailed.

"Ulric! What the fuck?!" At the sound of my name, my eyes snapped up to see my Commander and closest friend since birth, Renfred, seething in my face. "Are you fucking abandoning us? You're our King!" Renfred screamed, blood coating his elongated canines.

"I am not abandoning my people! We are being

slaughtered out there and I'm trying the only solution I can come up with!" I screamed back. "Now get the fuck out of my way and let me handle this."

I started sprinting through the field of death again as I threw back over my shoulder, "Oh, and sorry about the arm!" It should reform with his fae strength in a matter of minutes.

Creature after vile creature attempted to stop me in my path towards the temple. Thrusting out my magic, I reveled in the way their decrepit bones snapped and popped, making them falter in their efforts. The muscles in my legs coiled as my boots pounded against the crimson colored dirt and the screams of more of my people meeting their demise saturated the air.

I was running out of time and the well of my magic was almost depleted into nothing. The undead were already rising from the ground and reforming their dismembered limbs with snarls sent my way. Their black eyes seeped into my soul as they reached out to grab me again with clawed hands and I used the last of my magic to push back their advances and dash to the Temple of Haco.

The Temple of the Divine came into view, the white stairs lined with lit torches leading up to a white–pillared glass dome with a large gaping hole in the center of it. I made my way up the marble steps, into the temple, and followed the path to the center of the dome where the night sky shone through the hole.

The sounds of battle still raged on in the distance as I grabbed my emerald-hilted dagger from my belt, got on my knees, and did the one last thing I could think of to have a shot at beating this darkness overtaking our realm. I made a cut into my palm, an offering, and watched the blood drip onto the cold stones as I prayed to our Gods.

"I call upon the King of Gods, Haco. I leave this blood as an offering to show my devotion to you. Please hear my call."

A drop of my blood hit the stone below.

"I call up Reombarth and leave this blood as an offering to show my devotion. Please hear my call."

Another drop.

With my blood, I called upon all nine of our Gods, each with a different ability, offering each of them my blood as payment.

I opened my eyes to the sound of fire lighting the empty torches, fueled by Haco's power which formed a circle of light around me. Shooting up from my position, I held my dagger at the ready for whatever could enter the temple. The ground started to shake as the temple cracked along with the earth below my feet as Ragnar answered my prayer. Haco's fire flickered into larger flames while thunder rumbled through the sky, the sign of Evander coming to meet me as well. Bright light, almost as strong as the sun, blurred my vision from Samael's answer. Nine answering strikes of lightning fired off around me in a complete circle, showcasing that all nine Gods had joined me in my time of need.

All movement from the God's call ceased.

I could've sworn I saw the flash of a green flower-filled meadow, causing my body to relax instantly as the scent of fresh air filled my nostrils. For a moment, I was not in this destroyed sacred place, but somewhere peaceful filled with life. Blinking my eyes again, the vision cleared and I realized it was just Bomris' illusions seeping into my brain to calm my racing heart.

There was dust and smoke everywhere; my ears were still ringing from Reombarth's energy affecting my hearing but at least the ground didn't feel like it would split open and swallow me whole anymore. A chilling wind from the Goddess Aither whipped around and moved the debris of the temple as Kano's soft rain started to patter in through the opening above. The rain that was washing away my earlier sins turned into ice as it fell from the skies and punctured my open skin as Eirwen's might settled around me.

A deep voice boomed through the debris, "Who has summoned us all, mere mortal?"

Before I could see the owner of the voice, I fell back down on both my knees, with my head down and palms up in submission as I said, "I am King Ulric Daivat of Menodore and I have called upon our great Gods to ask for help against the evil forces taking over our realm."

The smoke finally dissipated as I peeked from beneath my black hair that had fallen over my eyes as I bowed. What I saw before me stole the breath from my lungs. It was glorious, beautiful, and terrifying.

Black iridescent scales glimmered under the double moons, covering a large dragon's body with black leather-like wings. Deep golden eyes with vertical pupils and power pulsing behind them pierced my skin with their glare. Long white fangs that could gobble down three carriages in one bite glistened in the moonlight and sent a shiver of fear racing down my spine.

"Ah, yes. And what would you have us do to help you, oh mighty King Ulric?" The King of Gods, Haco, answered my prayers.

"Whatever you may give me to help, my King; I will give anything to stop this. Pay any price to save my country, to save my people," I replied while trying to hold the deadly Dragon God's gaze.

Haco looked from me to the other Gods surrounding the circle, a telepathic question in his eyes. They nodded their heads in agreement and those golden eyes locked back onto mine and I bowed my head again in submission, palms facing up in offering.

"*Anything,* you say? Well my little Kingling, I will make you a deal," the fire God beckoned.

Looking back up with hope in my emerald eyes, I vowed, "Whatever will save my country and my people."

Haco gave a feral smile as he explained, "As you are aware, my fellow Gods and I have been trapped in our realm of the Divine, only allowed to walk this earth if called upon by your kind, and even then we don't get to roam freely. We are shackled to the temple in which you summon us, we have no power here, and we can only give our power through our blessings on your kind. We simply want what every living being wishes for. The ability to live. To be free."

I cocked my head to the side, trying to understand what he was asking.

The God continued on, "Bind yourself to me, to *us*. Swear a blood oath to us with an exchange of power from us to you.

Once we are bound, we can be fully corporeal bodies in this world, rather than having to watch from above and never experience. Surely you've heard of the different blood oaths, particularly the exchange of power between beings?"

"Yes, I know what that blood oath entails. Say a short oath, combine our bloods together and we share our powers. I don't mean to question you, Your Holiness, but my kind was always warned away from any form of dark magic; power exchange blood oaths included. The cost of the exchange can absorb the magical life force. Will it be safe to practice in those dark arts?" I queried.

"The oath is of blood magic, dark magic, the kind that demands a price since it is taken from another life force. Our immortality mixing with yours won't pull from your life force, so it won't affect you the way it does the others.

"We know of the forces attacking your realm. Those creatures you're fighting come from something *darker* than this blood magic." The image of a corpse, rising from the blood of battle with no sign of ever stopping popped into my mind. "They can only be killed by a power greater than any in your realm. By a power only *we* possess. We have never offered this to a mere mortal before, so make your decision swifty before we change our minds and more of your people are lost," the dragon explained with feigned confidence. He either meant the threat or was bluffing. From the way his golden eyes glanced at the other Gods in question, I would say the latter.

The Gods of the Divine needed me just like I needed all of them, only Haco wasn't going to admit that to me—*a mere mortal.* Biting my tongue, I held back from correcting the Death God and calling him out on his blatant lie.

I was *High Fae*, not a human. I possessed the power they needed to make the blood-oath and only they retained the power to defeat those creatures.

I looked at the mighty Gods surrounding me, their golden gazes burning into my skin.

They were my only fucking option…

"Tick tock, Kingling. Your time is running out," Haco probed as I shot another glance at the double moons above coming together to form one magical force.

My palms started to sweat from the pressure of the choice. Either tie myself to these nine Gods forever, or watch those I loved *and* the Kingdom I swore to safeguard perish right before my eyes.

I swore an oath of loyalty to the people of Menodore the day I took the throne. I swore to defend them, to *protect* them and to never stop fighting for their lives and freedom.

These Gods said they could stop the slaughter of not only my people, but of the entire continent of Ladon.

Fuck it.

"I'll do it," I said with determination as I met the Death God's gaze.

"Hand me your blade, Sir Ulric," the Dragon God's teeth gleamed in what looked like a vicious smile as I held my dagger out to him.

Haco's sharp, black claws wrapped around the hilt of my dagger as he removed it from my grasp. He then took the blade and sliced his scaly palm, letting the golden blood of our

Gods descend into a chalice covered in gems that appeared out of thin air. Each God proceeded the same routine, one by one, until the chalice was in front of me and the dagger back in my hand.

"Cut your right palm and let the blood drain into the cup," Haco instructed.

The cold bite of the blade slashed across my palm and I didn't wince from the slight sting of pain as I watched my blood drip into the golden liquid, melding the two together. I looked back up at Haco in question as he extended his taloned arm back towards the cup.

"Do as I do and say as I say," the God said with fire in his golden eyes.

"From blood to blood, from ashes to ashes, from dawn to dusk, until both light and darkness die, I, Haco, King of Gods, bind and willingly give myself to King Ulric Daivat of Menodore." He then dipped his long reptilian tongue into the chalice and passed it along to the others. They all repeated the vows binding themselves to me and then the cup was suddenly in front of me.

I took a deep breath before I spoke, "From blood to blood, from ashes to ashes, from dawn to dusk, until both light and darkness die, I, Ulric Daivat, King of Menodore, bind and willingly give myself to Haco, Reombarth, Samael, Aither, Kano, Bomris, Eirwen, Ragnar, and Evander, the Nine Gods of the Divine." Then I downed what was left in the cup before I could let the taste settle on my tongue.

"You will no longer be named after your ancestors. You will abandon the name Ulric Daivat and ascend into a new being of the Divine. You will be now known as Choryrth from this day forward, the High Fae King with dragon blood in veins, with the ability to crush any person or thing that poses a threat to you and your people. On this night of the Moons of the Divine, we will now be known as the Great Divine of *Ten*," Haco proclaimed at the same moment lightning struck the remaining glass dome.

The Temple of the Divine started to shake again; the walls tumbled down around us, and the glass dome cracked above, revealing the double moons intertwined among the stars. The Gods surrounded me, their taloned arms outstretched in the moonlight as their powers fused, making everything come down around us.

A shooting pain worked its way up my back as I keeled over and let out a hollow cry. The torment was everywhere. In my arms, my legs, my head. *Everywhere*. I was burning alive, every bone snapping in my body and reforming into something greater. There was fire in my blood, flowing through my veins and I couldn't get it out. I screamed and bellowed from the agony, from the transformation taking place, before I blacked out in a broken, bloody heap in the dirt.

I came to consciousness with the temple in shambles and the Gods around me, watching and waiting for me to rise. My hearing was now even more sensitive to the world around me. I could hear the clash of swords and shields in the distance still rioting in battle, along with every command Renfred was screaming at our soldiers.

I went to put my hand down to level myself up, only to see it had been replaced with claws and talons. I looked down at the body that was no longer mine, but one of green iridescent scales and leather. My eyes snapped up to Haco, who was still right in front of me, only he was not towering over me anymore.

We met eye to eye now.

I could feel the power emanating off me, feel it pulsing in my blood like a scorching hot fire running through me. Basking in its wonderful glory, I stretched out my new body on the rough dirt and adjusted to it. The ground beneath my new claws crumbled with every step as I bellowed out a stream of deadly fire into the night air. Haco matched the flames with his own as one of the other Gods—Reombarth, I think—started to chuckle from the display of power.

"Let's go kill those demon fucks," I snarled through my new razor sharp teeth.

The Gods of the Divine all nodded in agreement, blood thirsty expressions painting their reptilian faces as we all took to the skies to reclaim our realm.

CHAPTER 1
PRESENT DAY

"*Baby, keep your eyes closed. It'll be over soon," whispered a soft and familiar voice.*

I continued scrunching my eyes until I could feel them ache, concentrating on keeping my chattering teeth from making too much noise. Then I felt warm hands wrap around my wrists and bring my hands up to my ears to cover the muffled screams coming from up above us.

Not even a moment later, those comforting hands were suddenly ripped away from my wrists and I flung open my eyes to see what took the warmth from me so aggressively. My nose scrunched from the scent of something rotten and what I imagined death would smell like invaded my senses before my eyes adjusted to what stood before me.

The dark creature blended into the shadows of the night, flashing its mouth full of yellow jagged teeth before a wave of blackness and shadows overtook me.

I woke up to sweat-drenched sheets clenched in my fists. My hair stuck to my face from the moisture as I gasped for breath.

Not real. Just a dream.

Not. Real.

Worse than a dream though, a memory.

"You are safe," I whispered as I felt a warm tear run down my cheek.

I sat up to catch my breath and calm my racing heart. The moon was shining bright, casting a glow that lit up my bedroom chamber, so bright that the remaining candle burning on my nightstand was barely needed. It would be dawn in a few hours. Gripping the small painting of my parents next to the candle, I stared at it as love bloomed in my chest. They were so happy and full of life. Not anymore. Never again.

Taking another steadying breath, I quickly blew out the candle before hopping out of bed. Gently, I set the portrait back down before rushing to the open window.

From the angle of my bedroom at the top of the tower, I could see the large courtyard right outside my window. With a lush garden and a pathway leading to the training yard looming in the distance, I could also see that they were both completely empty.

Bellator Fortress—or the warrior school, as I liked to call it—sat atop the Argyllian eastern cliffs, a huge expanse of stone buildings enclosed by a large formidable wall and protected by intimidating but cocky faerie soldiers in full armor. While faerie was just a term to reference all magical beings, they came in a multitude of shapes, sizes, and magical abilities. Only the strongest were selected to train here. They were filled with lust, greed, wrath, pride and power. Their magical blood kept them immortal with quick healing and the ability for some to harness their magic externally as well.

No one came in or left this giant fortress without the knowledge of the High Fae overseers. Who I'd still never seen myself. No one on the outside knew how many trained here, how they trained, or even where they came from. They were always on strict schedules, so I knew by now they were in the barracks resting or on watch near the wall, waiting for any outside threat to tempt The Fates.

Now was as perfect a time as any to get some practice in. I moved to the closet doors and creaked them open slowly, trying not to make too much noise. I reached in to grab an oversized tunic, matching linen pants that would only stay up with a belt, and some wool socks before I walked back over to my bed. Throwing my nightgown over my head, I quickly changed into attire better suited to blend into the shadows of the night.

I then moved to the floor under my bed, searching for that crack in the darkness until my fingers gripped a hold of the loose wooden plank. Silently easing the floorboard up, I slipped my hand in to grab my belt that I had stashed away. The four silver daggers sheathed within the belt gleamed in the moonlight as I buckled it to my waist while smiling to myself. Yes, it definitely looked prettier on my waist than on that ogre of a guard I stole it off of while he was sleeping on duty.

Finders keepers, right?

Throwing my hooded cloak over my shoulders, I then slid

my feet into my too-large leather boots. Another courtesy of a smaller guard not paying attention. Over the years, I had stolen more than my fair share of weapons, clothes, and pretty much anything I could get off one of the many lazy guards. I may have been surrounded by some of the greatest fae warriors but because of that greatness, no one would be stupid enough to try and invade the fortress, making it so guards on duty were mostly for looks and not actual security. That led to a lot of dozing off or just not even caring while on the job. It gave me the advantage to get what I needed and they could only blame their own carelessness when they realized half their weapons or even their own shoes were missing.

I double checked the lock to my chambers quietly then made my way back to the window. Peering outside, I checked below the balcony for any sign of movement. Once again, no guards patrolled on this side. Plus the only other entrance and exit on this side of the fortress was to either climb up or jump down the thousand-plus-foot drop into the dangerous Circadian waters known to be filled with beautifully murderous sirens waiting to feast on any flesh readily available. Yup, no one was coming in that way either. Any guards on duty right now were surely stuck patrolling the front gate of the wall or having much sweeter dreams than I, atop it.

I tucked my long dark brown braid into my cloak and threw the hood over my head, concealing my eyes and nose with a shadow of darkness. Opening the tiny jar of tar that I stole from the kitchens, I scooped some out onto my fingers. Carefully closing the jar, trying not to touch it with the glob I had on my other hand, I shoved it in my pocket for later.

I quickly rubbed my hands together to spread the tar. Then using my forearms, I dropped from the ledge of the window, my feet dangling while I reached with my sticky hands to grip the stone ledge. Continuing to grip the cold edges of stone with my fingers, I silently made my way down the tower, landing with a soft thud on the balls of my feet.

Gritting my teeth together against the silence of the night, I looked both ways around the tower to make sure no guard was wandering the grounds aimlessly. All clear. Taking the opportunity to sprint into the courtyard, I used the overgrown hedges as cover while I walked up the path to the empty training yard.

Rinsing my hands in a nearby fountain to get rid of the leftover tar, I could smell the fresh scent of the ocean on the summer breeze and hear the waves crashing against the rocks of the cliff.

Letting out a breath of relief, I gripped the leftover quiver filled with arrows and the bow alongside it. Fastening the strap around my chest, I let my eyes adjust to the three-ringed target ahead of me. I knocked my arrow, closing my eyes for a moment to let the tranquil sounds of the ocean and darkness take over my restless thoughts. Taking one more deep breath, I opened my eyes and began another night full of what I liked to call: self preservation.

I woke back up with my head throbbing and eyes burning from lack of sleep.

"Cassandra! It's time to get up! Breakfast is waiting!"

"Coming!" I groaned and rolled out of bed. Looking down, I realized I never changed out of my clothes from last night. "Fuck," I muttered under my breath.

"What was that?" Evia, my nursemaid, scolded through the door.

"Nothing!" I shouted back. That damn fae hearing could hear me curse from a mile away. Well, not actually. But pretty damn close. It wasn't ladylike to swear, or so I had been taught. Nor was it ladylike to flip people off after they made some shitty comment about my body under their breath. But what would you expect from an orphan girl who was raised surrounded by fae warriors who cussed and made vulgar gestures like their lives depended on it?

Keeping my mouth shut, I ripped the clothes off as quickly as I could and shoved them to the bottom of the laundry bin. Then I quickly ran over, threw open the closet doors, grabbed the first dress I saw, and threw it over my head. Running my hands quickly down my hair to flatten the bedhead from my braid falling apart as I slept, I walked to the door of my room and threw it open.

"What took you so long, Evia? I've been up for hours," I asked with false exasperation to my nursemaid, as she narrowed her brown eyes at my wrinkled lavender dress and then worked her way up to my flushed cheeks and unbrushed hair. I cracked a smile as she glared at me.

"Really, Cassandra? It looks like you just rolled out of bed," Evia retorted while scrunching her nose in the direction of the mountains of book stacks near my nightstand. "Perhaps if you hadn't been reading at all hours of the night you wouldn't look so exhausted. Go. Sit." She pointed to the chair in front of the vanity in the corner. "Let's fix this mess."

Giving her a sheepish grin, I scurried to my spot. Catching a glimpse of myself in the mirror, I couldn't help but stare at the purple bags underneath my eyes, bringing out the bright green hue of them. My tawny skin against my dark hair made the dark hues appear deeper in the morning light. I'd have to deal with the exhaustion and the reprimand of not prioritizing my beauty sleep first, per Evia's beliefs. But I needed to get as much training in over the next few nights before I left this place for good.

Evia cleared her throat and interrupted my train of thought. "If you're going to lie, at least put the effort into it and make it believable," she said while reaching for the hairbrush and started to tame the dark brown beast on my head that could be considered hair. I met her brown eyes in the mirror and she smiled with her too-white teeth gleaming past the red lip stain while working through the knots, and I couldn't help but return it. Out of obedience or fondness, I couldn't tell.

When she smiled like that, she looked excessively fae. Her elongated canines made the smile look almost animalistic and slightly feral. The High Fae were quite similar to humans as far as appearance with their mostly slender but graceful bodies. It was the sharpened canine teeth, delicately pointed ears, and their huge, shimmering eyes that make them look terrifyingly beautiful. Oh and you couldn't forget the extra strength, speed, senses, and quick healing ability that almost all average fae had as well. But the High Fae were the most similar looking to humans, to my kind.

Evia was the closest thing I had to a mother growing up. She was prudent but beneath that icy exterior and her bitter words—deep down in her soul—I knew she had some semblance of love for me. She was my instructor, my mentor, and the one person who could actually talk to me. Almost everyone else ignored my presence, like I was a forgotten ghost roaming these halls. The ones who didn't were just jackasses who thought they had the right to comment on the form of my ass. Hence the use of unladylike gestures I had learned about over my eighteen years here.

No fortress workers, training instructors, or guards were supposed to speak to me because according to Evia, it would disrupt my progress in becoming the perfect wife. My smile faltered at the thought.

Would I be ready to be married off and play the part of the perfect wife to form the alliance my aunt and uncle had been working to secure for over a century? Or would all of this have been for nothing?

I fiddled with the bracelet on my wrist while I let my thoughts drift. The gold glinted in the sunlight as I turned it around my wrist: that was the most it could move, and it wouldn't come off, for my own protection. It was supposed to protect me from any form of magic.

The High Fae were, conceivably, the most powerful species. Unlike other species who were limited to only a single power, High Fae could possess multiple magical affinities and my bracelet came quite in handy with the given fact that I was the only human in this whole fortress, surrounded by said fae and other elemental creatures with astonishing magical gifts. Nobody around me wore a bracelet like the one I had—they had no need—but Evia informed me that only the luckiest of humans were granted this protection. It still hurt that no one else around me needed such protection.

Nope. Just me. The *weak human*.

"There. All finished. Now you look like the princess you're supposed to be," Evia said as she pinned the last of my braided hair to the nape of my neck. "You need to hurry and eat breakfast. Lessons start in half an hour. We have a lot to go over still, and such little time before your introduction to the Crown Prince of Gambriel," she prattled on while walking to the door.

I immediately got up and followed her to the stairs that would take us down to the dining hall. Staring at my slippered feet as we descended the endless stairs of the tower, I walked as slowly as possible, avoiding the inevitability of another day full of my wrong doings and how to properly behave as the perfect docile wife to my future husband, the soon to be King of Gambriel.

CHAPTER 2

Crack!

Four more days. Four more days.

I kept chanting in my head as my knuckles throbbed from the yard stick Evia wacked my hand with during another drawn-out lesson. It wasn't as bad as the other forms of punishment that she deemed fit for the process of becoming a proper lady. From small lashes by her hand to having my meals taken away, this form of discipline had been the easiest. Evia would never do anything so harsh as to leave a scar on my skin because she didn't want it to be *tainted*, but there were many other ways to hurt somebody without leaving a mark.

"Pay attention!" She demanded as she hit the other hand.

Crack!

I held back the whimper that was building in my throat and readjusted my posture in the chair. Shoulders back, chin up, core tight and centered just like she taught me. I refocused my attention to the beautiful but shrewd High Fae pointing with the same yardstick used to bruise my knuckles, at the board in front of me. She did this because it was her job, her duty to the people of Argyll. Just like it was my job to become the best possible version of myself and be married off to some stranger. Evia may have been coarse with her methods of turning me into the perfect wife, but I knew she did have a soft spot for me and how important this alliance was for Argyll.

Evia narrowed her gaze at me while she asked, "Cassandra, can you list off the qualities that a wife fit for the Crown Prince would possess?"

"Yes, my lady," I said with as much sweetness as I could muster up. "She should always look and act presentable, be well educated and well read, never question her husband's judgment, speak when spoken to, and never talk back."

"Yes, precisely. Although, the no talking back applies mostly to you," Evia threw her golden hair back in laughter. "You need to be as perfect and agreeable to him as possible. This marriage will be the start of a new alliance between two nations making their way to restore the peace to our continent." Her gaze turned serious again. "If this doesn't go as planned, our people will suffer the consequences and all that we've been working towards will be lost."

I flinched at the last remark. "Yes, my lady. I will do my duty for the people of Argyll." For the people of a nation I had never met nor seen, to bring peace to the continent I'd never gotten to explore more than the courtyard outside. I was always told how important I was for this alliance, for this Kingdom, but my opinion rarely mattered and neither did my questions.

Evia sighed in acceptance, not disappointment. Her job had been doomed since I was first brought here. She had to train and turn a lowly human who came from the rubble of a fallen kingdom into a proper lady fit for a royal marriage with the High Fae. She had raised me since I was five years old, hounded me about what I needed to become, but I couldn't help that I wanted to be *more* than just a pawn in their royal game of chess.

Over those eighteen years, I grew closer with Evia and looked up to her like I would my own mother. A memory of her worried face leaning over my body as I twisted and turned in my sheets during another one of those horrific nightmares filled my mind. I would wake up and cling to her as she quieted my frightened sobs and stayed the whole night with me, keeping the monsters at bay. She would always pray with me to the God of nightmares, Bomris, asking for him to give me a night filled with peace instead of the incessant psychological torture.

Those prayers were always left unanswered.

Rubbing my sore knuckles, I looked down at them and my fragile human hands that were laced with calluses from my secret training. I clenched them into tight fists as I gritted my teeth; *this* was my purpose. I could do this, I had to do this. If throwing my freedom away meant I could unite the fae and humankind together under a reign of peace, my freedom would be worth it.

"Now back to our lesson. Let's review the history of Gambriel again and how it came to be the greatest ruling kingdom on this continent," Evia trailed off, pointing back at the board marked with the same things I'd gone over since I was brought here.

I had to learn about the movements of the stars in the sky and how to use them as a map; the medicinal and magical properties of herbs; how the fae's magic was linked to the land and the one that rules over it; the composition of music; and of course, court etiquette. But first and foremost, how the great Kingdoms of Gambriel and Argyll saved our continent from destruction and how to make said kingdoms even greater than before.

Over the last few years, since our Gods had abandoned us to our own devices, the lands had begun wilting without their magical blessings. Ladon was dying, slowly rotting from deep within the earth and killing any living thing that could sprout from it. Some of the fae had to use their own magic to fertilize the soil and come by every week to help our crops sprout and grow into what we needed to survive. We had some Gambriellian High Fae that were gifted with magic from the God of earth to thank for the food that sat upon our tables. It was a quick fix, but not a forever solution that we could rely on, especially the humans who weren't blessed with any magical affinity.

Ragnar, the God of the earth, had blessed our soil since the beginning of time. His power was infused with the very fibers of our earth, keeping the soil healthy and sustainable. Without him or the other Gods' blessings, the magic the fae carried had lessened, and so had our supply of goods. Everyday, we still prayed to the Gods in hopes that they would return to bless us and our land once more.

But before that could happen, we needed to become united as one and not divided as a species like we currently were.

I sighed and tried to act as attentive as possible while Evia rattled on once again.

Four more days.

That was it.

Just four more days and then I'd be free of this prison, only to be put into my next cage.

After supper I took the stairs two steps at a time, rushing up to reach my serenity of a room and to make sure any other evidence of last night's escapade was hidden. My knife belt was still under the floorboard, black training clothes still stuffed in the laundry bin and boots hidden behind my stacks of books. Thank the Gods. I didn't want to have to go on another scavenger hunt for more clothes that were suitable for training. Only being allowed to own dresses and heeled shoes was yet another mold I was forced into. Not that I hated beautiful dresses or that I wasn't thankful, but I would definitely love clothes more suitable for easy movement or at least the option of picking something for myself. It just left me to sneak and steal any left over casual clothes not taken by the guards or staff in this fortress.

Taking the pins out of my hair, I walked over to my vanity to take a seat. I rubbed the back of my head; it ached from the pins digging into my scalp all day. Letting my hair free from the tight knot that secured it, I took a sigh of relief,

"Finally." Running my brush through the dark brown tresses that reached my ribs, I couldn't help but drift off into my own thoughts.

Would I meet the Crown Prince first? What would the Kingdom of Gambriel be like? Would we get married immediately? Would I have more freedom than here and get to wear the clothes of my choosing? Would I still be able to train at night? Would a union between a human and a fae actually bring peace to our continent? I still didn't understand how one single marriage would stop a war that had been going on for over two decades.

Shaking my head to slow the endless questions, I set the brush back down on the vanity. I needed to stop thinking about all those things. They would happen no matter what I did or didn't do, no matter how much my anxious thoughts filled my head. In almost three days now, I would be moving to Gambriel to begin my duty for the people of Argyll.

Whether I was ready or not.

I fanned my face against the late summer heat and the anxiety building in my chest.

I needed some air.

Grabbing a book off the top of the stacks next to my bed, I pressed it tightly to my chest. Books were the only luxury that I was allowed because a good wife was always well read, per Evia. They were also my perfect escape, because I couldn't physically leave this place—but when I read and became engrossed in a story about dashing knights and their long lost loves, I was mentally in another world far better than my own.

I ran down the stairs of my tower to the garden in the

courtyard to get some light reading in before sundown. Clutching my book in hand as I walked to my usual bench, I took a seat, opened my book, and before I could escape my endless thoughts, the sound of steel clashing against steel pulled me away from the open novel. I looked to my side where the hedge broke away just a crack to see the fae warriors doing their exercises out in the training yard.

Each series of steps and movements they went through were as precise as they were lethal. I found that I was holding my breath as I watched them fight. Their lithe but muscular bodies whirled back and forth across the training square with deathly grace as if it were a dance. So swift and powerful. If I wasn't watching with my own eyes, I wouldn't be able to believe anyone could move like that, let alone armies of them.

I watched them run through drill after drill, taking mental notes of their footsteps and movements, until the summer sun went down over the water and they started to clear out of the courtyard.

Walking back to my chambers, I heard a loud smacking noise come from the small room where Evia and I took our meals. I crept over on the balls of my feet until I was pressed against the stone wall, hidden from their sight as I listened to hushed voices arguing.

"You blathering idiot!" Another smack of skin against skin filled the air along with the sharp intake of breath. My heart sped up. It was Evia, reprimanding one of the lower fae staff members. Her voice came again, sharper than the first time. "We only have *three more days* of having to deal with all of this and you decide to fuck it up when we're so close to being finished?"

"I-I'm sorry, my lady," the fae stuttered as my mind raced with what in the Gods they were talking about. It clearly had to do with my being here because I only had three days left. What was Evia so pissed about and why did she sound so relieved about me leaving this place behind?

"Get out of my sight!" Evia shouted, with an ear-piercing crash of glass shattering on the floor. I ran as quickly as I could, back up the stairs and into my room before Evia could scold *me* for eavesdropping.

My heart beat rapidly from the adrenaline but also broke at the thought of my nursemaid feeling relief by my upcoming departure. After all those years under her care and the long nights of her by my side, soothing me. I assumed she came to care for me as I have for her but from the sounds of it—I was just another job.

I braced my hands on my trembling thighs and closed my eyes, giving myself a moment to catch my breath. I needed to keep going. I would not be weak. I would not be left defenseless like my parents.

It had been eighteen years since I lost them. Or more like since they were taken away from me. At five-years-old, they were slaughtered by the same demons that haunted my nightmares, along with most of the people of Menodore. Only a few survived by hiding long enough until the warriors of Argyll, my adopted aunt and uncle's kingdom, arrived to take away any survivors from the village or castle.

A human child, the daughter of a castle servant and a blacksmith worker, survived the Great Siege of Menodore by hiding in a small spot under the floorboards in the castle. Thousands of fae and humans alike died that day, but some were able to escape or were taken to safety by Argyllian and Gambriellian armies.

I still didn't remember that day or much before it, but I remembered the onslaught of emotions; the fear, sadness, desperation, and feeling of horror during those events. My brain clearly blocked most of it out from the trauma that affected thousands of us during that time. I barely even remembered my own parents; the only thing I had to recall them by was the small portrait sitting on my nightstand. My mother with her bright green eyes to match mine, fiery red hair, and a smile as bright as the sun. My father had warm skin with a strong nose that was similar to my own to match his black hair and chocolate brown eyes. My heart clenched in my chest. What I wouldn't give to see them now. Their features had already faded from my memory but the last picture I had of them helped keep their washed out memory alive and burning in my brain.

Most of what I remembered from that day was meeting who would become my aunt, Radha Lennox, and how she took me from the ashes and piles of rubble. She took me and made me her own, to save me from the life of an orphan scrounging for basic necessities, and to use me as her way to unite two kingdoms and two kinds on this continent. I now had a purpose, thanks to my Aunt Radha and Uncle Arron Lennox, the King of Argyll. They came to Menodore's call during the siege and helped in a time of need, but I'd never forget that they were still fae, still akin to those enslaving my kind.

I also would never understand how one marriage between a human and a High Fae could forgive their old sins and decades-long bloodshed of my kind. But anything would be worth trying to lessen that bloodshed from continuing and give humans the chance at a real life, at *freedom*.

Gravel crunching under boots alerted me as I pulled my body back up and looked around to where the noise was coming from. Rambunctious male laughter filled the night air as those steps sounded closer, coming from the hedges. I held back from muttering *fuck*, trying to not alert them of my location. Sprinting to the edge of the training yard, I crouched down behind a stand that held wooden practice swords and waited.

Their voices carried on the wind, "Graham's a fucking fool."

"How does a male as smart as him lose his Godsdamned boots?" The other faerie barked in laughter. I peeked down to my leather-covered feet and bit down on my lip to hold in my snickering.

Thank you for the lovely boots, Graham.

Peeking through the gaps of the stand, I could see the two faerie males, one with long red hair and the other with cropped blonde hair, bantering back and forth about more nonsense as they inched closer to me. I stiffened as they kept moving forward, their bodies angled directly at my hiding spot. My body started shaking uncontrollably with dread as my palms grew sweaty.

Did they know I was here? Were they coming to grab me and report me back to Evia?

No fucking way.

Wiping my wet hands on my pants, I held my breath as they came closer. My lungs started to burn from holding it in as they took their sweet time walking across the yard.

Were they moving in slow motion or was I just that scared that they were going to find me?

The red-haired fae stopped walking right next to my discarded bow and stared at it as the blonde-haired one kept on track towards the swords. Red whistled while staring at my bow, "Commander's going to beat someone's ass for leaving this out."

Blondie inched closer as my hands started to itch to reach down for one of the daggers on my waist. I didn't know what I would do with it, especially against a trained warrior like the one before me, but I wouldn't go down without a fight.

My hand grazed the cool metal of the hilt as Blondie turned his head to look at Red, "What are you going on about?"

"Someone left out a bow and a quiver of arrows. Right on the fucking ground." Red reached down and picked it up, waving it around in the air. Still holding my breath, I prayed to the Gods that this male wouldn't find me.

"Leave it there. We'll let the Commander find it in the morning and whoever was dumb enough to do that, won't make the same mistake again when he's through with them." Blondie rolled his eyes and grabbed a metal sword off the shelf that was right next to me. I could feel my heart pounding in my ribcage, the erratic thump filling my ears with nothing but its unsteady beat as I waited for the moment his eyes would travel over to my hiding spot.

My chest was on fire from the lack of air as dangerous thoughts flooded my mind. I was going to be caught and *punished*. I have had the unwanted luxury to see what those punishments would entail when one of the guards stepped out of line. Even with the fae and their fast healing, there was nothing but blood and bruises covering their bodies when the Commander was finished with his form of discipline.

I didn't know what would happen to me and I didn't want to find out. It was just my luck that I was so close to being caught for the first time, and with only a few more days of being trapped in this place. Closing my eyes, I sent a quick prayer up to our Gods in hopes that they might answer me just this once.

I promise I won't say fuck as much if you don't let these guards find me. Please, please, please don't let me get caught tonight.

My eyes snapped open to the sound of he quiver and bow clattering against the dirt as Red dropped them without a care. Blondie swaggered away with sword in hand as Red followed close behind, yammering on about bad bow etiquette. Crawling out of my hiding spot, I dusted off the dirt and thanked my lucky stars that the almost-encounter didn't go down differently.

"That was fucking close," I muttered under my breath as I picked up the bow.

Shit.

The whole not saying fuck thing didn't last very long. Looking at the night sky, I whispered a soft, "I'm sorry," to them and the promise I already broke. The guilt in my gut quickly faded away into panic as I started pacing on the dirt.

Double shit.

What would Evia have to say if she caught me out here, dressed in random male's clothing, galavanting around with daggers on my waist? I stopped moving and rubbed my free hand down my face in frustration.

Oh my Gods.

What would my *Aunt Radha* have to say if she saw me like this? I could already see the disappointment lining her sparkling black eyes as she glared down at me in my current state. I was her shining example that not all humans were filth, like the fae grew up believing. Radha would always say that I was the *hope* for our people, that I needed to be what everyone expected of me. She would always tell me how important I was to her and to the people of Argyll. But when she scowled at me like I was some sort of inconvenience, I didn't feel all that important any longer.

I would forever be thankful for my Aunt saving me and giving me a better life, though. No matter what that cost may be. She may have been the wife of the King of Argyll, but she was not the Queen of Argyll. We had no Queens in the great continent of Ladon, we only honored royal male bloodlines when it came down to who ruled over our territories. There were, however, some Queens in the Eastern continents, but they didn't follow the same traditions that we did in Ladon.

With the High Fae and their long life spans, they were almost always able to produce a male heir to inherit the kingdom and if they weren't able to, the kingdom would go to the next male family member with any drop of that royal blood in his veins. There were princesses of course, but they could not ascend into queendom, only a Royal Consort at best. Their main job was to produce heirs and help handle most of the social aspects of ruling, like planning feasts, balls, or any other celebrations in the kingdom.

That would be my job. Playing the part of the perfect wife to a soon-to-be King and to make him as many little demi-faes as I could until my short mortal life span was up. Not a completely atrocious way for a human girl with no family to spend her life. But most definitely not my first choice.

Taking a seat on the hard ground, I stretched my sore muscles from this evening's training and let the moonlight kiss my face with its soft warmth. I sat there for a long time, watching the single moon on this side of the world gild the star-filled sky, listening to the waves crash against the boulders below, and thought about what I had lost and what I still had to gain. I would do anything to help this continent and my people have a chance at a better life, my freedom and choices be damned in the process.

CHAPTER 3

The next few days flew by quickly between the endless lessons with Evia and trying to squeeze in as much training for myself before I had to leave this place, hopefully, forever. I stuffed my knives, training clothes, and anything else I wanted to keep hidden at the bottom of the trunk filled with some of my casual dresses. I took a mental note of exactly which trunk they were in so I could get that sent directly up to wherever I'd be staying and hide them in that room as soon as I got in.

I stood outside the front doors of the stone building that led to my room, and waited for my Aunt and Uncle's carriage to pull in after the long retinue of horses with carts and Argyllian guards as they came through the gates to gather my things. I spotted the eight enormous white Galdur horses before I saw the golden carriage they were pulling. Galdurs were descendants of a type of Pegasus, as large as they were pure with lifespans to match the fae. No large wings adorned their sides like their ancestors, but they were as quick as the wind with their long strides and enormous bodies. They were an endangered species but of course, Aunt Radha and Uncle Arron had a stable full of the majestic beasts.

Letting my hand glide over one of their soft snouts when they came to a stop, the horse snickered while I cooed at it, causing its long white mane to flow in the wind. One of the others reached over and started licking my hand, asking for attention as I let out a laugh from its ticklish tongue. They were truly magnificent but loving creatures.

After fawning over the gorgeous horses for the millionth time, I turned my gaze to the gilded carriage as the footman hopped down and opened the door to it. My Aunt Radha may have not been a Queen, but she looked every part of one from my books on the Eastern continents as she descended down the golden steps. Her long chestnut brown hair was swept back from her moon-pale face with small neat braids woven through a tiara of golden spikes, looking as if it were a part of her. High apple cheekbones, delicately arched ears, dark sparkling black eyes and crimson full lips to match her long sleeve, blood red gown.

Radha only looked to be about thirty years-old in human years but she was actually over two hundred years old, still relatively young for fae standards. With the fae's elongated life span, they aged differently as well. From birth, they aged normally like a human would and once they reached around the age of twenty and were close to being done developing, they aged significantly slower. That was also when their powers started to fully develop and showed their true potential. You could see small spurts of power when they were children, but their power matured just like their bodies. Hundreds of years of difference looked only like a couple years to a human's eyes.

"Cassandra, darling! Oh, how I've missed you, my little flower," Radha exclaimed as she touched my cheek with her warm palm. I closed my eyes and leaned into the touch. Gods, just that single touch sent a wave of warmth through me and I instantly felt calmer in her presence. I opened my eyes and smiled up at my stunning Aunt. She was only a couple inches taller than my five foot, nine inches but it always felt like she was towering over me with the power that emanated off of her.

"I've missed you for far too long! Where is Uncle? Is he meeting us there or will he be coming later on?" I asked excitedly as she smoothed my light pink gown with her soft caresses. I hadn't gotten to see her in a little over six months; she would usually come to visit every few months to spend a couple days with me.

The last time she was here, I was so exhausted from our activities during those few days that I passed out in bed and missed her departure, which was pretty common for when she would visit. Radha always filled the days with amazing meals, little activities that we could do around the fortress, trunks full of dresses she picked for me, and all the shoes a girl could dream of. I did wish for more variety in the clothes, not just dresses and slippers fit for a Princess, but I didn't want to seem ungrateful by asking for anything else from her.

She had already given me so much and I felt like I hadn't given anything back for her generosity. I was always so tired by the end of it, but every busy second was worth spending with my Aunt—and sometimes my Uncle when he had time to come with her.

My heart ached from the thoughts of my Uncle Arron; I missed him tremendously. For being a King, he was always so unremarkably kind to everyone no matter the circumstances or what they were. It had been years since I'd last seen him, but I could still remember the way his rich dark skin crinkled up next to his warm brown eyes when he smiled down at me and his hearty laughter that could light up a room. He was full High Fae as well, blessed with the power of emotional manipulation. Even without his powers, just his personality alone would make you feel at ease.

"Sweet Uncle Arron has fallen ill and will be staying at Castle Argyll with a healer until he starts to come around. He was too unfit to even travel by carriage! Poor thing will get better in no time though. You need not to worry about him, dear," Radha explained while she walked with me to the front doors, her slender hand wrapped around my arm. "Why don't you go and make sure they got everything from upstairs while I talk to Evia?"

Before I even got the chance to ask more about Uncle Arron, Radha was gone. Nonetheless, she went and searched for Evia among the moving chaos. I'd ask her more about my uncle on the journey to Gambriel.

The hair on the back of my neck started to stand up as I felt someone's gaze burning into my back. Swiftly turning around, I saw Falkur, the right hand to the King of Argyll, standing beside the carriage. Usually the High Fae were beautiful with their symmetrical features and the power they radiated, but Falkur, with his sickly pale skin and stringy black hair, was not what I would consider appealing. He flashed me a savage grin as his beady black eyes trailed over my body, assessing me as he drummed his ring-filled fingers against his forearm. I returned his smile with a demure one of my own before I curtsied and rushed back inside the fortress and away from his lingering gaze.

I wouldn't let that creep ruin my day.

Beyond nervous and anxious to leave this place, I scurried up the stairs to my tower bedroom to do one last check. For it only being mid-morning, the sun was shining bright and illuminated the whole bedroom through my single window. It looked relatively the same, even without all my things scattered about. I did a quick check throughout the room and the bathing chamber to make sure everything was packed and I wasn't leaving anything important behind.

The mountain of books was still by my nightstand but they would be staying here and eventually be returned back to the library they had come from. I plucked one with a light green cover off the top; it was one of my favorites about star-crossed lovers and the open sea, full of adventures and that perfect slow burn romance that my heart yearned for.

Holding the book close to my chest, I made up my mind. Yup, definitely taking it with me, you'd have to pry it from my cold dead hands before I left it behind. I didn't even know if I would have access to a library in Gambriel, so having at least one book—even though it was stolen like most of my other acquired goods—was a fantastic idea.

I sprinted down the steps, my slippered feet padding against the stone floor with each movement. Coming to an abrupt halt at the entrance, I feigned elegance and walked gracefully back to the gilded carriage where Aunt Radha was already waiting for me inside. The entire thing was luxurious and golden, with black velvet seats, wood paneled walls with the Argyllian crest of the Dragon Goddess Reombarth carved into the side of them, and soft woven carpet. Big enough for six people to sit comfortably, but it seemed to be just Radha and I traveling in it.

"Isn't Evia coming with us?" I asked as I repositioned my pink skirts to sit comfortably, keeping the book still clutched to my chest.

"No, my flower. She had other business that she needed to attend to," Radha explained as she wiped her hands off on a black handkerchief and stuffed it into the pocket of her red skirt.

I nodded as my stomach turned from the guilt. Evia was tight-fisted, but I loved her either way and didn't get the chance to say a proper goodbye. Clutching the book tighter until my knuckles turned white, I hoped I would see her again soon. The door to the carriage opened again and to my surprise, Falkur stepped inside and sat across from my aunt. I assumed he would be riding with someone else, giving Aunt Radha and I some time to catch up. But like many things I assumed, I was wrong again.

The carriage jerked forward powerfully and we were off at last.

I gave the fortress one last look through the curtained window and thanked the Gods that I was out of there. But I couldn't help the sick feeling in my stomach. Was I just nervous or was I scared for this new adventure? Or I could just be feeling extra guilty about not saying goodbye to my life-long nursemaid.

I let out a deep breath as I silenced the guilt that was gnawing at me and turned back to Radha. She was looking out the other carriage window in deep thought. The sunlight reflected off her necklace, making the gold glimmer and a large black stone ricocheted a confetti of colors and light across the carriage. It was a locket of heavy gold, etched with symbols I had never seen before but they swirled around the black stone in an enticing manner. I bet she felt my eyes on her because she turned to look at me, catching me staring at the bewitching necklace.

She smirked a little and held it up to the light, "Beautiful isn't it?" It caught the light again and I could've sworn I saw the symbols near the center stone move like they were dancing with the sun. I wondered if it was enchanted.

"Yes, it's stunning. What type of stone is that in the middle?" I asked while ignoring Falkur's gaze on me. I'd never seen that type of stone elsewhere, which wasn't saying much because I hadn't seen a lot of things. But, every time I had seen my Aunt, she always had the necklace on.

Radha laughed and shook her head, "I don't remember what it's called, it was given to me by someone long ago and I can't seem to part with it." She looked back down at the necklace with adoration in her eyes.

I smiled as I reached out with my free hand, "Well it's beautiful, whatever it is. Can I see it?"

Radha went still, her black eyes went from sparkling with

joy to cold and bitter. "No, you may not, and never ask me that again," she snapped as she grasped the locket in her hand tightly.

I flinched from the sudden outburst and put my head down in shame, long brown tresses hiding my reddened face. I couldn't stand when she was mad or disappointed in me. I owed her my life because she saved me that day in Menodore. Without her I was nothing, and I spent every day trying to prove to her that I was worthy of the time that she invested in me.

"I'm sorry," I whispered. "It won't happen again."

I felt the shift of the mood in the air. It was thick with tension now. Radha had always had a short fuse, so I was used to walking on eggshells when I was around her. I peered back up at her through my hair and she was already back to looking out the window as we left the fortress far behind us. Falkur was shuffling papers in his lap, with one leg crossed over the other in a casual manner but I didn't miss the way he gripped the papers with white knuckles.

Sighing, I looked out the window and studied the landscape before me. We were passing a small pond filled with fish that reflected the bright summer sun. Lady Kano, the Dragon Goddess of Water, helped rule over the court called Aestas that was located on the Western continent of Atrium. She also ruled over all bodies of water surrounding both of our continents. She was who we had to thank for the gorgeous lakes and little ponds teeming with life. A smile slowly graced my lips as I thought of the water Goddess blessing our realm once more. The smile quickly dropped when we passed a dead field, reminding me that our Gods were nowhere to be found and that we were on our own now.

At the rate we were going, it would only take about a week and a half to two weeks to reach Gambriel by carriage. It was going to be a long trip, an even longer trip considering this was the longest I had ever been allowed out of that fortress.

Eighteen years.

I spent eighteen out of my twenty-three years within the walls of that place. And now I just wanted to see everything, and not behind the glass of a window but out in the open with the world all around me. I wanted to see every kingdom and all the lands that the Gods had blessed with their magic. Each one used to live and protect a territory while they were still in this world, before they left us eighteen years ago during the Siege of Menodore. But for now, the carriage window would have to do.

The world also wasn't a safe place for a human to just be wandering around and exploring. Especially on the continent of Ladon, where it was mostly populated by other mystical beings with only some humans.

In Ladon, we did allow more freedoms for the humans. Not all humans here were slaves, some had normal jobs according to Evia, and some even worked side by side with the fae. That's where I came in and why my job was so important not just for the people of Argyll and Gambriel, but for the continent of Ladon. This would be the first royal marriage between a human and a High Fae. There, of course, had already been a few fae and human marriages. Even though to some that was frowned upon, and the marriages were never on this level of royal politics.

Our marriage would hopefully be the foundation of a new world. A world where it wouldn't matter what type of being you were. A world where everyone would have the chance at happiness. A world where it would be safe for a human like me to wander and explore without the fear of being taken and sold into a life of slavery for just simply *being*. Ladon had been ruthless to my kind, but certainly kinder than other places in our world.

Like Atrium, our neighboring continent across the Circadian Seas. Atrium was ruled over by High King Seraphim. Not just a High Lord and not just a King, but a High King whose territory was divided into five courts where his word was law. The courts were once ruled over individually by the High Lords of that court until High Lord Seraphim of the Umbra Court found that being only a High Lord was not enough for his existence, and conquered the other courts of Atrium until they fell under one rule.

One High King to rule over them all.

Five out of the nine Gods helped protect and bless the continent of Atrium, and without their presence, I was unsure of how well they were faring over there without their powerful magic blessing the land.

The Dragon God Bomris, who ruled over the Umbra Court—home of the High King Seraphim—had the power to manipulate your mind and make all your worst nightmares seem real. It didn't surprise me that the court the God of illusions ruled over was now the source of the living nightmares plaguing that continent.

Atrium was a rough and brutal place, even more so since King Seraphim took over the entire continent, only letting High Fae Lords work through him as partial ruler of their courts. Humans have never existed freely in his territory, only as slaves. I had even heard some of the guards saying how High King Seraphim's throne was made from the bones of his human slaves.

Just the thought alone made my stomach churn in disgust. High King Seraphim got to live lavishly while the humans he enslaved lived in filth and suffered at his iron fist. It was ironic because Atrium was built off the blood and bones of those same humans and yet they were treated worse than the livestock.

Only humans suffered such harshness from the other magical creatures. Our short life spans, lack of magic in our blood, and fragile bodies made us easier targets for them to take advantage of. This marriage was going to bridge the gap between our kinds and hopefully set an example for the other continents that humans deserve freedom and not to be stuck under the thumb of some High Fae ruler as their slaves or pets.

I looked back towards my Aunt who was now reading through a stack of inked parchment. Radha caught my stare and reached out her slender hand to rest on my knee and gave it a few small pats of affection. I met her black eyes with a small smile that she returned with a quick flash of her pearly white elongated canines. My heart filled with pure bliss from the simple gesture that showed my aunt wasn't mad at me anymore, before she went back to studying her pile of papers very intently.

Falkur was still reading through his own stack but I could feel him revert his attention back to me and then over to my aunt. The tension was still so thick that I could cut it with a knife. I had so many questions for Radha but I didn't feel comfortable voicing them in front of the Right Hand to the King. He always made me feel on edge and I never understood what my Uncle Arron, King of Argyll, saw in the slippery bastard.

Holding back a sigh, I looked back out the window at the redwood forest we were passing through. We'd only been traveling for a few hours and my muscles were already aching to be stretched out and to just go *do something*. This was going to be a long, quiet, and boring trip. But I was going to make the most of being out in the open and not locked into one place. Hopefully I would get to see more of this great continent before I was trapped in another fortress of my future husband's choice.

Well, I would make the most out of what Aunt Radha and Falkur would let me do, anyway.

CHAPTER 4

For two weeks, we made our way through the southern part of the continent to the Kingdom of Gambriel. We passed through the green rolling hills of Taernsby, the great central waters of Lacus and through the tall Inverness Mountains that seemed to kiss the sky. We stopped and camped out at night, the guards pitching a large tent for Radha and I to share. I reread the same small green book I took from my old room to keep me company throughout the long journey while Radha was busy with Falkur, going through endless stacks of parchment. The days became shorter while nights became colder and longer.

Fall was coming, and change was too.

Everyday we got closer to Gambriel, and I could feel the unrest simmering in the air the longer it took to reach our destination. More than a few nights, I would wake up in mine and Radha's tent alone. Each time, I would get out of my makeshift bed and watch the shadows of the Argyllian soldiers walking through the camp, keeping it secure. Peeking through the tent opening, I could see the soldiers' steel armor, with the sigil of the Goddess Reombarth adorning them.

Reombarth was the Goddess of Sound and had the power to take away your ability to speak or even your sense of hearing. She could disable your whole body with one screech alone, leaving you frozen and at her mercy. Reombarth was fierce and cunning, the perfect symbol for Argyll.

The Arygllian soldiers never slacked in their security measures, so I didn't get a chance to leave the tent just like my aunt was. I kept wondering where Radha was running off to and I wanted to find her. One night I gained enough courage to ask her, and all I got was a scolding for not minding my own business *and* not getting a proper amount of rest. From then on, I never asked again, and the disappointment that lingered in my aunt's eyes slowly dissipated.

My mind kept drifting back to the first night I woke up alone. I waited for hours, pacing around the tent, thinking of all the horrible scenarios where my aunt was taken from me. She was the one person who had come to my rescue and pulled me from the ashes to make me her own. She saved me and I didn't know what I would do without her. I didn't know *who I would be* without her.

Radha ended up returning just a few hours before dawn and I finally stopped my incessant pacing to wait for her by the front of the tent. She wasn't alone though. Falkur was standing with her speaking in hushed tones, so I couldn't make out their conversation but I didn't miss that it sounded like they were arguing about something. Was she meeting with Falkur every night after that? They could've just been working through more of the never-ending paperwork I always saw gracing their hands.

The smell of fire and smoke and something bitter in the air that brought me back to my senses of the present. I swiped back the curtain of the carriage and what greeted me ripped my heart from my chest. There was something burning alright. It was a pile of mangled dead bodies burning together, and others were still scattered about the side of the road. That bitter and metallic smell was the blood of the fallen rich in the air. It made my nose crinkle in disgust and I could practically *taste* the rotten death on my tongue.

The bodies were hardly recognizable from the deep gashes in their skin and severed limbs. Most were human, from what I could see of what was leftover of them, and I could've sworn there were a couple of fae in the midst of the dead. There were soldiers walking around in golden armor with carts to pick up bodies and toss them into the heaps of burning flesh. I peeked ahead to see there were more pyres, already burning furiously with black smoke dissipating into the air.

Bile crawled up my throat from the stench and my eyes started to burn with unshed tears for the dead before me. These were people's families, their *loved ones,* and here they were, cut up and discarded on the side of the road, their lifeless bodies waiting to be thrown into another pyre until they no longer existed in this realm. Nausea churned in my gut and my throat clenched as I swiped away the mournful tears that began to fall.

I recognized the sigil on the gold chest plate of one of the soldiers pushing a cart piled high with the deceased. Lady Aither: the legendary Dragon Goddess known for her strength, and the fastest flier among the Gods with her almost-golden reptilian scales. It was the official sigil for Gambriel. They were a part of King Roderick Harrington's army and they were… *killing people?*

"What's going on?" I asked, my voice shaky from the horrors in front of me.

"That is why you're here," Aunt Radha simply stated, as if I should already know that.

I turned and just stared at her, waiting for her to further explain what in the Gods' names she was spouting off.

"It's the Rebellion. They attempted an attack on the Castle of Gambriel, but as you can see, their effort didn't go as planned," she gestured to the massacre just a couple of feet from our carriage. "This is why you're here, to restore good faith to humans, to show that we see them as equals now."

"Me marrying the Prince of Gambriel will make them stop?" I questioned, still trying to process how that could possibly stop all of this death.

"That's what we're hoping for," Radha sighed. "This marriage will be the first between a royal High Fae bloodline and a human. It will be the first step to represent a united nation between the human race and the other beings, not just the High Fae."

I looked back out the window at all the bloodshed. You weren't innocent when you sat by and watched all of this bloody carnage happen. You were just as guilty as the ones holding the blades over their heads. You were complacent and still had their blood on your hands, especially if you were in the position to do something about it. I wanted to jump from the moving carriage and stop the King's Guard from killing the lone survivors moaning out for help. I moved my shaking hand to the handle but Radha gripped it in her own and shook her head at me to stop.

Gulping back the ball in my throat, I brushed away the now angry tears. I sent a quick prayer to the God of Death, Haco, who ruled over my home Kingdom of Menodore. I asked him to help those who had fallen pass into the Vale with ease. May his comforting darkness of death bring them peace at last. I clenched my hands into fists on my lap. Whatever it would take to end this madness, to make the death stop, I would do it.

The sweet smell of impending rain cut through the stench of burning death. I looked up towards the heavy gray clouds and could see the downpour begin. The Gods may not have been here in person, but they still answered my prayers in their own way this time. I sent a thank you to Kano and Evander, the Goddess of Water and the God of Lightning, for coming together to wash away the blood, the ruination, and to take care of the souls that we had lost.

Through the lashing rain and low hanging clouds, I saw the capital city of Gambriel, Rimont, approach as we traveled further away from the pyres. The narrow cobblestone streets were filled with pale two-story houses made of wood and stone, closely tucked together with shops intermingled amongst some of them. The first to appear was a metalsmith, the chimney expelling large puffs of smoke into the early evening. My lips tilted up into a small smile, thinking of my father who was a blacksmith and worked someplace similar.

We passed by a carriage repair shop, then a dress shop, and on and on they went. Their signs were all the same print and size as the others, hanging above large doors, most of which were shut and locked up for the night already.

There were a few lower fae milling about the streets, trying to take cover from the rain. Pixies with their tiny wings fighting against rain in their flights, nymphs with bark colored skin and bright green hair to match lively leaves used their magic of the forest to create tree-like umbrellas to shield from the downpour and a few more types of fae stopped in their passages as the Galdur horses hooves echoed on the stones. They turned their heads with wide eyes to study the procession of horses and carriages going down the avenue. We went through the streets at a steady pace until we edged closer to the Gambriellian docks leading out to the Circadian Seas and the endless array of ships waiting in the harbor.

Despite the rain, there was a crowd of people, every shape and color, near the docks. I careened my head to get a better look and noticed that there were countless human slaves in chains working the docks. There were some that were so badly beaten, I couldn't make out the features of their faces, staggering down the plank of a merchant ship.

What I saw next made the whole world slow for a moment. There were human children with their ankles and hands bound together in chains. *Actual children.* Some of them couldn't be older than six years old. Blood and dirt caked onto their skin and the rain washed away some of the pain marred into their too skinny bodies. Their small hands were bound with long chains while they worked together to shovel coal onto a vessel and moved boxes that were bigger than they were.

I stopped hearing the sounds of their work, of the rain, of my own heartbeat. My breaths came in short ragged gasps. I couldn't breathe. Couldn't expel the air trapped in my lungs. Tears burned my eyes and threatened to fall upon the black velvet seats on the carriage.

I had to do something.

Anything.

They couldn't do this to them.

Those were *children*, innocents.

Radha grabbed my hand again and brought me back to her attention.

"You need to be worrying about this alliance and not those slaves over there," my aunt sighed, her eyes showing no emotion to what was playing out in front of us. I wanted to reach over and throttle her at that moment. I wanted her to feel the pain that my kind had felt everyday, for *generations*.

How could she be so careless about those people's suffering? This alliance was supposedly about making all of us equals, so why *wouldn't* I care about what was happening right in front of us? Those humans staggering, with large hopeless eyes, were still supposed to be under the Crown's responsibility and here, one of the rulers of Ladon sat and watched with nothing but impassiveness in her eyes.

"I'm supposed to just ignore what's going on here? What's happening to people like me? What's happening to those *children*?" I retorted with seething hate lacing my words. I could feel my blood starting to boil under my skin from the anger pulsing through it. At that moment, I wished I could sprout claws and shred everything, *everyone*, in front of me and get to those children.

"Not ignore, just push to the side for now and then you can worry about them all you want when you have the power to do something," Radha said while stroking my shaking hand with hers.

Before I could argue any further, Radha placed her hand on my chin roughly and moved my head to look back out the window. Gleaming in the gray light, was the great Castle of Gambriel. The fire churning in my gut ceased to a small, flickering flame as I stared at my new home. The large stone castle towered over the whole city. High turrets adorned the tall towers, the tips puncturing the sky, the clouds bleeding their rain upon us. Ten bright yellow flags with the Goddess Aither upon them flew amongst the clouds and rain, creating a contrast in the gray glum.

My palms started to sweat, and I fought the urge to wipe them on my apricot colored skirts. This was really happening. The iron gates of the castle appeared before us, intricate metal doors with a latticework of flowers adorning them. They opened to reveal dozens of the King's Guard holding circular shields, swords drawn at their sides, and their golden helmets concealing their slightly arched fae ears.

They were flanking the cobblestone path we currently traveled down until we reached the massive castle doors. Instead of stopping in front of those, the carriage kept moving to the side of the castle, near what must've been a side entrance. Another large set of wooden doors were at the side, but not nearly as big as the main ones up front.

The carriage came to an abrupt halt. I could already feel eyes on the carriage, *eyes on me.* I definitely preferred to keep myself tucked safely into the shadows and not in front of a gaping crowd of people. Those same shadows had always been my closest companions in my lonely life, one of the few things that kept me calm.

I took a deep breath to calm my erratic breathing and closed my eyes, listening to the padding of the rain falling upon the roof of the carriage before I began my new life, my duty for my people.

You can do this. This is what you've been preparing for your whole life.

CHAPTER 5

he Goddess Aither's cold, wet air whipped the dark
fallen strands that escaped the intricate updo my
aunt's handmaiden spent over an hour on earlier this
morning. My skirts were slightly wrinkled from the journey
here and the sleeves on my gown were disheveled.

So much for the perfect first impression.

Turning on my heels to look at Radha, she still looked
like the epitome of elegance in her burnt orange dress flowing
behind her in a fiery wave. The golden spiked tiara sat atop
her head, with her chestnut hair pulled back to the nape of
her neck in a low braided bun.

She held out her hand for me to take as she led me to the
smaller castle doors. The flutter in my stomach quickly became
a quake the closer we got to those doors. Concentrating on
controlling my breathing, my foot almost slipped on the wet
rocks but Radha caught my arm and kept me straight.

"You must be the perfect Argyllian lady from this moment
on," she instructed as she gave my flesh a not-so-gentle
squeeze, biting into my skin with her nails. "Remember, this

is for our people and our country. You *cannot* ruin this."

Before I could muster a response, the doors opened before us revealing the monstrosity of a castle within. My eyes struggled to take in everything in front of me. Large stone walls with wooden doors that were scattered about, high stone pillars punctuated the foyer, and the ceiling touched the sky itself as firelight danced on the walls and even in the air, clearly controlled by magic.

Paintings hung on the stone walls within golden frames, everyone in them looking regal and important with crowns or small tiaras upon their heads. Careening my head to the side, I attempted to get a closer look at the portraits. I had never seen the King of Gambriel or his son, but my attention was pulled away by Radha's hand gripping mine tightly, pulling me back to the center of the foyer lined with the King's Guard.

My eyes caught on something adorning the walls above the paintings—well, not *just* something. A gigantic dragon skull was hung on the stone wall as if it were just an ornament. A descendent from our own Gods, used as a decoration.

My heart dropped to the pit of my stomach at the sight.

In the Gods' immortality, they grew bored of this life, of this land. No longer giving a damn about their people, they abandoned us and their children when they no longer wanted to fight for our country or our people. They left us to fend for ourselves, only until the great Kingdoms of Gambriel and Argyll came to help stave off the demons plaguing Menodore with their highly advanced fire torches.

The remaining dragons, the children of our Gods, were hunted down and slaughtered for their supposed threat to society. Once our Gods abandoned us, they had no say over their children and what we as a society did to them. I always knew that there were few and far between still alive to this day, but to see one's skull on the wall like a mere painting was otherworldly. That fire increased to a raging inferno and burned through my middle as disgust filled every fiber of my being.

People in great power tended to destroy things that they feared could take that power from them.

I had heard the stories that the fae warriors told in passing when they would visit the homes of the nobles or the castles. Some of the more powerful nobles began collecting the dragons as pets or trophies. The more dragons you captured, the more powerful you were for taming one. Taming a dragon to listen to your every beck and call was believed to be the highest achievement amongst the nobles and royals. If you could capture and control a beast of that magnitude, what *couldn't* you do?

But of course the dragons hadn't taken well to being captured, abused into submission, and held captive when they were used to roaming the lands, soaring through the skies, and enjoying the basic right we all wanted: *freedom*.

Their numbers dwindled over the last eighteen years from being hunted and if not tamed, then killed outright for being a threat. I was sure that the dragon's skull adorning the castle of Gambriel's walls was a failed attempt at a fancy pet.

My heart couldn't help but hurt for those dragons who were murdered for just existing as something different. I couldn't help but see the similarity between us and those mighty creatures.

Hunted. Captured. Killed or enslaved for being something different.

It was also known that after the siege of Menodore, the remaining dragons burned down the villages and the castle out of anger for the Gods' abandonment of themselves and our people. It gave the royals and nobles all the reason to go about their sadistic ways. A small tear started to fall from my eye but I batted it away before anyone caught my sadness.

To show emotions like that would be weak while surrounded by monsters.

"Three ballrooms, four hundred rooms, multiple guard's and servant's quarters, one giant library, and six separate gardens," said a booming voice that took me from my melancholy thoughts.

My glossy eyes snapped up and my breath caught in my throat. Standing before me had to be the most devastatingly beautiful man I had ever seen. No, not a man, but a High Fae male.

He was overtly masculine but tall and slim, his skin a lustrous golden brown tone. He wore a casual yellow tunic with black pants and leather boots. His slightly curly brown hair was pushed off of his face to reveal his alluring features and perfectly tousled from running his hand through it. Full lips, arched fae ears, sharp jawline that could cut glass, and *those eyes*.

My Gods, those eyes were something otherworldly. As blue as the Circadian waters, I could get lost in the deepest depths of the ocean in those eyes. His lips curled up into a half smile that flashed the sharp tip of his canine.

Radha quickly squeezed my hand again and brought me out of the trance-like daze I fell into.

"This is the Crown Prince of Gambriel, Wesley Harrington," my aunt remarked as she released my hand. Before my hand could fall back to my side, the Crown Prince wrapped his fingers around it and brought it to his lips.

His mouth gently brushed over the knuckles as he said, "It's lovely to meet you, Lady Cassandra." I held back the shiver building in my bones from the contact.

I dropped into a curtsy as I pulled my eyes down to the stone floor and replied automatically, "The pleasure is mine, Your Highness."

The prince dropped my hand, gripped my chin with a feather light touch, and brought my gaze from the floor back to his. My stomach pooled with warmth when our eyes met again. I'd never had someone touch me other than Radha or Evia and those touches weren't as light nor as caring as his. He smiled as he explained,"I would like to apologize on behalf of my father. The King is off dealing with an unexpected border conflict in the East for the next week. In the meantime, we can get you used to the castle while we wait for his arrival."

I nodded, my chin still held in his hand. He smiled at me again and I could've sworn my heart stopped beating for a second. The Crown Prince was beautiful. Charming. Gods, he was *dazzling*.

My heart pattered in my chest as the blood rushed to my ears. A male with charm could be a very precarious thing.

He released his grip on me and turned towards my aunt.

I could feel the anger pulsating off of Radha by the way she clenched her jaw. It was well known to address another noble before you address a commoner like myself but the Prince of Gambriel didn't seem to care about those formalities.

"How wonderful to see you again, Your Grace," Wesley said in a courteous manner as he took her hand and pressed a light kiss to it.

"You as well, Your Highness." Radha rearranged her expression of annoyance to one of pure bliss in a matter of seconds before she curtsied.

Prince Harrington turned towards Falkur and gave him a slight tilt of his head as Falkur bowed before him. Trying to hold back from fidgeting during this very strange encounter, I pulled my hands behind my back and stood straight while keeping a pleasant expression on my face.

"I do have some rather unfortunate news. My sweet Arron is still ill, so Falkur will be coming in his place as the King's Advisor." Radha gestured to Falkur as he turned a golden ring around his finger. "The weather delayed our travel by a couple of days, so we're actually running behind schedule. We are supposed to be in Lochlan for a meeting tonight with the Regency Council."

"All the way in Lochlan? That's a few hours by carriage from here," Wesley exclaimed as he turned towards the guard standing post near the doors. "Go alert the stables to get Her Grace fresh horses and to ready a carriage to Lochlan."

"Oh, thank you. You are too kind," my aunt said with a note of relief on her face as she turned back towards me and cupped my cheek with her slender hand. "My dear, I will see you again in about a week if all goes smoothly." She patted my cheek again before her black eyes turned cold for a split second. "Remember what I told you."

"Yes, Aunt Radha," I simply replied. I knew better than to ask questions, especially when she was all flustered about being late. Like where the hell was I staying and what the hell was going on? Why was she leaving me here so quickly? Did I have to share a room, *share a bed*, with a complete stranger? A stunning stranger at least, but nope. That was not happening.

"Sire!" A voice yelled, "The carriage is ready!"

"If you'll excuse me, Your Highness," Radha nodded and curtsied once more to the Crown Prince. Falkur murmured his goodbyes, rather rudely, as he bowed once again. Wesley ignored the slight and nodded his head in agreement before my aunt and Falkur disappeared back through the doors to the rain once more.

Intertwining my fingers behind my back, I squeezed them hard to distract myself from the uncomfortable situation my aunt just left me in. I understood that this male was meant to be my husband, but it didn't make it any less weird that we were standing there alone, just staring at each other. I didn't expect Radha to just drop me off and abandon me so quickly. She could've at least helped me get settled into wherever I would be staying.

"You must be exhausted from your journey," Wesley implied while he held his hand out in an 'after you' gesture. "Let's get you to your chambers to get more comfortable and then we can reconvene for dinner in a few hours?"

"I would gladly go to my chambers, if I knew where

they were," I laughed as I looked at his outstretched hand. Forgetting I was supposed to act like a docile pet, I mimed his gesture as I crooned, "Lead the way, Your Majesty."

He matched my smile with a beaming one of his own as he shook his head. "My apologies. You could say I'm a little nervous about this arrangement and I'm not too sure how to act. Please, if you'll follow me, I'll show you to your rooms."

The prince held out his arm for me to take and I gripped it, praying that he couldn't feel my sweaty palm through his shirt. We started walking down a corridor off to the side of the foyer, the stone walls filled with more paintings of the royal line. Above my head, crystal chandeliers hung from the rafters, reflecting the candlelight in a warm hue of colors. Despite it being a stone castle, there was a warmth to the air—no doubt controlled by magic as well.

The only sound was our footsteps as I cleared my throat to render the silence. "So why would you be nervous?"

He let out a breathy laugh, and heat pooled in my stomach again from that sultry sound. "It may be normal for arranged marriages amongst the royals and nobles but it doesn't stop it from being quite…hmm, what's the word I'm looking for?" Wesley pondered as he looked down at me with humor in those large blue eyes. "Awkward."

"Awkward?" I questioned with a laugh of my own, already feeling more at ease in his presence. There was just something about him that made me feel more comfortable. Like the eggshells I usually walked upon had turned to soft grass, welcoming every step I took.

"Yes, we're strangers and yet we're to be married, supposed

to spend the rest of our days together. What if we hated one another upon meeting?" He smiled with those bright teeth, a small dimple peeking through his right cheek. "Now that would be awkward."

I slapped his arm playfully with my free hand, once again forgetting what I was supposed to act like. "Let's hope it doesn't come to that. For both our sakes."

"Yes, let's hope." He let out that sultry laugh again as he stopped us in our tracks. "These are your rooms."

I scrunched my eyebrows, probably not the most lady-like gesture, but I couldn't help myself again when it came to this male.

Rooms?

CHAPTER 6

We stopped in front of large wooden doors with intricate carvings of dragons soaring through the skies over a flower-filled meadow. The dark wood was smooth and warm to the touch as I traced the artwork. Wesley gripped the golden handle and pushed the door open into the room. To call it a *room* was definitely an understatement. Now I understood exactly what he meant when he referred to it as *rooms*.

A wave of that warm air hit me as I stepped into the lavish sanctuary. Wesley dropped his arm. "This is where I leave you. Your chambermaid should be in there unpacking your things and will help you settle in. I'll come back to retrieve you for dinner in a few hours," he bowed at the waist and I held back a laugh at the gesture. "Until I see you again, Cassandra."

"I'll see you in a few hours, Your Highness." I dropped into a curtsy but he stopped the movement with his slender hands on my waist.

"You don't have to curtsy to me. I am to be your husband, not your master," he said with a soft smile as he released me and turned away to walk back down the hallway.

Standing there dumbfounded by what he had just said, I could feel the ghost of his hands warmth around my middle. I had never had anyone speak to me that way before. Like I was a person and not just some pawn in their royal games. All the training I received over the past eighteen years seemed to melt away from those few words.

He didn't want to *own* me. He wanted a partner in this alliance, and not just some pretty face he could boss around like I expected. I was taught to be submissive and always agreeable, but now I had no idea *how* to act around him.

Turning back into the room with a flutter of butterflies going insane in my chest, I took everything in. The first room looked like it was some sort of sitting or dining room. A deep brown worn leather couch with matching armchairs sat in front of a crackling fireplace and a small dining table that could seat four people was off to the side of it. I could already imagine myself curling up with a book and a blanket there during a thunderstorm. At the end of the sitting room was another door that led to the bedroom with an attached dressing room and a separate bathing chamber.

A canopy-covered bed that could easily sleep a family of seven sat in the center of the bedroom, bedecked in soft yellow and cream-colored blankets and pillows. The linens matched the yellow silk curtains that framed the windows perfectly. I ran my hand along the soft cotton sheets as I made my way to the stained glass doors leading out to my own balcony.

Small candelabras dangled from the ceiling and walls, bathing the room in their soft light. The rooms were lavish, fit for a king, but warm and cozy nonetheless. I padded excitedly over to the balcony on the other side of the bedroom and opened the double glass doors.

A fine sheet of rain consistently fell from the sky, the gray clouds overhead rumbling like a ravenous beast about to devour his prey. A flash of lightning struck, like the God of Thunder, Evander, was answering the roar moving through the clouds. My balcony overlooked one of the six gardens with neatly trimmed bushes, benches throughout the paths, and bright blooming flowers of all sorts soaking up the rain from overhead.

It was like something out of a dream.

Some of the flowers couldn't even bloom in this area—especially with this bad of weather and the rotten soil plaguing the land—let alone prosper like they have. Whoever was this castle's gardener needed a raise and a giant glass of wine.

Closing the balcony doors, I turned back around to continue exploring my new rooms. There was another fireplace in front of my bed, loaded with wood already burning into dancing embers. To the right of the fireplace was the door for the bathing chamber that was already ajar, and to the left was a dressing room which led to my closet.

My closet. Fuck.

I needed to find that trunk with my training gear before anyone else did.

Rushing to the dressing room, I threw back the closet door in a hurry to find a small woman with blonde ringlet curls going through my trunks and dispersing the items throughout a closet that was bigger than my old bedroom.

The little woman yelped and dropped the dress she was about to hang up and looked up at me with large, startled gray eyes. She dropped into a curtsy, her curls bouncing from the movement as she stuttered, "I- I- I'm so sorry, my lady." She quickly grabbed the fallen dress and smoothed it back out with ghostly pale hands before hanging it on the rack. "I was just putting all your things away. I am Minka, your chambermaid. I am here to make sure you're bathed, fed, dressed and well rested."

I put out my hand to Minka as I introduced myself, "It's lovely to meet you, Minka. I'm Cassandra and I apologize for scaring you earlier. Prince Wesley did mention I would be meeting you somewhere in my rooms and I got a little taken away with the exploring," I explained as I smiled warmly at her.

Minka stared at my outstretched hand as if introductions were a foreign concept. I put it back at my side before I could make this interaction anymore uncomfortable than it already was. The fact that I towered over her probably didn't help that I was trying to be warm and inviting, not intimidating. She was truly tiny, probably only five feet tall with a few extra inches compared to my almost six foot height. She wore a black matching servant's uniform with a white apron tapering to her small waist with matching tattered shoes.

"I don't mean to be rude, my lady. It's just that I'm not used to serving another human, let alone someone who is as kind as you," my chambermaid voiced as her gray eyes began to soften.

"Please, call me Cassandra. None of that 'my lady'

bullshit." I laughed as her eyes almost bulged out of her head from my casual use of a curse word. "I came in here looking for a specific trunk that is very personal to me. Do you mind if I have a look around for it and unpack it myself?"

"Not at all. I'll give you some privacy to go through it and get you a nice bath going so you can freshen up before dinner, my la—errr, I mean, Cassandra," Minka quickly corrected herself before leaving the closet in a hurry.

I waited until I could hear the door click shut behind me before I sprang into action. In under five minutes, I had already located the trunk, threw the dresses out of it, hung up my training clothes and shoved the knives, tar, and boots in the bottom drawer of one of the dressers along the wall.

"I'll be seeing you very soon," I whispered to the inanimate objects encasing my sanity before I headed to the bathing room.

Throughout most of my life, all of my choices had been made for me. I never had control over what I got to wear, eat, learn, read, or even who I was allowed to talk to. But every night when I would sneak out and practice, I could finally take that control back. It was the only thing that I had chosen for myself in the past eighteen years and it was the only thing keeping me from spiraling from the loss of control over my life.

Minka leaned over the largest claw-foot bathtub I had ever seen, pouring in different types of oils and soaps that perfumed the air with the soft smells of lavender and vanilla. The aroma instantly put my mind at ease before I noticed the gigantic window upon the ceiling above the bathtub that would show a perfect view of the night sky, if not for the incessant downpour.

I took a seat at the vanity in the corner and started the task of unpinning my wind blown hair. The sound of the water filling the tub abruptly came to a stop as soft footsteps came closer to me. My new chambermaid was behind me, removing the pins herself as she insisted, "My—" she corrected herself, "—Cassandra, let me help you. This is a part of my duties, after all."

"Thank you." I shot her a bright smile that took her by surprise. I was probably already being too much, too friendly and I didn't want to scare her with my loud personality. Laying my hands in my lap, I let Minka go to town on my hair while I studied my reflection. I once read in a book that the eyes were a window to the soul, but every time I looked into my eyes, I didn't even see a glimpse of my soul. The soft demure lady who looked back at me didn't match the constant fire burning in my chest. Eventually, you just stopped looking for the one you would recognize and became acquainted with the stranger staring back at you.

Minka finished unpinning my hair, brushed out any remaining tangles, and started to help untie my dress from the back. I caught the dress before it could slide down my shoulders and shooed her out of the room as I said with a trickle of laughter, "I draw the line at helping me bathe myself."

Minka giggled at that, the sound like a soft melody filling the air. "As you wish. I'm going to finish putting everything away in the closet but please don't hesitate to call for me if you need anything," she trilled back as the door closed behind her.

My dress fell to the ground while I made my way over to the steaming tub of heaven. I popped the tight joints in my neck, arms, and fingers as the heat of the water bit at my now pink skin in a sinfully exquisite way.

My endless thoughts raced through my mind as my tired body relaxed. Every time I closed my eyes I saw those piles of burning bodies just outside the city. Did the Crown Prince know about them? How would he feel knowing that his own soldiers were the cause of all of that death?

I needed to figure out a way to stop the ruination of this kingdom. I was supposed to be a pillar of hope, of change, and I needed that change to happen quickly before any more lives were lost. Radha's stoic face while looking at the demise of hundreds popped into my brain next. How was I supposed to implement the change we needed in this continent when its own rulers seemed like they couldn't care less?

Shoulders loosening, I released a ruffled sigh. I had always loved the rain and brutal storms that followed. It showed that even the sky and Gods living within them, needed to scream out of frustration sometimes. Tipping my head back to stare at the gleaming sprinkle of stars trying to peek through the endless downfall, I attempted to bask in a moment of peace before dinner with the handsome stranger I was supposed to marry.

CHAPTER 7

The windows of the castle trembled from the thunder rolling across the skies as Minka escorted me to the dining room. I ran a nervous, sweaty palm down the citrine yellow gown my chambermaid insisted I wear tonight. I still was not too sure how I was supposed to sit at a table and eat a complete meal in this monstrosity of a dress.

I glared down at the corset that was keeping my ribs prisoner and hoisting my breasts up to my chin, making every step all the more difficult to breathe. The matching yellow skirts were built of layers upon layers of both tulle and silk, causing a swishing noise with every step I took. My long brown hair was pulled back into a mess of curls on top of my head with pearls and gems woven throughout. Soft curled tendrils framed my face that Minka dusted with matching glitter and light pink blush.

She groomed me within an inch of my life after my relaxing bath. Skin scrubbed a raw pink, hair plucked and so heavily perfumed in the different oils and balms that it brought a slight burning to my nose when I inhaled.

"You look like a princess," Minka commented as we made our way down the hall. "But you must stop fidgeting in that dress. Is it too uncomfortable? Should we go back and try another one on?"

"No," I answered too abruptly. We just spent the last hour trying on dress after dress until Minka had convinced me to wear this yellow ball of fabric thinking the representation of Gambriel's colors would please the Prince at our dinner. "Once I am out of this dress, you will not be able to put me back in this one or any other for the rest of the evening," I joked as my chambermaid fussed over the skirts.

"Can I get that in writing?" A masculine voice asked from a distance.

My head immediately shot to the figure who commented, ready to tell him where he could shove that remark before I realized who was now walking towards us.

"Prince Wesley." I quickly looked down and bent into a curtsy out of habit.

A warm, soft hand wrapped around mine and brought me back up to my normal height so we were now eye to eye—well, more like my eyes to his neck. He was dressed in the same attire as earlier but his brown skin glowed in the candlelight, making him seem so ethereal.

"Cassandra, you look absolutely delightful," he purred my name and I couldn't help the shiver that radiated down my arm that he currently encased in his. I didn't know if I would ever get used to all this free touching, no matter how much I adored it. "I hope you were able to settle in and relax some before dinner. Are the accommodations to your liking so far?"

"Yes, my rooms are beyond anything I expected. I must thank you for the kindness and generosity you've already bestowed upon me, Your Majesty."

"You should get used to it. You are to be my wife—and please, call me Wesley." He grinned down at me, his blue eyes twinkling as he patted my arm. "Come. I will escort you and Minka can finish preparing your rooms."

I turned to thank Minka but she bowed to the Prince with a timid, "If you'll excuse me, Your Highness," before scampering back down the hall.

Wesley led me down the corridor until we came upon a room full of music and laughter. I stopped and craned my neck to get a better look. It was the entrance of a vast throne room filled with fae of all types; more tiny pixies fluttering about, goblins chugging ale, forest nymphs moving slowly like branches in a soft wind, and High Fae in elegant but revealing gowns and intricate two-piece outfits for the males mingling amongst each other. Fae of every color, shape and size gyrated in splendor with one another. Not a care in the world for them because they were *free*. Holding back from clenching my fists, I bit my tongue instead because just outside this castle was nothing but death of those that wanted what these fae so easily had.

Grunts and lust filled moans littered the air alongside their seductive music. A few couples were not so hidden in the alcoves of the room, kissing, sucking and... my cheeks heated as I looked away. My breathing quickened with the realization that they were having sex in front of everyone. I knew the fae gave in to their inhibitions, but never at this rate.

Wesley turned my gaze from the floor and back to his. "We will be dining in another room, Cassandra. This is one of the never-ending parties my mother throws."

"Your mother?" I squeaked out.

"Yes, she is the Consort of the King. So it is a part of her duties to host parties in the good nature of our kingdom," he replied with a laugh. "Some of them get a little more wild than the others."

"Are they always so... intimate?"

"Well, that is completely up to those in attendance. Some parties stay on the more modest side, but sometimes they are for giving into our natural selves, our instincts. It would be a dishonor to turn our back on our truest selves and what the Gods have blessed us with. Our lives, our youth, our *fertility*." Wesley chuckled the last word. "But not everyone has to participate. My mother has gotten more into her parties over the last few years," his voice started to trail off with a hint of sadness behind it.

My cheeks started to catch aflame as I looked down, too embarrassed to make eye contact with him again. He gave my arm a quick tug away from the entrance. "I apologize if that made you uncomfortable. I know humans are raised sometimes to act more modestly but it is quite normal for my kind to witness such things," Wesley divulged. "But still quite weird to think of my own mother being involved. I steer clear of them at the off chance I could see her doing something I most definitely don't want to witness."

I met his cool blue gaze as I explained, "No need for an apology. Just something I'm not used to yet. As you may know, I was raised very sheltered from the world; so a lot may come as a surprise to me."

He smiled, that same dimple showing on his right cheek. "Duly noted. I'll try to lessen the blow of the surprises as much as I can."

I matched his smile with a soft one of my own, trying to act as demure as I possibly could. My arm still in his, he then led me to a dining room just a few doors down from the throne room, but far enough away that it drowned out the noise from the orgy happening in the next room.

A long banquet table sat in the center of the room along with a roaring fireplace and a leather couch directly in front of it. A black rug with gold interlaced fibers ran underfoot, with more portraits of male royals upon the walls, and candles everywhere illuminating the room with their soft glow. The table was only set for two but could easily sit a large family and had a smattering of all types of foods. My mouth started to water from the enticing scents of roasted chicken, seasoned potatoes, fluffy rolls, and endless amounts of fresh fruits and cooked vegetables.

Wesley helped me to my seat by pulling the chair out for me as I sat. I fixed myself to the correct position, hands in lap, shoulders back and feet tucked under my chair. Human servants dressed in matching black and yellow attire rushed to fill my glass and the Prince's with faerie wine.

Wesley thanked the server before he lifted the glass in a cheer to me with a bright smile, so comfortable in his own skin; I wish I knew how that felt. I returned the smile but reached for the water in front of me instead.

"Is something the matter with the wine?" He asked with curiosity before taking a sip of his.

"It's just… It's… faerie wine," I replied, trying to not sound ungrateful. Humans couldn't just consume faerie wine without facing the consequences. Our bodies were not made to handle the same level of magic as the fae. To them, it was just a light buzz like any normal drink; but for humans, it was dangerous. It removed all of our inhibitions, showed our deepest desires, and caused us to forget everything that we may have done.

My bracelet may protect me from their magic but I never tested how it worked against literally *consuming* magic. I was not about to black out from one sip and do something absolutely embarrassing that Radha would have to come here and wring my neck for.

"Ah, yes. I almost forgot," Wesley said as he pushed a container of salt my way. "Put a sprinkle of the salt in and it'll neutralize the magic that's in it and make it to where it won't affect you that way."

I eyed the salt in front of me in dismay as he continued on, "Salt has iron in it, and iron is the one thing that can suppress magic. So if you put just a pinch, not enough to ruin the taste, it will take away the magical properties that cause those effects on humans. We have countless humans who enjoy our wine that way."

My eyes went wide at the declaration of humans enjoying the faerie wine. I did learn in my lessons how some humans had normal day to day jobs and weren't enslaved like most. This alliance was about giving more humans that same freedom. But to think of those lucky enough to not be in chains, enjoying the products made by the same fae enslaving our kind left me baffled.

I pushed that thought to the back of my mind as I took a small pinch of the salt, just like he instructed, and stirred it into the glass with my spoon. Staring at the swirling liquid, I forced my shoulders to relax and gripped the glass in front of me.

Fuck it.

I took a cautious sip, and the Prince eyed me as he sipped his own. I let the smooth liquid make its way down my esophagus, warming my stomach immediately. The servants started pilling all types of the food onto my plate as I enjoyed another sip of the sweet red faerie wine. "It's delicious," I murmured above my glass.

The Prince smiled again, flashing the sharp tip of his canine before he brought his own glass back up and downed the whole thing with a wink. I couldn't help but let out a giggle at how improper it was in a formal dining setting. Evia would've confiscated that wine glass so quickly if she saw.

Evia.

My heart swelled in my chest for her because I didn't think I would miss her crass, abrasive self so quickly. I still felt unbelievably guilty for not saying goodbye to her. Hopefully she would be here for the wedding and I could see her again soon.

Another servant came up and placed a small roll on the side of my plate. His too skinny and pale arm reaching forward pushed forth the memory of a blood covered, limp hand laying in the dirt as Gambriellian soldiers picked up the body and discarded it into one of those carts. My gaze shifted to the glass of red wine in front of me and all I saw was the blood of those murdered disgracing the inside of it.

My stomach twisted and turned despite my hunger. Bile started to rise up my throat, creating a burning sensation throughout my chest. I wanted to ask Wesley about all of those people but after Radha's constant berating of my questions, I bit my tongue once again.

Wesley noticed the change in my expression and he probed while refilling his own glass, "Is something the matter, Cassandra?"

Radha's remarks circled through my mind on repeat, filling it with the reminder of what I needed to do.

Of *who* I needed to be.

You must be the perfect Argyllian lady from this moment on.

Your flaws and misgivings are a direct representation of Argyll; of your uncle and I.

Don't show them your imperfections.

You cannot ruin this.

You must be perfect.

I forced the bile back down and plastered a fake smile on my face as I lied, "No, nothing at all."

Pushing more of those gut wrenching questions to the back of my brain, I wondered if it would explode from filling it with so many unanswered and worrisome thoughts. Wesley was still staring at me with his azure eyes, like he was studying me.

Before he could question any further, I lightly cut up my chicken and I bit back a moan from the deliciousness as it settled on my tongue. My hunger was back in full force as I took another drink of wine, causing my body and mind to relax again. I wanted to gorge myself and shove all this amazing food straight down my throat but I knew that was not very *lady-like.* So I took my small, dainty bites and concentrated on still trying to look as lovely as possible while eating. I wanted to sigh as I ate and do a little shimmy in my chair as the delicious flavors danced across my tongue.

"It's sadly too late in the evening to take you on a tour of the castle after we finish eating but I would love to take you on one after breakfast tomorrow morning, if that is something you would like?" Wesley inquired as he speared a piece of chicken without looking.

I finished my bite and swallowed before I responded, "Yes, that would be lovely. I've never been to a castle before, let alone one quite this beautiful, so a tour would be very helpful in not getting lost trying to find the dining room."

His melodic laughter filled the air as he joked, "I've lived here for my whole life and I still get lost sometimes, whether I have myself to blame or the wine," he held up his second glass of said wine. "It'll take some getting used to but I have no doubt that you'll manage. It only took my sister fifty years to get the hang of it, so I should be there in no time."

"Fifty years?" I laughed. "Wait, your sister? I didn't know you had a sister."

Wesley's blue eyes turned into pools of sadness as he nodded, "Her name was Carina."

My heart dropped along with my silverware. "Was?"

"She died in the Siege of Menodore, trying to help pull survivors out of the destruction in the village. Ever since then, my mother has thrown more parties as a way of distracting herself from losing her first child. She was my older sister and my best friend, despite being a hundred years older than I." He pushed the food along his plate with one hand as he sipped the wine with the other. "She was an amazing person but she is with our Gods now."

I held my glass up with a trembling smile, holding back the tears from falling. "To Carina, savior of Menodore."

His eyes warmed as they met mine and he clinked my glass with his own. "To Carina."

Downing my remaining wine in sync with him, then filling our glasses back up myself, I asked, "So how old are you exactly?"

He flashed me a smile full of white teeth. "One hundred and fifteen years old."

I couldn't help my expression as my eyes practically bulged out of my head. "One hundred and fifteen?" I asked in disbelief.

Wesley nodded, his brown hair fell forward with the movement and he brushed it back with his hand. Maybe it was the wine but I mumbled with a smile, "positively ancient if you ask me."

He let out a loud laugh. "And how old are you, Cassandra? Clearly not a day over eighty," he said with a wink.

I wanted to throw my napkin at him for that comment but I only rolled my eyes. "I'm almost twenty three. Well, I will be in less than a month."

"We're practically the same age... If we're counting yours in dog years, maybe." He waggled his brown eyebrows at me.

It was my turn to laugh. "Did you just call me a dog?"

"Bark, bark, Cassandra." He lifted his glass, "Cheers."

"You're closer related to a dog than I am, faerie," I said with a teasing glare.

He lifted both his eyebrows, "Touché." I clinked my glass against his and again he went on, "This might not be as awkward I initially thought it would. You're very easy to get along with, Cassandra. And truly gorgeous as well."

My cheeks warmed from the compliment that I wasn't used to receiving, or from the third glass of wine, as I looked back down at my plate and ate more of the delicious food before me. Over the course of dinner, Wesley went over the different parts of the castle and what their functions were, his kingdom, and his people. He wasn't what I expected of a future faerie ruler, he was kind and thought very highly of all of his people, humans included.

I was raised with the similar prejudice that the fae held towards humans except for me, I was taught to *fear* the High Fae. Because of their magic and greed and cunning words, I had to protect myself not only with the magic repelling bracelet but also with my nightly training. I wasn't sure how Wesley was brought up, but he seemed to not hold any disdain towards my kind.

He graciously thanked the servants each time they brought him something and I know that should be common courtesy but that wasn't the usual treatment for people like myself.

We eventually made our way to the couch in front of the fireplace with another fresh glass of wine as we moved away from the subject of his kingdom and onto what we liked to do in our spare time.

It turned out the Crown Prince of Gambriel was an avid reader, such as myself, and the castle had a gigantic library that he promised to take me to first thing after breakfast. He loved spending his time outside, riding horses, hunting game, and going on new adventures. It was truly hard not to admire him. His unyielding sense of dedication to his kingdom, his love for life and everything surrounding it.

As the evening went on, we gradually got closer to one another on the couch. The troubling thoughts that plagued my mind, drifted away from the playful banter Wesley kept up. We swapped tales and jokes as our thighs slowly began to touch from sitting too closely to one another. I savored his warmth soaking into my skin through the skirts of my yellow gown and the way his cerulean eyes watched my movement with kindness and something else I couldn't name.

My thoughts came easily and naturally with him, not having to worry and stumble over every word while being afraid of saying something outrageous. If I did, he would match my jest with something even more far fetched or even so inappropriate that Evia would have blushed from hearing it before swatting him.

I could've gotten used to nights like this. Not being what I was told to be, but being someone I *wanted* to be.

CHAPTER 8

After dinner and far too many glasses of faerie wine, Wesley walked me back to my room with my hand tucked into his arm. He leaned down and pressed a soft kiss on my cheek as he whispered, "I'll see you tomorrow morning, Cassandra."

Blushing from the contact, all I could do was nod before he walked away. I moved my hand to my face, directly where his lips touched, and could still feel the warmth of his kiss. I smiled to myself before turning into my room.

Minka was waiting for me in my bedroom, silk nightgown in hand and a small smile on her exhausted face. She gestured towards the vanity for me to take a seat so she could start the process of undoing her marvelous work from earlier. I scampered over to my seat and plopped down, less gracefully than I initially intended.

Damned faerie wine.

As Minka removed pin after pin in comfortable silence, I studied my reflection. The girl who stared back at me was different from the one from earlier. My green eyes were shining bright, cheeks full of color and life, pink lips still tipped up into a smile, and even the tip of my nose had some rosy color to it.

That girl was different, she was happy and alive.

Alive. Not dead. Unlike thousands, if not millions, of other humans in this realm.

My smile dropped from the reminder.

I peeked up at Minka hard at work on my hair still. Her gray eyes looked washed out, with dark circles under them and her cheekbones hollow. When was *her* last meal? Or the last time *she* got to rest?

I couldn't help the sick feeling in my stomach. The never-ending *guilt*. Here I was galavanting around a gorgeous castle with a beautiful faerie prince, sipping wine, eating the finest of foods and wearing phenomenal gowns crafted for royalty. While others like myself would never know such luxury, only pain and famine caused by the family of monsters I was marrying into.

I cleared my throat before I asked, "Minka, if you don't mind my asking. When was the last time you had something to eat?"

My chambermaids eyes went large as we stared at each other in the mirror. Her hands stopped their work as she just stared at me in shock.

"Minka?" I probed again.

"I'm sorry. It's just... I... No one here has ever asked me a question like that," she stuttered as her hands returned to grooming me. "Us servants get one meal a day, around our break time, so the last time I ate would be earlier this morning."

"You only get one meal a day?" I questioned, trying to hide the indignation in my voice. No wonder she looked so exhausted and worn down.

Minka nodded in response as she turned her concentration to the back of my head.

"How many breaks a day do you get? Only the one for the meal?"

She nodded again and my stomach turned in disgust, the meal from earlier trying to make its way back up my throat.

That was barbaric.

Before I could ask any more questions, Minka gestured for me to stand and helped me out of the piles of yellow fabric that were considered a dress. I slipped on the silk nightgown as Minka gathered everything off the floor and headed to the door.

"I will be back in the morning, my lady," she whispered while looking down at her tattered shoes. "If you need anything before then, just ring the golden bell near the fireplace in the sitting room."

"Thank y—" I tried to get out but she was out the door immediately and I was completely alone.

Fuck. Fuck. Fuck.

It hadn't even been a day and there already needed to be serious changes around here. Was I supposed to just turn a blind eye to what was happening here as well? My mind was already full of unanswered questions and the need to fix this absolute shitshow of a continent. How was I supposed to act like I was perfectly fine becoming a part of the royal group that mistreated my kind so horribly?

Shit. Fuck. Dammit.

I couldn't lose focus on why I was here.

Yes, for marrying the Prince, but that was to create a better world. A place where fae, humans, and any person could live in harmony. Not one where human slaves got one meal and break a day.

Clenching my fists in anger as I gritted my teeth, I started to pace again.

That was my purpose and I needed to feel protected while surrounded by creatures that could kill me within a blink of an eye.

I took the opportunity of being left alone and rushed to the closet to pull out my dagger belt. I ran my warm hand over the cool metal of the blades before returning to the bedroom and standing before my floor length mirror. I needed to find a place to train from now on but this would have to do for tonight.

Sitting down to stretch my tight limbs on the floor, I savored the burning feeling of my muscles being pulled taunt. After countless stretches that loosened me up and helped with my flexibility, I unsheathed one of the blades and practiced my movements in the mirror. Back and forth, on my feet as I struck my opponent in the mirror. The anger and rage pulsed in my veins as Minka's words circled in on repeat.

Only one meal a day.

I ducked and feigned another strike as if it were a real duel. That raging inferno filled every fiber of my being when I saw those exhausted gray eyes filled my mind.

One meal a day.

Parry, strike, parry, strike, parry, strike.

I repeated the movements until sweat beaded down my forehead and moved on to my next set of exercises. Push ups, sit ups, squats, and anything I could do to strengthen my frail, human body.

I looked back into the mirror at the girl before me, nightgown drenched in sweat, face red and muscles aching. "You will not be weak," I repeated over and over until I worked my way into shaking exhaustion and fell into bed for another night full of the nightmares I needed to protect myself from.

But not only myself; I needed to protect my kind from them as well. I laid there for a while before drifting off to sleep, thinking of ways I could help Minka *before* I married into a position of power. I didn't know how soon that would be and how much power I would actually have—let alone how much time Minka would have, from the look of her body that was slowly breaking down.

CHAPTER 9

I awoke with another pounding headache; it seemed that just because the effects of the faerie wine weren't as extreme, it didn't mean the consequences would be any less severe. I reached for a glass of water that wasn't there and came back to the realization that I was not in my room at the Bellator Fortress in Argyll, but in the Great Castle of Gambriel.

I groaned while I got out of bed and made my way to the bathing chamber to relieve my too full bladder. There was a glass next to the sink and I poured myself some water to clear out the disgusting taste from my mouth. Upon leaving the chamber, I heard shuffling coming from my closet. I headed over and opened the door to reveal Minka rifling through the dresses, no doubt looking for what I should wear for the day.

"Good morning, Minka," I said while she was comparing two dresses side by side.

She turned her head towards me, gray eyes tired looking still. "Good Morning, Cassandra. Would you like to wear blue or red today?"

I smiled softly, "your choice. Whatever you think is best."

She settled upon a dark, navy gown that was a mixture of ruffles and lace, no corset this time. Thank the Gods. I didn't know how I'd go about the whole day not being able to breathe. Minka was quiet as she went about styling my hair with two small combs that swept the sides up, leaving the rest to trail behind me in a sea of dark brown tresses. I tried making conversation but her answers were short and clipped, so I didn't pry anymore. I really hoped I didn't embarrass her or something when asking about her meals yesterday.

A knock came at the door as Minka was helping me into the navy slippers that were the perfect match for the dress. I knew that they weren't mine because I had never seen them before, just like the yellow gown from last night. Radha must've sent some ahead of time for me to have here.

"That should be the Prince," Minka suggested as she smoothed the lace sleeves of my gown. "I believe he is taking you on a tour of the castle after breakfast. Is there anything I can get for you before you go?"

"No, thank you. I seem to be all set." I smiled down at her head full of blonde curls. She seemed more rested today, the circles under her eyes weren't as deep as they were the night before but I could still see the malnourishment in her hollow cheeks. Maybe I could ask the Prince about something we could do for her, or I could just figure out something myself.

I preferred the latter for the time being, until I knew how the Prince truly felt about the treatment of the humans he had here. Just one night of watching him treat us with common decency wasn't enough for me to trust him at that level.

Either way, there was no way I could just sit by and watch

someone fade away. If I was being complacent about their treatment, I was just as bad as the ones enslaving them. No fucking way in hell would I be a part of that.

Another rap on the door pulled me from my thoughts. Minka led me to the doors and opened them to reveal the Crown Prince clad in a light brown ensemble with gleaming brown leather boots and an award winning smile plastered on his perfectly fae face.

"Good Morning, Cassandra," he drawled as he gave me a look over. "You look absolutely ravishing today."

The Prince then held out his arm for me and I graciously took it as I smiled back, "Thank you, Your Highness. Minka is the one responsible for the choice in gown and hair. She truly is a gem and a wonderful help. I don't know how I would get on without her."

I planted the first seed. She deserved better treatment. They all did.

He looked at a blushing Minka and smiled genuinely, "Yes, she truly is. A wonderful help. Thank you, Minka."

My chambermaid curtsied at the Prince before excusing herself back into my rooms to clean up the aftermath of getting me ready this morning.

"Shall we go to breakfast?" Wesley offered.

I nodded my reply and he kept my arm in his as we walked to wherever breakfast was being held this morning. He made a sharp left turn where I could've sworn we should've taken a right to get to where we were the night before. We walked through another hallway with more paintings on the wall. I searched for one that might be similar to Wesley, hoping I could catch a glimpse of his departed sister, Carina.

Disappointment filled me at being surrounded only by older High Fae males, clearly the nobles in the Kingdom. I squeezed the Prince's arm nervously as I questioned, "Where are we going?"

"It's a beautiful day, I figured we could have breakfast in the Western Gardens and then I could take you to the library and give you the rest of the tour," he explained as he put his other hand over mine in a comforting gesture.

Gardens.

Perfect. I needed to get the layout of the gardens and courtyards if I wanted to get any training done not inside the confines of my rooms. Beautiful as they may be, I would still feel suffocated having to spend a majority of my time there. I focused on the steps we were taking and how to get back out here so I could explore further by myself later.

Two Gambriellian guards in gleaming gold armor stood in front of two giant wooden doors and opened them in sync as the Prince and I approached. Out of the corner of my eye I could see a small group of High Fae nobles standing off to the side. An older and tall red haired male dressed in jewels and golden finery kept his hazel eyes on us as we walked through the doors. I could feel his glare burning a hole into my back where mine and Wesley's bodies were touching.

He clearly had a dislike for my kind and for this arrangement. He wouldn't be the first to disagree, nor would he be the last, but people like me shouldn't have to live forever in fear.

We *deserved* our freedom.

Ignoring him and keeping my head high, we stepped out to see that the rain from the night before left everything in the gardens looking fresh and green. Bright sun shone down on us and the flowers around, perfuming the air with their exotic scents. Small marble statues were scattered about by the entrance of the castle, and a large white fountain with the Goddess Aither soaring through the skies was carved into the base of it.

"That fountain is gorgeous," I said as I stepped closer to it and marveled at the artist's work. It was the perfect depiction carved into the stone, looking identical to the few paintings I had seen in the castle.

"Yes, it is." Wesley admired it by my side, "I'll show you some of the other ones he's done as well. The artist's name is Carden Amour, he's done most of the statues in this garden too. Truly remarkable work. He's been working for my father for about four hundred years now. Before the Gods left us, my father loved having depictions of the Goddess Aither surrounding him as a reminder and a thanks for her magical blessing."

I gripped Wesley's arm again as we started walking further into the gardens. "What is the King's magical blessing?"

"He is blessed after Aither, with the power of the winds and all the air surrounding us." A cold gust of wind swept through my hair and ruffled my dress as he went on, "Just like I am."

I looked up at him, azure eyes dancing with delight as he held his free hand up and swirls of small leaves turned in his palm like a mini tornado. "I'm not as magically strong as him though, he's had hundreds of years to perfect his magic, but mine is getting stronger and better everyday."

I watched the tornado swirl and go higher until it disappeared in a snap, the leaves falling into the palm of his hand as I murmured in awe, "Truly remarkable." I fiddled with the bracelet at my wrist, thankful for its protection as I wondered how dangerous that type of magic was. So far, the Crown Prince's kindness showed that he wasn't going to attempt to kill me with it.

Wesley grinned, "Come on, there's someone I want you to meet."

We rounded a corner of more shrubbery that seemed to climb higher the further into the garden we went. I spotted a High Fae female standing near one of the bushes of roses, rich brown hands outstretched, stroking the petals, making the flowers bloom in her hands. Her gorgeous face was turned down in a sad frown as she concentrated on the flower, a hint of sorrow peeking through her strong demeanor. She wore a pale blue dress that gathered low on the swells of her breasts, nearly translucent with a golden underdress beneath it. Her raven black hair was in individual braids with different colors weaving through them creating a rainbow on top of her head and trailing down to the center of her back.

She was *beautiful.*

"Mother," Wesley chimed as he walked us over to her. "How are your girls doing after the rain from last night?"

Oh shit. This was his mother. The Consort to the King of Gambriel.

I immediately did a once over to check my posture and

gave her a warm smile. The sadness from earlier was gone from her expression as she stared with love shining in her blue eyes at her son. "They seemed to have loved it. I have been out here all morning, going around and checking through them to make sure they're okay and thriving."

I was assuming by girls, they both meant her plants. She was a foliage faerie from the look of it, the type that could influence the earth and anything that grew from it. The kind that were keeping our continent alive and well through the slow death of our lands.

Their magic came from the God of the Earth and had the power of geokinesis—also known as the power to manipulate the lands, rocks, plants, and animals. Ragnar helped rule over the court of Fons, on the continent of Atrium, which was known for their luscious gardens teeming with life.

I had read about her before when studying Gambriel's history. Her name was Keva Harrington, Consort to the King for the past two hundred and fifty years. I wondered how much Carina, Wesley's sister, looked like her, and what type of magic she had been blessed with.

The Consort was definitely in that crowd we saw in the throne room last night. My cheeks started to heat once more from the memory of it, but I pushed those thoughts down with everything else and focused on the present.

"I'm happy to hear that," the prince told his mother as she turned to me, waiting for the introduction even though I already knew who she was and she, I. "Cassandra, this is my mother, Keva."

Not the Consort of Gambriel or wife to the King.

But his mother, Keva.

I took my arm from his and curtsied as I looked down, "It's lovely to meet you, Your Grace." I came out of my curtsy and gave her the best smile I could muster up, "Your gardens are absolutely breathtaking."

That seemed to make the Consort smile even more, flashing an elongated canine. "Thank you, dear. They are my pride and joy." She stroked another bush of roses, causing them to bloom and perfume the air with their intoxicating scent. "If you'll excuse me, I have much to attend to as I have only gone through the Western Gardens this morning and need to check on the others."

Keva patted her son's cheek with love and turned to me with bright blue eyes. "It's lovely to meet you officially, Cassandra."

I curtsied again as she departed and turned to Wesley. "You have her eyes." I was surprised by how the Consort actually greeted me and didn't sneer at me like the noble inside. I could already see where Wesley got his kindness and alluring good looks from.

"Indeed I do, I wish I had her influence over nature as well. But alas, we can't have everything," the prince winked at me and my heart stuttered for a moment before he continued, "Come, the table is set right over here."

We took another few turns through the luscious garden until we came up to a small metal table covered in bacon, assortments of cut fruit, sweet rolls, eggs, potatoes, and different meats I didn't even know the name of.

Wesley pulled my chair out for me as I said, "Well you

know what they say, if you have a garden and a library, you have everything you need."

"Wait until you see the library then," he gave me a conspiratorial grin that I matched with my own.

We ate our breakfast in comfortable companionship, talking about different types of magic as my headache slowly faded with the amazing food I stuffed my face with. The large cups of tea with ridiculous amounts of sugar certainly helped it fade as well.

After breakfast we walked around the gardens some more. Wesley showed me his favorite parts of it and I spotted a dirt trail that led out to a smaller building near the forest outside of the castle. I took a mental note to check that out later and see if that could be my new spot for training.

After that, it was time to see the library that the castle had to offer. I was bristling with excitement at the thought of being surrounded by books and the ability to pick them out for myself, finally.

More guards were stationed outside the large double doors, muscles shifting as they pushed against the worn oak. It was moderately bright, the large crystal chandelier hanging from the center of the ceiling illuminating the white marble floors. There were two roaring fireplaces on each end of the room, as well as leather couches with blankets and pillows on them. Long wooden tables with matching high back chairs scattered about the room, whereas bridges, mezzanines, ladders and countless shelves of books went all the way to the chandelier. There had to be millions of books, all different shapes and sizes—it was a *literal dream*. Not a lot of things left me speechless, but this magnificent space filled with a world full of knowledge was mesmerizing.

"I… I don't even know where to begin." My eyes scoured over the books, "I could stay here for the rest of my life and be perfectly content."

There were goblins milling about with parchment and stacks of books in their gnarled green hands. They had large black eyes with matching black hair pulled back as they worked through the library. They were considered lower fae, not as respected as the High Fae, but still not treated as poorly as humans because they possessed magical abilities.

Wesley laughed softly and that simple noise sent a bolt of heat down my spine. "What's your favorite genre? We can pick a few out for you to bring back to your rooms."

I looked down at my navy slippers. How could I say romance without saying romance? Evia would always make fun of me for my taste. She would blame my human heart, always yearning for something I couldn't have.

Actual *love.*

I've had an arranged marriage since I could remember, so romance was never in my cards.

Fuck it.

If I wanted to read romance, I would read romance and he could make fun of me too.

"I enjoy love stories, but ones with adventure," I explained with pride in my voice.

"Ah, a fellow fiction lover. Come, this way. We have a whole section and I'm sure there are a few in there with the love stories you desire." He held out his hand for me to take and led me towards the back of the library, near the fireplace. "So you like to read a lot?"

"Yes, I absolutely love it." I answered quickly, surprised that he didn't make fun of me too. "It was one of the few luxuries my nursemaid allowed. She would bring me some from the royal selection." Reading was like being able to escape into a different world, able to live a different life from the one I was currently stuck in. My eyes trailed over all the new options I would have free reign to pick through. I was overwhelmed with the possibilities of finding something else I would love as much as the green book I took from the fortress. Holding in a squeal of excitement, I turned back to the Crown Prince.

Wesley looked at me with a small amount of sadness in his eyes but he quickly pushed it down with a small smile. "You can take as many as you like and come here as often as you want to. If you can't find what you're looking for, then you can ask one of the workers to help. They know where everything is in here and won't hesitate to help you find the perfect book."

"Thank you for the generosity," I wiped my sweaty palms on my navy skirt. I really needed to control my nervousness. "I would love to know what *you* like to read," I said with a bright smile. "How about you pick something out for me and I pick something for you, along with our own choices for ourselves?"

"You got it." He ran his hand through his brown curls as he looked down with a mocking grin, "I bet I'll pick something better than you do."

I rolled my eyes as I crossed my arms over my chest,

"You're so on."

The fire crackled as I scoured the shelves for a title that popped out at me. I snagged a few that seemed pretty good, skimming some pages of them, looking for one with extra spicy romance that would have Wesley keeling over. I turned to check and see where he went but he was scouring the shelves himself, a fat stack of books already in his arms.

He turned my way and we locked eyes for a second, and I could see the blue in his flare to life as he smiled, "Got anything good? I always get a little taken away when I come in here."

My eyes crinkled in laughter, "I can see that." I brought my stack over the table and set them down to review my options. The prince brought his pile over and we exchanged the books to see what the other picked. I also grabbed the ones he picked out for himself to see what he actually liked.

Color me surprised, but the Crown Prince of Gambriel had a love for adventure books as well. He actually did have good taste and I might've needed to borrow a couple of them when he was finished. The book he picked for me, surprisingly, had some of the romance in it that I usually wanted. I started reading that one first but Wesley made a noise of amusement that stopped me. "What?" I asked as he laughed again.

"My, my Cassandra. Who knew that you would pick such a... what's the word I'm looking for?" His blue eyes twinkled with amusement and flirtation, "*Dirty* book?"

I grinned at him, then pulled my eyes back down to the one he picked out. "You're welcome. Feel free to take some notes," I said nonchalantly with a wave of my hand.

I peeked back up at his shocked expression. "Duly noted, my lady."

About an hour or so later, a set of human servants came in and set out some tea and biscuits in the center of the table for us to enjoy. Wesley and I both thanked them before they departed. I couldn't help but notice their eyes were dark, cheeks hollow and too skinny, just like Minka.

My stomach churned in guilt and shame again. I needed to think of a way to help at least one of them, not sit here and reap the benefits of their hard work while they were being hurt like that. I stared at the book in front of me, not reading but trying to think of a way to bring it up to Wesley. He said he had a love for his people, all kinds of them, and he treated them with respect rather than rudely dismissing them, from what I had seen so far.

He must've noticed the change in my mood because he set his book down and poured me a cup of tea as he asked, "Are you okay?" He cut a biscuit in half and spread strawberry preserves over it.

"Just something that I noticed," I said and set a biscuit on my plate as Wesley passed me the knife, hilt towards me. Working up the confidence to ask him about their treatment, I reached for the knife and smiled at him, "Thank y—"

Gong.

Gong.

Gong.

A large bell started to go off, so loud I could feel the floor move and I had to cover my ears so fast that my hand flicked the knife away from me and at the prince. My heart was pounding out of my chest from the incessant noise. "What in the Gods names *is* that?" I yelled at him over the loud gongs.

The bell stopped ringing. "Shit," he muttered with a drawn look on his usually happy face, "It's high noon; everyday the bell rings at noon to signify the middle of the day."

A flash of crimson pulled my attention to his hand.

Oh, *fuck*.

His hand was bleeding. I cut the prince. I cut the fucking Prince of Gambriel because I

got scared by a damn bell. I rushed over, pulled a handkerchief out of my dress pocket and quickly wrapped it around his bloody hand. Crimson seeped through the white linen cloth as he stared down at me, smirking with the light back in his eyes.

"What's so funny? I just cut you!" I demanded as I pressed the cloth firmly into his gushing hand.

Wesley grabbed my hand softly and pulled it away, unwrapping the cloth to reveal a perfectly healed hand, as if nothing even happened. "Fae healing," he held up his hand and gave his long fingers a little wiggle.

I blushed, embarrassed, and looked down as I shoved the bloody handkerchief back into my pocket quickly. He just acted so *human* sometimes, I completely forgot we're a different species with a whole different set of abilities.

"Well then, I'm not *as* sorry," I retorted with a laugh as I sat back in my seat.

Wesley rolled his eyes at me. "Just because I can heal quickly, doesn't mean you can go around stabbing me, Cassandra." He poured himself a cup of tea with his freshly healed hand.

"Duly noted," I repeated his same words as he dove back into his *dirty* book while we enjoyed the silence of each other's company for a little bit longer.

CHAPTER 10

After an eventful day full of walking around the castle grounds hand in hand with the prince, I took dinner in my room as Minka tidied up the sitting room I was eating in. I was already out of my navy gown and into a cotton nightgown after my bath. Minka looked even worse than this morning and she was moving at a sluggish pace as she went around and dusted the candelabras.

"Minka?" I voiced.

"Yes, my lady?" the chambermaid responded.

"Please, call me Cassandra," I corrected her again as she looked down. "Will you please come have a seat?" I asked in a soft voice.

Her head shot up, eyes blazing with a million questions as I gestured to the chair directly in front of me. She hesitantly took the chair and stared at me in question as I pushed a plate of bread towards her. I then piled some more potatoes, vegetables and meat onto a separate plate and pushed that in front of her as well.

Minka looked down at the plates and then back up again

at me as I smiled, "I couldn't possibly finish all of this. Plus, I would love some company as I ate."

"Oh, no, My Lad— Cassandra. I really shouldn't. It's not right for me to dine with someone above me," she stuttered as her hungry eyes looked back at the plate in front her.

"I'm afraid I must insist," I gave another encouraging smile. "Please, join me," I said before I put another fork full of potatoes in my mouth.

It really didn't take much convincing before she started to shovel the food into her mouth as if she was starving. Well no, she literally *was* starving. I pushed a glass of water in front of her and smiled while she graciously took the glass.

We ate in silence, and I kept piling more food onto her plate until she shook her head in exasperation, "I don't think I can take another bite. I might just explode now."

I let out a light laugh, "Me too." I patted my full stomach. "If you don't mind me asking, where are you from?"

Minka took a sip of water. "I'm actually from Menodore. I was taken here after the siege when I was seven years old." Her eyes were sad from the mention of it and I couldn't help but see the similarities between us.

We both lost our homes and families during the Siege of Menodore and then we were taken as children by the kingdoms who came to Menodore's aid. We were both humans, pulled from the ashes to serve the High Fae for different reasons. What if the roles were reversed and my Aunt Radha had taken Minka instead of I? Would I be sitting here, gaunt faced and too skinny, just like Minka? A pang of guilt ran through my chest that there were so many others like me, but

I was lucky enough to be taken in by Radha rather than being left to become a slave to the High Fae.

Minka's small voice spoke again, "Thank you for dinner, Cassandra. It was amazing."

"Thank you for joining me. I truly hate dining alone," I lied, but she needed to eat more. I wasn't going to sit back and watch her starve as I lived lavishly. "Now that I'm stuffed as well, I'm going to get ready for bed and call it a night."

She smiled brightly and I could slowly see the light returning to her eyes after just one full meal. It would take a lot more than just one meal to bring some color and life into her pale face and scrawny body but it would happen soon enough. She got up and started to clear up the table as I helped her. "You don't have to do that, My Lad—Cassandra," she quickly corrected herself.

"I enjoy helping, it makes me feel a little better after gorging myself on that dinner," I said as I stacked the dirty plates and set the silverware on top.

She nodded as she picked up the stack. "I'll see you in the morning." Her face lit up with a stunning smile, "Thank you again."

"Of course, Minka. I would love to dine with you again." That time, I didn't lie. "You truly are great company."

I went into my bedroom while I listened to the sound of Minka putting everything into a basket to take it from my room and waited to hear the click of the front door when she exited. I looked at the clock near my bed, but it was only a little after ten at night. The moonlight sucked up the darkness from the night. I would need to wait a little longer before I went out and searched for a new training place; there would probably still be random faeries milling about the grounds.

Well, no shit.

There were always going to be, because it was a freaking castle that hosted orgies every other night. It wasn't like the fortress I was raised in—I would have a lot more freedom here. I was sure I was allowed to go on a walk in the evenings. If someone saw me, that would be my excuse.

Couldn't sleep. Needed to walk it off.

Yup, that would work for now.

I rushed into my closet and quickly changed into my black training clothes. Throwing the hooded cloak over my face to obscure anyone's view of who was beneath it, I buckled the knife belt to my waist—under my shirt—to conceal it in case someone questioned me. The comfortable training clothes could be easily excused for something that I would wear that required no assistance from a chambermaid, but not a belt full of knives.

I creeped out of my room and looked from side to side in the hallway.

All clear.

Now to remember how to get to the gardens.

I retraced mine and Wesley's steps until I came face to face with those same large doors, where there were no guards this time but a couple of High Fae standing near a portrait on the wall, drinks in their hands. A female with long black hair and olive complexion looked my way while the others kept up the conversation. I walked by quickly, trying to ignore the sneer she sent my way. Shoving the heavy wooden door open with my shoulder, I cut straight into the gardens and headed in the direction of where I saw a courtyard earlier this morning.

A cool breeze played with the hem of my black tunic, prickling my skin from the cold touch as I came up on the stone building I spotted earlier. I hid in the pockets of shadow at the wall's base as I listened for any sound of movement coming from within. My nerves melted away almost instantly as I felt more comfortable hiding in the darkness already. Most people were afraid of it but for me, it had been the one consistent thing that had always been there for me.

When you spend most of your life staying secluded in that darkness, you begin to befriend it and all the shadows it offers. The only time I was able to have control over my body and choices was in the dark of the night, dancing with my blades through the shadows.

I didn't hear any sounds coming from the building so I took a chance and rushed to the front door and creaked it open slowly.

A gasp left my mouth as I took it all in.

It was *perfect*.

The building was empty but scattered about were wooden swords for training, bows and quivers filled with arrows, stacks of padded practice armor and even some metal armor with matching iron swords. There was another door towards the back of the room, so I headed to check that out before I made use of everything in this glorious room.

The back door led to an outdoor training yard that had dummies standing around in various spots, some archery targets, and a small arena that had more swords leaning against the wooden posts. Smiling to myself, I walked closer to the arena to see what else it had to offer when a large hand clamped over my mouth and I was pressed against a warm body that reeked of stale alcohol and cigar smoke.

Trying to scream as the stranger's hand muffled the sound, I jammed out my elbow and punched the stranger right in the ribs. I heard a loud manly grunt from the impact and my spine stiffened against that sound.

Male.

My body shivered with fear as dark thoughts raced in of what this person would do to me if they got ahold of my body. I needed to escape, I needed to get out but before I could make another move, he wrapped his free hand around my arms to stop me from elbowing him any further. I started kicking my feet out, trying to gain leverage as his hot breath touched my ear and whispered, "Feisty little thing aren't ya?"

The hand covering my mouth started to wander to my breasts as I let out a scream, still fighting his every move. I kicked out backwards and his legs went out from underneath him, and we both fell into a heap on the ground. His greedy hands tried to find their way in between my legs and I clamped my knees together to block it.

"Get the fuck off me!" I screamed as he laughed, still trying to work his hands onto any part of my body he could reach as I flailed. Any training I practiced went out the window as my breathing accelerated and I started to sweat from the sense of panic overriding me.

He was going to rape me if I didn't get my shit together.

But my body kept trembling as my instincts froze in the face of horror.

He brought his fist up and decked me square in the face so hard that I saw stars and then he gripped my throat as he tried to reach in between my legs again as he whispered with hatred, "You stupid bitch. You'll learn that a woman's place is beneath a man."

CHAPTER 11

No fucking way was this happening.

My head cleared before I snapped my teeth at the hand that barred my throat, and he started raining blows down near my face, my chest, everywhere he had access to. He was clearly intoxicated, judging by the way he was fighting. Frenzied, messy, and with no actual thought for his movements besides to strike and strike.

I could overpower incompetence.

I let my limbs fall flat, like I had given up in the fight. He stopped because of my stillness, probably worried he killed me before he got what he wanted. "That's it. Now you'll learn," he said as he leaned down to my face to probably spout off some more bullshit in my ear. I took that moment to slowly glide my hand to my now exposed waist while he was distracted by himself. "Now be a good bitch and—"

His words were cut off as I shoved my dagger straight into his throat and his warm blood sprayed across my hand. That same fire and something akin to power filled my middle as I twisted and turned the dagger deeper into his neck until his body went limp over mine.

Disgusting.

The smell of his blood mixed with booze burned my nose as I pushed his heavy body off of mine.

Shit. Fuck. Dammit.

I just killed someone.

I just fucking *killed* someone.

What was I supposed to do? Just leave him there? Go back and explain what happened?

No. Stupid. Fuck.

I couldn't do that. Then that would lead to questions about why I was out here. I supposed I could say I was exploring the gardens when I was attacked?

Sitting up, I looked at my blood-covered hands. They didn't disgust me like I thought they would. The crimson only increased my anger and the rage from someone trying to *hurt* me, trying to *take* something from me. My entire body started to ache from his brutal punches as I attempted to stand and glared over at his still gushing corpse. My own blood dripped down from my nose where he hit me, mingling ours together and I wanted to stab him all over again. My vision cleared as the feeling of terror of someone catching me swept in again. I put my arm over my eyes as I rocked back and forth on the hard ground, fighting the internal desire to make the man pay again.

Think, Cassandra. Think.

Footsteps approaching interrupted my train of thought and before I had time to react there was another man standing directly in front of me.

No, not a man. But a male faerie.

His movements were graceful and sleek, just like his dark clothes. He radiated raw and carnal power, and I could practically taste the magic on my tongue. My mind started to race with alarm that he was going to fuck me over and turn me in for murdering my assailant. The male was every part the predator as he stalked toward me and by the way he was looking at me, *I* was the prey.

His shoulder length black hair blended in with the shadows that were dancing across his reddish-brown skin. Molten, golden-amber eyes stared down at my blood covered form and his elongated canines glinted off the moonlight as he spoke, his voice like a smoky caress. "Look at you." His eyes darkened, "My little monster. Don't you look positively ravishing, covered in the blood of those who wronged you."

My green eyes shot back from the man I just killed to the one before me. The High Fae male gave a vicious smile and turned his head to look at the oozing corpse next to me as I noticed a large scar that started at his forehead and went through his right eyebrow to his cheekbone. That gnarly scar only heightened his beauty and gave into his predatory look. Slightly arched ears were peeking out from under his deep onyx mane that flowed in soft waves down past a sharp jawline. He was more broad than some of the other High Fae males I had seen, and a lot taller too. More shadows crawled up from behind his back, slithering towards me like wispy snakes.

He looked back to me with those mystical eyes in a way that made heat rise along my spine. Something within me stirred as he stared at me with approval and pride. The faerie lifted his long and scarred fingers towards the dead man and the body disintegrated into nothingness, not even a speck of ash or dust left behind. I let my mouth fall open, awestruck by what in the hell he had just done. His golden eyes twinkled in the starlight as he smirked once more at my dumbfounded expression.

His ebony, sleeveless tunic did nothing to hide his muscular frame and he smiled again as I stared at him, showing two small dimples as he held his tanned and scarred arm out for me to take. I looked from the large calloused hand, to his face, and back to the hand again before I decided to help myself up.

He arched a midnight eyebrow my way as I pushed myself up, reddened dagger still in hand in case this faerie stranger tried to pull the same stunt. Adrenaline pulsed through my veins as I came face to face with this beast of prey before me. Pointing my blade in his direction I blurted, "What did you do to the body?"

The stranger chuckled, "Gone. Not something you need to worry about anymore."

"I… I killed him," I admitted, not knowing why in the Gods' names I just told him that.

"You defended yourself, from the look of it," the faerie countered with pleasure in his deep voice.

"Defended or not, I still killed him." A shiver trailed down my back from the confession. "What's going to happen to me now?"

"You did the world a favor. One less vermin for us to

worry about."

I scrunched my nose at his blatant disregard for life. For *human* life.

Typical High Fae asshole. Not caring about anything but his own *kind*.

"I still took someone's life. That's someone's father, husband, or child," I ranted as I pointed to where the dead body was a few seconds before. That man would've raped and killed me, leaving me to become nothing but a bloody heap in the dirt but I couldn't help but to defend his death because *I* had been the one to kill him.

But maybe the High Fae and humans weren't so different after all? That man was human but he still attacked me and would've taken what he wanted without a second thought. He was selfish and egotistical, just like the High Fae. Whereas Wesley was High Fae but so far he had been nothing but kind and generous to me. The Crown Prince was warm hearted and sympathetic, and held no disdain for my kind.

Maybe it truly didn't matter *what* you were but it really mattered how much of an *asshole* you acted like.

And this male in front me, radiated asshole energy.

"Ah, yes. But it was a life he forfeited when he deemed it necessary to hurt you, to take something from you without your permission, and possibly kill you." His voice got darker as he continued, almost like he was enraged but not letting his body show it. "Nothing is going to happen to you. I will take care of *that* and you will tell me why you were out here, *alone*."

I crossed my bloody arms across my chest—dagger still in

hand—and put my bruised chin up, holding his gaze. "I don't have to tell *you* anything."

Churning tendrils of shadows outlined his face as he leaned down to ask again, his voice much softer now. "Why are you out here, sweetheart?"

I wanted to throw my dagger at his face for the condescending use of a pet name.

Fucking *asshole*.

He had to be almost seven feet tall, and even leaning down his height was still lording over me. I held his menacing gaze and ignored the demeaning nickname as I narrowed my eyes. "Why were *you* out here?" I mimicked his question.

"I heard a scream. But it seems you have already taken care of the issue," he gestured to my blood covered body.

No shit I took care of the issue. What was I supposed to do? Wait for someone to hear my scream ten minutes too late as I lay assaulted and dead in the dirt?

I wasn't about to wait for my knight in shining armor to ride up and save the fucking day. With my luck, the knight would probably show up with rusted metal, covered in shit, and would've just let me down in the end. Why hope and wait for someone to save you when it would be worthless?

I would save myself time and time again. *I* would never let myself down.

Glaring at the faerie I said, "Yes, as you can see. The issue is resolved, so I will be on my way now." I went to step around him, already feeling better before his large hand came down on my shoulder and stopped me.

Without even a second thought, I reacted on instinct

and brought my dagger down on his wrist. The blade went straight through his arm and he didn't even flinch. I brought my startled eyes up to his golden ones to find the High Fae male smiling down at me, his dense shadows now dancing across my shoulder down to my forearm. Enveloping me in a floral and dark teakwood scent that made my muscles relax without my permission.

"Can you control your little friends?" I asked, exasperated.

"They have a mind of their own, little monster."

Yup. Smug asshole.

Hand still on the grip of the blade, I slowly extracted the dagger from his wrist, not breaking the stare down we were obviously now competing in. He removed his hand from my shoulder as he repeated, "Why were you out here? Alone?"

"Couldn't sleep," I lied all too easily. "Thought a nice walk would make me tired and then I was attacked."

He arched an ebony eyebrow my way. "A nice walk dressed in all black attire and a belt full of knives?"

Giving him a vicious smile, I simply nodded my reply.

"You're a terrible liar, little dove," he admitted, dimple peeking through with his grin.

"And you're terribly nosey," I retorted back, pointing the bloody dagger at him while I ignored yet another stupid pet name.

He grinned, showing off those alarmingly white teeth, sharp fangs gently poking his bottom lip.

"So I've been told. Apology accepted by the way."

"I haven't apologized?"

What in the fuck was the crazy faerie talking about?

"I know. I thought I'd get the jump start on that for you. You stabbed me," he pointed to his already healed wrist. Damn fae healing; I was hoping it would scar along with the other ones that littered his tanned arm. "Now it's only common courtesy for you to apologize."

I just stared, dumbfounded once more. Now I would definitely not apologize for stabbing that prick.

His dark laugh filled the air, "Well this is going swimmingly. Now, one more time. What are you doing out here?"

A sigh escaped me, my expression annoyed. But maybe he would fuck off if I threatened him. He did just find me with a dead body, so I could clearly make certain on that promise. "Training myself. So when I'm cornered by people like *you*," I waved my blade at him, "I can defend myself by any means *necessary*."

He clicked his tongue as his gaze swept over my entire body again. I was going to stab out those pretty eyes next if he didn't quit staring at me like I was his next meal. The faerie gave a smug smile as he snapped his fingers again and all the blood and dirt was removed from my clothes, but not from my skin. His smirk quickly faded as his eyes narrowed down at me and then went to the bracelet around my wrist. Those golden eyes went wide with the realization that his magic wouldn't work on me. His expression turned neutral with understanding before he flicked his eyes back to mine.

Smiling with all my teeth, I probably looked insane but I didn't care. His magic wouldn't work on me and that gave me the upper hand.

"Training, you say?" My smile dropped. "Then let's do some training," he disappeared in a puff of shadows and reappeared within a second, two swords by his side now. I tried to stay as expressionless as possible but I couldn't help the stunned look on my face from this High Fae's immense powers.

I had never seen magic like that used before. It frightened and excited me all at once.

Somewhere deep within my soul, I knew he wouldn't hurt me. He would've done that already if he truly wanted to. But I wouldn't let that feeling control my instincts and let my guard down around this male though.

He extended the sword to me, so I gripped the hilt and stared at him in question. He then bowed at the waist, raven hair falling forward. I was hyped on adrenaline, body ready to take this asshole down. This thing inside me was careening at the sight of a challenge and I wanted his blood on my hands next. He stared at me with that same challenge lining those golden eyes, waiting to see if I was up for a fight. So, I matched his bow with one of my own as I sheathed the dagger at my waist and then he struck.

Our swords met with a resounding clash. "Good. Very good," he murmured as my shoulders barked from the sore muscles as his strength pushed against them. He struck again and I matched his movements blow for blow, never taking my eyes off his weapon. He advanced again and I ducked beneath his arm while taking a long swing at him that he met with equally brute force. His dark laugh came again as we parried in circles until sweat was beading down my blood crusted forehead.

A smile broke across my face because I was actually dueling *someone* for once. Not a stuffed dummy or a wooden post and most definitely not myself in the mirror. I was practicing with someone for once and from the look of it, a High Fae *warrior*. Adrenaline pulsed through my veins once more as I fell into the rhythm he created with our dancing blades.

He quickly grabbed the wrist of the hand that the sword was encased in, pushing on the pressure point so that I dropped the sword. That raging inferno filled my gut and I wanted to reach for one of my daggers to slice into him. Fighting back that instinct, I met his warm, amber eyes as he dropped his own sword and asked, "Who trained you? Your skills are mediocre but your footwork is pretty spot on."

Mediocre? I'd show him mediocre. This time, I did start to reach for one of my daggers to fling at his face until his scar covered hand gripped my own to stop me.

I shot a glare up at him as I retorted through my own barred teeth, "I taught myself these *mediocre* skills."

His eyebrows shot up with surprise, "We're going to have to change that."

"I don't need nor want your help," I said as his rich teakwood smell invaded my senses again.

"Oh, you need it alright." He released his hold on my hand.

The cool metal of the blade calmed my racing heart as I held onto it. I shot him a feral grin as I spoke, "I don't make deals with the fae." Rule number one: never make a bargain with any faerie creature. It was the same as making a death wish for yourself.

"No deal necessary, I'll find you again to work on your mediocre skills," the strange male laughed as he disappeared into a blend of shadows before I could refuse him once more.

"Asshole faerie," I muttered as I walked; well more like *limped* back to my rooms. The burst of energy slowly faded with every step I took before I collapsed in exhaustion and excitement on my bed.

CHAPTER 12

The sunlight streamed into my bedroom through the gaudy yellow curtains as I tried to sit myself up, muscles barking in resistance. I guessed that the adrenaline from the night before had worn off because I felt like living death. I slept in my now spotless training clothes, too tired to remove them the night before.

I managed to get myself out of the bed and sit in front of the vanity to try to clean out some of the cuts on my body. I wasn't as injured as I thought I would've been, but I *looked* as bad as I felt. My eyes were bloodshot, skin smattered with bruises and cuts alike, my lips swollen with dried blood crusted on them. Shit, how was I supposed to excuse all of that?

A loud gasp and the clatter of a metal tray interrupted my thoughts and I turned to see a wide-eyed Minka, shocked with her pale hand over her mouth in the doorway.

"What... What happened?" My chambermaid asked as she rushed over the fallen tray to me.

My first instinct was to lie and tell her an elaborate story, but my second was telling me to trust her and see what she could do to fix this and prevent any questions from the others. I quickly chose the latter.

Trust went both ways, and I wanted her to trust me because trust was going to be vital for there to be any change to how our kind was treated in this kingdom. Your word didn't mean shit if there was no honor behind it.

She listened intently as I explained my life events to her, what led me to want to train myself and of the events that happened the night before—not including the run in with the fae male, for some reason that felt more private and personal to me. I wasn't quite ready to disclose that yet.

"I can't bring in a healer because their magic won't work on you," she explained as she eyed my bracelet. "But I can get a few things to help with the pain and lessen the look of your bruises and cuts. I'll be right back."

Minka bounded through the room to the door and tossed over her shoulder, "Thank you for trusting me, Cassandra. You've been nothing but kind to me and I will do whatever I can to return that kindness."

Standing there dumbfounded by Minka's tenderness and trust, my heart swelled to the size of the moon at the gesture of friendship. I'd never had anybody I could confide in before, let alone another human that I could at the very least, *talk* to. Despite the pain in my muscles, a warm fluttery feeling filled my aching limbs with hope. A smile stretched across my face until it hurt because I had a friend now.

A real life *friend*.

With a delighted expression, I went into the bathing

room and relieved myself before I peeled off the rest of my black clothes with a groan. That warm fuzzy feeling in my stomach quickly ceased as the feeling of pain took over once more. Every move I made pulled on the multitude of cuts and bruises, so I ignored the discomfort and pulled them off quickly to just get it over with.

I then turned on the faucet and let the hot, steamy water fill the claw-footed tub. Grabbing a bottle of lavender oil off the shelf, I poured a dash into the luscious warmth waiting for me. I eased my sore body into the tub, hissing through my teeth at the sting of pain from the cuts cleaning themselves out as the heat seeped into my sore muscles.

Minka walked in with a basket full of tins and bottles as she came to the tub to sprinkle in an odd powder mixture as she explained, "This should help with the sore muscles as well as disinfect the smaller cuts and we will apply the different salves once your body is all clean."

I nodded my head in agreement as she worked her way through the bathroom, picking up the dirty clothes that were no longer stained in the blood of the man I killed just mere hours ago.

Minka brought me a small towel that she dunked in the warm water to put over my eyes to ease the ache building behind them. Before she rested it on my face, her gray ones searched mine as she whispered, "Are you alright? I know the answer for physically but I mean… In here?" She put her hand over her heart.

Blinking back the tears, "I… don't know. I…" stuttering to get the words out. "I killed him."

She tilted her head in question. "Do you feel bad that you protected yourself?"

"No." I shook my head quickly. "I liked it. I felt in control for once and that's what scares me the most."

Her eyes softened at my confession, "You did what you had to do, Cassandra." Putting the cloth over my eyes, she squeezed my arm in reassurance. "I'll be right back with some other things that'll help," she stated as I heard the door shut behind her.

The events of the night before came rushing back in a frenzy. Focusing on my breathing, I calmed the anxiety building in my bones from the near death experience. I fought back the sob building in my throat because I just kept imagining what would've happened to me if I hadn't ended up killing that man. What he probably did to other women before he targeted me as his next victim.

The guilt from the night before was long gone, just as his body. Maybe I should've felt guilty about killing him now but I didn't and I don't think I ever could. I didn't know if the lack of remorse or the fact that I murdered someone disturbed me more. Definitely the murder part, but I couldn't bring myself to feel bad about it because it was just like what that weird but beautiful fae male said: one less vermin to worry about. He would've raped and probably killed me and gone on to do it to however many people he felt he had the right to.

I would not feel guilty for saving more innocent lives. But there was this gnawing thing in my gut, like there was this beast inside of me who sang when I took control and made it out of that situation.

It felt almost *liberating*.

But I still couldn't stop the tears from falling from the way that man still tainted me. Tainted my soul with his death at my hands that would stay with me for as long as I lived.

I did what I had to do to survive.

It turned out that the prince was busy today, so I was left to my own devices for the day and evening. After the bath—and what seemed like endless coddling from Minka over my wounds—I threw on a clean robe, already feeling better. We ate a quick breakfast, which I once again insisted she joined me for and we discussed what we liked to do in our free time. More guilt flooded my bones from the fact that free time didn't actually exist for her. She used to love to listen to bedtime stories told by her mother, dancing under the moonlight and painting while laying in the sunshine meadows of Menodore.

Now there was nothing but dust and the blood of our families in those once flower filled meadows.

Next on my never ending list was to find a way for Minka to have even a moment for herself and the chance to paint again. She had brought me a special tonic that was made from the poppies that surrounded the palace gardens and it numbed the pain almost instantly. I was feeling a little more like myself so I decided I would go back to the library and grab some more books that caught my eye and search for some paints for her.

Minka helped me into a soft velvet gown that covered

almost all of my skin in case I ran into anyone on the way to the library. She also styled my hair to where it was all down but could easily conceal my face if I turned my head at just the right angle. After she cleaned up all the cuts, applied the salves and even iced them, my face wasn't as marred up as I thought it would be. There were a few minor cuts still there and a light bruise on my cheek, but with enough makeup we could blend that bruise into my complexion and conceal it.

As I was walking back along the long hallways to the library, I ran my hand along the wall and a change in the cool smooth texture caught my attention. It felt warm and rough right under my finger tips rather than the usual coolness that the stone put off. I stopped right in the middle of the hallway and got down onto the level where the warmth was coming from.

The stone didn't look any different than the other spots but when I traced it with my fingertips again, I could still feel that warmth. I started to run my hand along the area to see if it felt similar anywhere else. My fingertips could only make out some different lines and shapes in the wall, almost like symbols. I closed my eyes and traced the warmth with my fingertips, picturing what it would look like in my head.

I probably looked like a crazy person, crouching in the hallway, feeling the walls with my eyes closed. Now self conscious, I got up and hurried along to the library as I kept my hand on the stone wall—like I was staying to the side of the hallway and out of people's way—so I wouldn't look as crazy as a few minutes ago. The change in texture and temperature kept happening as I moved along and I knew exactly what book I was going to try to find.

I wanted to grab any book that had to do with this castle or the symbols that might be along these walls, and what they could have meant. The way the stone changed in texture to the touch made me believe that they were enchanted. I already knew that the castle had wards on it placed by the King himself but usually those were placed on the outside of the castle's walls. Not on the inside.

Entering the library, I found that it was not as empty as the day before. There were a couple of High Fae sitting at some of the tables or on the couches, books in hand, not even looking up as I entered the room. A black haired goblin was shelving books off to the side, so he would know where I could find the type of books I was looking for.

He stopped his shelving when he heard my approach and quickly turned and dropped down into a bow as he asked, "My lady, is there anything I can help you with?"

I stared in shock for a moment but quickly recovered. This lower fae just addressed me as 'my lady' instead of insulting me or outright ignoring me. I gave him my best smile, despite the slight pain still lingering in my limbs. "Yes, actually you could be of great assistance. I was wondering if there is a section on any symbols, or the construction of the castle?"

The goblin looked at me with his own shocked expression and stammered, "The, the castle?" He shook his head, his hair loosening from the leather strap as he went on. "We do not have access to records such as that but there is a section on language and different symbols still used today. Follow me this way and I'll happily assist you."

"Thank you, I really appreciate it," I smiled brightly again at him. "Oh and do you know where I could find some paints?"

His eyes went wide again at my thanks and he nodded as he led me to a corner section of the library. He only had to have been about three feet tall. He was just up to my waist in height and had matching arched ears like the other fae. Most lower fae, like goblins, still had a dislike for humans because of our lack of magic. Goblins weren't as powerful as the High Fae but they did have a small form of magic coursing through their short bodies.

From the expressions this goblin was giving me, it seemed like he wasn't used to people actually thanking him for assistance. Maybe the lower fae weren't as respected as I originally thought?

He started speaking again, showing me the different sections and which one contained all the books on symbols, just like I had asked for. There were only about two shelves full of them so it hopefully wouldn't take me too long to find what I was searching for.

Before he turned away to go back to his work I quickly asked, "I don't mean to be a bother but is there possibly some extra parchment and ink that I could use?"

"Yes, of course, my lady. I will set some up over on this table when you are ready to use it. I will also leave some of the paint as well." His wrinkled finger pointed over to a small table just a couple feet away from the shelves I needed.

"Thank you—" I stopped myself because I didn't even know his name. "I apologize, I never caught your name."

He bowed at the waist again, "It is Igor and it is my

pleasure to serve you, Lady Cassandra."

"Thank you, Igor. I appreciate your help," I beamed at him and I could've sworn I saw a blush breakout across his green cheeks before he turned away.

I scoured the shelves, looking for a title that might have one of the symbols on it but I wasn't that lucky. I grabbed a couple off the shelf and brought them over to the table and skimmed through, hoping to see one of the symbols.

Once again, not that lucky. I returned that stack of books to their proper spot on the shelves and grabbed the next few. After a couple of failed attempts, I came upon a single book where the symbols in it looked pretty similar to the ones on the walls, but I would have to compare them to be sure.

Smiling at the palette of paint he left behind, I left the book on the table and grabbed the parchment and ink. Walking quickly, I went into the hallway to trace what I could of the symbols etched into the stone so I could try to match them with the ones in the book. I put the parchment against the stone and felt with my fingertips through it until I felt that same warmth, then put my finger in the bottle of ink and traced the symbols onto the paper carefully.

I held up the paper and admired my work. A little sloppy, but it would get the job done anyway. Today was obviously the day that the entire castle would think I had gone insane, first from feeling the walls while sitting on the floor with my eyes closed and now to dipping my hands in ink and tracing them like a toddler learning to finger paint.

Better to be crazy than boring right?

No, Cassandra. No amount of crazy is supposed to be

good.

I shook my head with a slight smile as I wiped my inky fingers off on another piece of parchment and walked back into the library and over to my corner table. I then laid my art work of the traced symbols side by side with the open book and—

Oh my Gods.

It worked. It actually fucking worked!

I made a slight squealing noise of excitement that caught the attention of Igor, the library goblin, who just looked at me with his large black eyes and cracked a smile at me as I gave him a small wave with my stained fingers. He shook his head and turned back to shelving the stack of books in his little green arms.

I couldn't help the large grin on my face as I flipped the book back over to the cover that read *Ancient Runes*. I quickly read a few paragraphs and digested the gist of it.

They were similar to the wards that the High Fae set to keep others in or out and most were sealed with the blood of who put them there. I didn't know too much about setting wards but I didn't think they used their blood to set them. Plus, Gambriel already had wards on the outside of the castle. The particular runes that I matched with the ones in the book were said to shroud something. From my knowledge, we used shrouds to bury our dead in, as a way to honor them. Could those symbols on the walls just be another way to honor our deceased with magic intertwined?

But the book said it was a way to keep others in or out. Maybe there was a royal burial site in the castle that needed that level of protecting?

My head kept reeling with the possibilities of what they could mean as excitement filled my veins.

But, why would the castle have runes on almost every wall on the inside when they already had a different magical ward protecting it? Were they just used as an extra type of ward to protect those in the castle from any intruders, if they were to make it past the initial ones? Or were they being used to honor something that was *hidden* within the castle?

It would take an extreme amount of power to break through King Harrington's wards because only the person who put the wards in place, would be able to take them down. I understood wanting to be extremely cautious and have a backup plan, but using a different type of magic just didn't make sense to me.

Also, using your blood to initiate a rune sounded like it was more on the side of dark magic, which was strictly forbidden for the fae or humans to dabble in. The cost of using said magic would be your own soul.

Why would the castle have blood magic throughout almost every wall?

Blood.

My eyes went wide at the thought and I just stared forward as my head reeled in circles once more.

I had an incredibly stupid but brilliant idea.

Grabbing the book, paints and the parchment I traced on, I made my way back to my room as quickly as I could without raising suspicion. I, of course, thanked Igor again on my way out and he gave me an award winning smile in return.

Minka was still in my room performing her usual duties. Her small body hustled through the extravagant sitting room as she folded blankets, picked random items up, and she was about to walk out with a pile of laundry that needed to be washed.

"Wait, I need something from there!" I shouted and she jumped from the boom in my voice as I rushed into the warm room.

She turned toward me as she wrinkled her little pale nose, "From the dirty laundry?" She set the basket down in front of me and gestured with her hands. "Have at it."

I tossed my book to the ground along with parchment and palette before I rifled through the pile of soiled clothes, tossing them to the side with excitement until I landed on exactly what I needed.

The handkerchief with Wesley's dried blood on it.

It was time to test my theory on the runes with blood magic and pray to the Gods that it would work for the sake of my own curiosity. "Can I have a glass of water, please?" I asked Minka as she stared at me like the crazed woman I was.

"Of course. There's a pitcher set up on the table. Give me a moment," Minka replied, curiosity in her voice.

She brought in the glass of water and I lightly dipped the handkerchief in the glass, to wet the blood that had already dried on it. I only dabbed it very quickly with a little water to make sure I didn't dilute the blood on it too much.

"Thanks for your help, Minka!" I shouted at her again as I scurried out of my room with only the handkerchief in hand. My slippers skidded as I came to a stop before the door closed, "That palette is yours by the way." Her quiet laughter was trailing behind me before a shocked gasp left her lips as my words sunk in.

The door clicked shut and I wanted to stay to see her reaction to her present but I didn't know if it would be a good or bad reaction and she probably would need the moment to herself. Emotions could be overwhelming, no matter how well you controlled them. Plus, I needed to find a more secluded spot that had those runes, so if the magic actually worked, it wouldn't be out in the open for everyone to see. Pushing off the wooden door, I turned the opposite way down the hall than I usually did when I left my room and kept one hand on the walls to feel for any more of those symbols.

The castle got quieter and darker the further I went down the corridor.

It was *perfect*.

I couldn't feel any of the runes yet, so I kept going until there was practically no light illuminating my path. The air around me was getting more brisk the farther I went as well. Thank the Gods Minka chose a warmer dress to cover the bruises because at least now I wouldn't freeze on my wild goose chase for those runes.

"Hurry up, boy. We can't keep them waiting any longer or they'll have our heads," a gruff, distant voice came from the other end of the dark pathway. My human ears strained to hear two sets of footsteps coming my way. One set seemed like a large man, judging by the sound of his leaden boots scuffing the floor and the second set was a patter, like small feet trying to keep up with the man.

I leaned into the wall, trying to conceal myself within the shadows as best as I could. I didn't know if this area was off limits and I wasn't about to find out.

The steps grew close enough to where I could see the man and small boy walking through the hallway, both carrying large baskets wafting off the smells of fresh bread and spices. I held my breath the closer they got and tried to sink back further into the wall, willing myself to disappear. I sent a quick prayer to the God Samael, with the ability to conceal within light and darkness, asking him to lend me his powers and cover me in his shadows.

They were both human servants, and the man was very large indeed and very bald. The little boy looked like he couldn't be more than eight years old, trying his best to keep up with the long strides of his companion. Luckily they were both preoccupied with their own thoughts and trying to get the food out as quickly as possible so they didn't even look in my direction.

I waited until they fully disappeared from my line of sight before I peeled myself off the wall. This must've been the way to the servants quarters. Of course they wouldn't keep it lit up. Why would they?

It was only for the humans after all.

I clenched my fists from the anger radiating off me. Fae bastards, only worrying about themselves. The fae had perfect eye sight, and were even able to see in the dark but they couldn't take the time to consider that the people they enslaved might need to be able to see in the dark to, ya know, do everything that was fucking demanded of them.

I shook my head to clear the angry thoughts and kept to the task at hand.

Find more runes.

Putting my hand back on the wall, I kept feeling for more texture changes in the stone as I kept on my path further down. A spike in the temperature stopped me immediately and I traced the symbols with my fingertips. They were similar to the ones from earlier, but not exactly the same.

Fuck it. I'd give it a try anyway.

I replaced my finger with the bloody handkerchief and worked on tracing all the symbols on that portion of the wall. The blood started to sizzle from the heat of the warm stones once I finished tracing all the ones I could feel in that small section.

It was working. Oh Gods. It was actually working.

I held back from doing a quick happy dance and kept my eyes on the dark walls, barely seeing anything through the darkness and my shitty eyesight.

The wall started to absorb the blood into it, slightly illuminating the runes with a faint red glow until it started to form a rectangular shape almost like an outline of a… a door? The runes started to glow brighter with the red coloring, and the sizzling came to an abrupt stop.

Those ancient runes created a door with the blood magic from the book.

In this case, shroud actually meant to conceal something and was not for honoring the dead. Maybe there was a tomb down there that they were keeping protected?

My heart started racing while my palms began to sweat.

I came this far and got it open, but I didn't know if I had enough courage to actually step into a potentially sealed off tomb. But if I didn't, the curiosity of what *could* be through there would slowly eat me alive until I got another chance to explore.

This might be your only chance, Cassandra.

I pushed on the stone doorway and to my surprise, it opened with ease and revealed a dark, old passageway lit with small candles hanging off the stone walls. It looked like it led into another hallway but went more or less down rather than straight. It smelled of dust and something metallic, and a little like stale murky water. I stole a glance over my shoulder, to double check no one was coming, and entered the dimly lit passage.

The air grew colder with every step I took down what was actually a ramp and not just a hallway. I followed the ramp down with a sharp turn towards the left, followed immediately by another, until I could finally see more lights. Sconces filled with dancing flames sat upon the side of the walls that lead to another tunnel.

A chill went down my spine as I headed towards the next tunnel. Keeping my steps light and quick, in case there was someone or something down there with me, I went through the small tunnel and it opened up to what looked like an office.

I was doubly wrong about this place being used as a tomb.

There was a large wooden desk in the center of the room, stacked with papers and mountains of books. Shelves all along the walls overflowed with more books, gold, and jewels.

Some chests sat off to the side with an overabundance of gold coins, while some were closed. The office had three wooden doorways on the opposite end of the room.

What was this place?

Heading over to one of the chests that was closest to me, I opened it to see it was filled with more gold and gemstones. I opened the next and it was filled with clothes; men's clothes at that. There were black tunics, breeches, and a black leather suit.

Wait. A leather suit?

What. The. Fuck.

I instantly pulled out the suit and it was heavier than I expected, as if there were rocks or something weighing it down. The long sleeves were especially heavy with a small button on the inside of the wrist. I pressed the button in and a long blade shot out of the sleeve and I let out a small yelp from the surprise.

My curiosity was definitely going to be the death of me.

Pressing the button again, the blade immediately sheathed itself back into the sleeve. It was astonishing. How could I get one of those for myself?

In every color, please and thank you.

Putting the suit back in the chest, I then closed the lid. My fingers itched to take it back up the tunnel and make it mine. But something that badass definitely had an owner somewhere that would be pissed if it went missing.

Shuffling lightly through the papers to see what they were, disappointment filled me when I didn't understand them. Most were just names with dates and numbers next to them. Some were dated back to hundreds of years ago and some were even from as recent as last month. A few of the names had lines crossed through them, marking them off the sheets of papers. Other papers were filled with drawings of our world's maps and their various leaders marked upon the territory they ruled over.

I grimaced when I saw King Seraphim's name scrawled under a depiction of Atrium. He was the reason so many died, including my parents, when he tried to take over this continent as well.

Flipping off the inanimate object that listed his name, I sent another prayer up- *may that asshole live a short and horrible life.*

I stuffed the paper back into the spot I originally found it before I went through with holding it up to the flames just to watch that asshole's name burn.

I really, really wanted to do that but this was someone's office and I couldn't just go around defiling people's property no matter how badly I wanted to.

Scanning the spines of the books on the desk, I found that the large gold lettering on most of them said *Medies*. Now, that was a subject I had never even heard of before. I flipped one of them open and it looked to be a book on the magic of spells, potions, and offerings. Most fae didn't dabble in that type of magic because they had their own flowing through their veins.

Magic like that was used by witches and mages. They had to call upon other forces such as the elements, because they didn't possess any magic in their blood but they still wanted to have access to some form of magic. Setting the book back down, I kept looking through the others. On the bottom of one of the stacks, in smaller black lettering, was a book on Menodore; *my home.*

I snatched that book up and shoved it down the front of my dress without a second thought. I was running out of time and I didn't want to be caught in here, perusing someone else's books. Gods, someone else's secret office. I'd quickly skim the book and return it the next chance I got.

I was not going to pass up the opportunity to learn more about where I was from. After the great Siege of Menodore, it was as if all the history of the kingdom was wiped off the earth. There were no books that Evia could bring me about the kingdom, and I had already looked in the library here when I was with Wesley.

Just nothing. As if Menodore never even existed. As if my life before this did not exist.

Like my parents never existed.

I bit back the sob building in my throat and wiped at the runaway tear that was sliding down my cheek.

Turning towards one of the three doors, I opened the one to my right to reveal yet another stone hallway. I only had time to take a quick peek before my luck ran out and someone caught me down here or worse, I got stuck in there.

A tingle worked its way down my spine when I stepped through the door. Stopping right at the entrance, I stilled, stunned in shock by what was before me. There were innumerous small statues, paintings and wooden figures all depicting our Gods. Everything about our Divine was piled into one room, pushed aside and hidden away just like our Gods had been since they left us. Taking a shaky step forward, I studied some of the paintings hung haphazardly on the walls.

Trailing my finger over the smooth paint, enchanted by magic to never fade, my heart started aching for this gorgeous piece just left down here. Eirwen, the Goddess of Ice, was illustrated on top of a snowy mountain. She was sitting proudly with her scaly white dragon body and wings spread out behind her. Even through the painting, you could see the power emanating off her.

Down the wall were more paintings of our Gods and what kingdoms they used to rule over. The King of Gods, Haco was depicted casting his deadly fire through the air as he soared high above Menodore. Evander, the God of Lightning and Thunder had his horned body perched atop a mountain in Cadere, a court in Atrium. I went through each picture, studying our mighty Gods and wondered what their thoughts were.

How could they have abandoned us when we still needed them so badly? Was it true what most people were saying, that they grew bored with immortality and just left, never to be seen or heard from again?

We had temples located in every kingdom, specifically for the God that blessed that High Fae ruler with their magic. It didn't make sense that all of these items used to worship them were down in a murky hidden corridor. Shouldn't they be in the temples, being treated with respect?

I left that hallway behind before all those questions

overwhelmed me. It wasn't like I could go and ask anyone about it. I would probably be thrown into some dungeon for even being near a place like this, let alone going through it all.

The next stone hallway was still lit up with more sconces, just barely dimmer than the ones in the office. The sound of chains rustling against metal put me on high alert. The hair on the back of my neck started to stand up as I continued down the dim hallway, getting closer to the sound of metal chains jingling.

The smell of urine, rotting flesh, and blood hit my nose before I saw the iron barred cells lining both sides of the long narrow hallway. The darkness stirred and I could feel the pain and anguish through the air. Each cell was filled with different faeries in soiled clothes, chains around their wrist and ankles bolted to the floor to minimize their movement. Iron collars were shackled to their necks with a small name etched into each of them that I couldn't make out from the distance.

One faerie male, with long disheveled red hair and a hollowed face locked his green eyes with mine and went to speak, but nothing but gargled noises came out. I stared back at him in horror and disbelief.

He didn't have a tongue to form the words, so only gargling choking sounds made their way out as he tried to speak to me. The iron cells and shackles kept their magic from healing them. More of the prisoners started to make the same noises, looking at me with scared, desperate eyes.

I could feel the emotions coming off every single one of them.

Pain. Desperation. Suffering.

There had to be hundreds of them. Those had to be the names that were on those sheets of paper in the office. They were all faeries. *None of them* were human.

There had to be some human prisoners, though. By the way they treated their servants, I wouldn't be surprised if they locked a lot of them up as well. Maybe they separated them by species, the fae needing the iron cells to stop any of their magic from coming through.

The trapped fairies all looked like they were fading away. Their chains started to rustle again, loud clanging against themselves like they were trying to break free of them. More moans came from even more of them this time, trying to get my attention.

I couldn't believe what I was seeing. Too shocked to talk, I just stared in alarm as my breathing came in uneven pants. My hands started to tremble with fear as a chill worked its way up my spine.

What the fuck is all of this?

I slowly backed away and ran back through the hallways as quickly as I could until I was back in the safety of my own room and away from that cold, dark place.

CHAPTER 13

Head pounding rapidly, I woke up drenched in my own sweat, sheets and nightgown soaking wet. I peeled back the blanket to cool off my too-hot skin and exposed the light pink, silk nightgown now covered in my own blood.

Fuck.

My monthly cycle.

At the realization, the cramps in my lower abdomen hit me, as if on cue. I hunched over, pressing my arm to the pain to try to ease it with the pressure. "Minka?" I called out to see if she was here already and could now help me with this disaster. We had stashed her paints within the sitting room yesterday after she thanked me endlessly when I returned and I wouldn't be too surprised to find her in there painting up a storm on the canvas I brought up later.

Shooting pain struck again and I gripped my middle, trying to reign it in. What I wouldn't give to be a faerie right about now. They only got their cycle once or maybe twice a year at most, rather than suffering monthly like most humans.

Luckily, mine had always been on the shorter side of only three to four days, so the suffering wasn't prolonged but it still sucked to get.

I got out of bed and headed into the bathroom when the doorway to my bedroom opened and Minka stepped in, going on about the weather, "It's going to rain again. I can feel it in my bones. So much for having another lovely da—" Her words stopped in her throat when she saw my blood covered nightgown and her eyes shot to the blood stained sheets. "Oh my. Here, Cassandra. Let's get you in the bath to clean up and I'll get you something to help with the pain again."

"I'm so sorry," I replied, slightly embarrassed. "Usually I keep track of it and don't ruin everything in sight."

"You're apologizing? For bleeding?" Minka laughed. "Most don't even keep track of it like that and it's a very common occurrence. Over half the population is female after all." She waved her pale hand, "It's bound to happen."

I sagged in relief at her words. Evia would always get annoyed when the time would come for me; she hated having to change the ruined linens if I didn't pay attention well enough. Like she was frustrated by something I couldn't even control.

"Now come on, let's get you cleaned up and relaxed." She pushed me further into the bathroom, "Then I'll change the sheets. How bad is the pain?"

"Scale of one to ten? About seventeen hundred." I winced dramatically from the knives stabbing into my stomach.

Minka chuckled, "So dramatic. Do you want to stay in your rooms for the day? I can let the Prince know that you're ill."

I checked my face in the mirror; those healing creams really did a number and the bruises were almost faded already. "Yes, that'd be best. My face still hasn't healed all the way and I don't want to raise any suspicions as well."

Minka started the bath and threw in some more of that weird mixture and some oils as she directed, "Now get yourself cleaned up and I'll go grab some more of that tonic for you to help with the cramps."

"Thank you so much, Minka. You truly are an angel."

"So I'm told." She winked as she left the bathroom.

Smiling at the way she had some pep in her step lately, I removed my soiled nightgown and sank myself into the warm running water. The ache in my stomach and back had already started to lessen as I let out a sigh of relief.

I guzzled down the poppy tonic Minka brought me while I was in the bath, pain already subsided. I needed to keep that shit on lock in my room at this rate. I now had a wad of thick absorbent material stuffed into my undergarments and I was already back in my bed with fresh sheets. Minka also brought me a light broth to sip with some warm buttered rolls.

Like I said before, literal angel.

The small fireplace in my room was stacked with wood and kept the room nice and cozy, despite the bad weather. I formed a comfortable pillow stack behind me to prop myself up and started to pour through the book I had snatched up the night before.

I plowed through the book all morning long until the noon bell tolled to alert me that it was time for lunch. I blinked rapidly, readjusting to my surroundings as I pulled my mind from the world that was contained in the book on Menodore.

So far, I found out that humans had existed in peace alongside the fae—well, used to, anyhow. In Menodore, the human 'slaves' were actually paid workers and not slaves at all. It made my heart so happy to know that my parents weren't subjected to the same treatment as most of the humans were here. Menodore also was the largest kingdom on the continent, the main one to illicit trade from neighboring countries, and they had even forged a treaty with the sirens in the Circadian waters. No wonder our supply chain had dwindled, leaving those not as fortunate to starve. It caused an uproar and more hatred towards the High Fae who had control over said trade routes and even the crops that needed their magic to keep growing.

I just didn't understand why all of the kingdoms in Ladon didn't follow the same customs that Menodore had. That kingdom was prosperous and well loved by its people, no matter who was ruling at the time. Their history was rich with culture and love for *all* living beings, no matter what their bloodline represented. Hell, they even had some noble families that married humans.

Learning any bit of this information made me seriously question why I was even needed here or why this alliance was necessary. They already had an example of a well run kingdom that didn't leave humans fighting for their freedom, but instead had humans working together in unity and everlasting peace.

The office I stumbled upon last night also showed that the castle's coffers weren't exactly hurting for money either. They could surely afford to pay the workers a livable wage, or at the very least *feed* them more than one meal a day.

The most interesting thing I learned was about how our Gods had truly abandoned us. They were once kind and considerate to all of us, so much so that they made a deal—a blood-oath to be exact—with King Choryrth himself to stop the dark forces that were attacking our realm over thirty thousand years ago. The blood-oath was so powerful because it occurred on the most sacred night that only blessed us every ten thousand years.

The Moons of the Divine.

On this side of the world, we only had one moon that would rise and fall as the days went on, and the same went for the other side of the world. As the ten thousand years passed between convergences, the moons slowly shifted until they met one another, interlocking among the stars, and creating a magical force that pushed down towards us. All carriers of magic in their blood would get an extra boost if they were lucky enough to be alive during the time that the moons intertwined. The Moons of the Divine fell on the longest night of the year. When we weren't celebrating Bruma, also known as the winter solstice, those lucky enough to be alive would get to witness the power of the double moons together. Sadly, I was born years after the last Moons of the Divine convergence and my mortal life would be up before I ever got to observe the glorious holiday.

King Choryrth of Menodore made his blood-oath with the Gods at the exact second the Moons of the Divine touched, giving him the power of the Gods and the ability to shapeshift into a dragon of death to defend his kingdom. Shortly after the moons interlocked, they would continue on their travels, leaving only one moon in the night sky on this side of the world and the other back on its original side.

I never knew how the Moons of the Divine affected the other side of the world, being left without a moon as it came towards us. Maybe they were washed in a wave of complete darkness during that time, or perhaps the sun never went down. But one day, I would know what happened.

But one question kept racing through my mind, though.

If the Gods cared so much then to make a blood-oath, why did they leave us when we still so clearly needed them now?

All the questions racking through my brain were starting to give me another headache. The Godsend of a tonic was clearly fading in its effectiveness.

I continued flicking through the pages, coming to the end where it was mostly drawings of the Great Castle of Menodore. It was so grand and made of dragonstone, the strongest stone known to all and impossible to break with any amount of force. Even dragon fire, the hottest fire that could burn through literally anything, could not penetrate dragonstone, hence where the name came from. It was recited in the book that dragonstone was blessed by the Gods themselves, to protect King Choryrth and his line. For when he made the deal, he was considered a God of the Divine but he could still be killed or die of old age, which for the High Fae was thousands of years old.

His blood-oath not only made him more powerful, but kept him connected to the Gods. They were bonded for life and had a sense of each other at all times. That type of oath heightened your sense of who was bound to you, allowing you to know when your blood-oath partner was endangered or hurting. They could even go as far as feeling the other person's emotions, such as happiness or pain, just as harshly as they would feel it themselves.

It was similar to the Mate bond that was decided by the Fates. Except with the blood-oath, that was considered dark magic and we didn't learn much about it because it sucked the life essence from one person to the other. The Mate bond was not a choice but predestined for you and it would not harm the other person if they accepted the bond.

To the Fates, it didn't matter what you were. Males could be Fated Mates with other males and the same for females. High Fae could even be a Fated Mate to a lower fae. The Fates didn't care about pure bloodlines, power, or even gender. As long as any form of magic flowed through their veins, they existed under one being to the Fates. They still had to accept the bond between two souls merging as one, but that was the only choice the fae had when it came to Mates.

The fae could still feel that person through the Mate bond, but not at the same level as the blood oath. The blood-oath was an exchange of power and life whereas the Mate bond was more of a joining of spirits. I had even read that some Mates could hear each other's thoughts or track that person's whereabouts for when they were in a time of need.

Rubbing my tired eyes that burned from reading for hours non-stop, I flipped past more illustrations of the greenest pine trees throughout the Kingdom of Menodore, of family trees dating back to King Choryrth himself, and of our mighty Gods with their fierceness seeping off the pages.

I came to a stop on the very last page of the most recent rulers of Menodore, the ones who died only eighteen years ago alongside my parents and most of their Kingdom. King Brodyn Choryrth, who had the ability to shift into a dragon representing Haco the King of Gods. But in his High Fae form he was one of the most beautiful fae males I had ever seen. Cropped blonde hair fell just above his arched ears, and deep green eyes with irises ringed in gold sparkled like emeralds in the sun. His light skin and long, dark blonde lashes framed those gemstone eyes. Standing at his side was Dalinda Choryrth, Consort to the King. Even though she hadn't come from a noble line, she had an amazing ability as a healer running through her magical blood. He still chose her as his wife and she was also his Fated Mate.

I ran my finger along her picture, tracing the outline of her. She was stunning, her warm skin complimenting her chocolate brown almond-shaped eyes and her dark hair was just one shade lighter than black. She was truly breathtaking. I stared at their picture with hope in my heart, of the last Choryrths of Menodore, hoping that one day we would have another set of rulers who were just as kind as them.

And from what I'd read, they were compassionate people. My heart hurt to know that they were kind fae rulers that lived alongside all other creatures in peace and harmony. Their kindness was most likely what led them to their deaths. Sadly, this world was too cold and dark for people like that. For people that were sunshine encased in a body. I sent a quick prayer up to the Gods and to the Caelum, the heavens, to thank them for their kindness towards my kind and prayed that they were resting in eternal peace.

Their kindness should never be forgotten.

A small tear escaped the corner of my eye. They were most likely kind to my parents. My fiery mother did work in the castle after all, and my father was a blacksmith who made some of the strongest swords used by the King's Guard of Menodore.

Another tear escaped. Gods, I missed them. I could barely remember much about them but when I closed my eyes, I could still imagine their warm hugs, the deep throaty laugh of my father, and the smell of my mother's verbena soap.

Minka interrupted my blubbering with her sing-songy voice, "Helloooooo, Cassandra. I brought you some lunch. Do you want it in the bedroom or in the sitting room?"

"Sitting room, please!" I called back as I hid the book under the covers and raced into the room to see her setting down a tray of sandwiches, cut up fruit, and more of that amazing tonic.

"I also have something else for you." She smirked in my direction as I took my seat and gestured across the table for her to take one as well. She beamed a beautiful smile my way as she took her own seat.

"And what's that?" I pondered before spearing a piece of

melon on my fork.

Minka held up three small books with gorgeous floral covers, one large book with a plain cover, and slid an envelope my way as she explained, "They're from the Prince." She smiled largely again as I dropped the fruit and quickly snatched the letter with excitement.

My eyes went wide with surprise as I opened the envelope that read,

> *Dearest Cassandra,*
>
> *I am so sorry to hear that you have fallen ill. I considered sending up some flowers with best wishes of feeling better but I assumed that you would appreciate some more light reading instead while you're laid up in bed. I have to say the book you picked for me was quite leg opening—I mean eye opening, and I did indeed take notes, as requested.*

I giggled out loud at that.

> *I thought I'd return the favor and pick some books as lovely as you. If the contents of those books aren't to your liking, you should enjoy the other one I added into the pile. I put my own notes in between the pages of that one. So maybe, don't send that one back to the library before taking all the notes out. I would hate for someone to stumble upon my sex notes—er, love letters.*
>
> *Sincerely,*
> *In need of a cold bath.*
> *P.S. Don't forget to take your own notes.*

I eyed the larger plain book, unable to stop the smile that was gracing my face and picked it up. Skimming through the various pages quickly, I stumbled upon a very detailed sex scene and snapped the book shut while my cheeks heated again.

He sent me books.

Books with flowers.

Rather than flowers that would just rot and die within a few days of being cut from their stems. This man—no, not a man—this male was something else. My cheeks started to burn from the blood pumping hot in my veins. I fanned myself with his letter as Minka asked around a mouthful of a sandwich, "What's it say?"

I handed her the note. She quickly skimmed it and put her hand against her forehead in a fake swoon, "That is so dreamy." She waggled her pale eyebrows. "And hot!"

I chuckled as she handed me the letter back then grabbed myself a sandwich to nibble on before I took another dose of the tonic. "Dreamy indeed."

The rest of the afternoon went by in a blur so I reread most of the book on Menodore while Minka painted in between her chores. Knowing that I would have to return the book tomorrow to its rightful owner, I couldn't help but to read it over and over. I also read some of that large book that Wesley brought, but had to put it down to fan my face again and again. I thought I would be the one making him squirm with what I picked, but he one-upped me with his raunchy choice.

Touché, Wesley. Touché.

Setting the book down on the nightstand, I walked over to my balcony. The night sky was clear and beautiful, a smattering of bright stars illuminating the garden below. My cramps had mostly subsided—the double doses of tonic really did the trick—so I decided I might as well get some more training in this evening before the pain started up again.

And if I ran into that annoying fae male again, I would just have to throw one of my knives at his scarred face. I quickly changed into my black clothes, braided my brown tresses out of my face and threw on my hooded cloak to hide my identity. It was way past dinner time and anyone left in the castle would once again be drunk out of their mind. I needed to keep my guard up and not be as sloppy as before, keep my ears and eyes peeled for anything coming my way.

I went down the dimly lit corridor and heard giggling coming from a well lit room on the left side of the hallway. I peeked past my hood and could see what looked to be another one of those sex parties but in a smaller room than the one from my first night in the castle.

There were people dancing in the center of the room—well, more like grinding on one another to the sensual music coming from the small orchestra in the corner. My heart started pounding in my chest, matching the beat of the drums. I could make out deep red velvet curtains from atop a raised dais where a handful of human women were in nothing but scraps of fabric surrounding a large, balding fae male. Most High Fae were beautiful but this male had a large pot belly, sweat glistening off his bald head down to his gray eyebrows, but he was dressed in the usual finery and covered in an obscene amount of gold jewelry.

Compensating much?

Something wasn't right about the human women though. Their expressions were cold and callous, unlike the ones in the center of the floor enjoying themselves in the midst of chaos. The women on the dais were almost slumped as if in a drunken stupor. Their eyes glazed over, looking at the grotesque fae male—no not looking *at* but almost *through* the male like he was merely an apparition.

My eyes bulged wide at the startling realization. Not drunk, but drugged. Their movements were sloppy and slow, words slurred as the fae male reached out for the one on his left side and had her settle into his lap. Her small frame fell slack against his body and her eyelids fluttered shut like she was falling asleep in his grip. Bile rose in my throat as my nostrils flared in anger.

Another fae male, taller and slender with short blonde hair and a lit cigar between his sparkling white teeth joined the little party in the corner. One of the girls moved to greet him with a sensual touch to his shoulder and in return he took one last puff from the lit cigar and proceeded to put it out on her outstretched arm. Her sensitive flesh started sizzling from the contact and her whimper of pain broke out over the music. He slapped his hand over her mouth to silence her noises as he dug the cigar further into her arm with a sick, twisted grin on his face.

Tears started to stream down the poor girl's face and he removed his hand from her mouth to pat her cheek and whispered something I couldn't make out, but it put the girl on high alert judging by her change in posture. She wiped her face and turned back towards the dais with the fae male's hand on her waist in a tight grip, bustling the thin fabric of her revealing dress.

Together, they walked up the dais and met the bald male holding out a gold encrusted container. The taller male took the container and spooned out a mound of brownish powder. He then put the powder into a pipe, and shoved it into the human girl's mouth as she stood with her shoulders back, her face not showing any emotion. The High Fae held a lit oil lamp under the pipe until the girl coughed, smoke leaking out of her mouth and nostrils.

Not even a minute later, her body started to go slack from the quickly working drug. Her once bright eyes glazed over into nothingness as the slender High Fae gripped her body and positioned her on his lap as he laughed with the bald male.

My stomach twisted and turned in disgust as my face contorted with rage. Knuckles popping from clenching my fists, I wanted nothing more than to go over and ram that oil lamp down that High Fae males throat.

Our pain was nothing but a sick game for most of those faeries.

I had to stop watching. Otherwise I'd do something incredibly stupid.

When you have power, you won't have to watch this happen.

When you have power, you can put an end to all of their

twisted games.

Turning my ass around, I walked as briskly as possible towards the training area repeating that mantra over and over in my head. I stuck close to the shadows of the night, basking in the comfort of dark anonymity to ease the thoughts of hurting them all.

Making it outside, I stared up at the stars, searching for their hidden answers to all the questions plaguing my thoughts as to why our continent had gone to complete and utter shit since the siege.

One of these days, the stars were going to have answers for me.

Staying on high alert, I stepped out into the training yard where I was attacked just a few nights before. I gripped one of the discarded swords by its hilt, the weight heavy in my hand, but a comfort nonetheless. I began going through my foot movements, sword in hand to manage the balance when I heard the snap of a twig come from behind me.

I quickly turned around to see the same fae male from a few nights ago step out of what looked to be a portal of shadow and smoke. He was wearing the same sleeveless black tunic that revealed his russet-brown muscled arms that were heavily scarred just like his face. His black hair mixed with the dark tendrils of shadows framing his face and along his tall body. One of them skirted out towards me again, curling around my wrist and the hand that was holding the sword.

I couldn't help but blurt out as I tried to shake the leechy shadow off my arm, "I thought fae had quick healing, wouldn't that make having scars like that practically impossible?"

The male smirked, crinkling the right side of his scarred face. "The magic in our blood does heal us but there are a multitude of ways for us to scar. There are potions to stop the magic from healing us and you can even go as far as rubbing salt in the wound, stopping the magic as well."

Hm. I guess rubbing salt in a wound wasn't just a figure of speech.

He continued while brushing the fallen black strands of hair out of his face, "There are a lot more ways to stop our magic from working." His amber eyes glanced down at my wrist where my gold bracelet was concealed by my black cloak. "They make iron chains that they can put on us to stop the magic from manifesting and to keep others' magic from affecting us. They can also drug us by lacing our food or drink directly with iron, leaving our magic depleted."

I shifted on my feet, feeling uncomfortable with his gaze that steadily burned through me like a thousand fires. I already knew what my bracelet protected me from. Evia said that there were a few rich humans who owned manacles like my own to protect themselves too. Quickly changing the subject so he wouldn't get any bright ideas to test his magic against my defenses, I held out my hand in greeting, "I'm Cassandra."

He stared at my outstretched hand as he scoffed, "I know exactly who you are. You are to be the Princeling's little pet."

"I am *no one's* pet," I snarled through my barred teeth as I snapped my hand back to my side. "I am to be his Consort, his *wife*."

"Is there a difference?" He retorted with humor in his

voice, his eyes flashing with a challenge.

A sound that I didn't recognize ripped out of my throat while I lunged with my sword in both hands—he met my blow with one of his own. I couldn't even fathom where he pulled his own sword from but I didn't care. I lunged over and over, and he met me blow for blow as the metal clashed against one another. I knew I would never beat him and I knew he was going easy on me. But that didn't stop me from trying and failing to break him again and again.

I was panting from exhaustion by the time he knocked the sword from my sweaty palms and said, "You must be strong enough to strike and strike again without tiring. Your opponent won't let up just because you're tired. They will take advantage of your weakness and kill you with a single strike of the blade. You need to learn how to be stronger and increase your stamina. You also need to learn how to pace yourself. Don't overexert yourself within the first few minutes or you're as good as dead."

I glared up at him with my hands on my shaking thighs as I panted, "Show me how to be stronger, then."

He flashed a vicious smile down at me, making his face seem younger and more handsome as he explained, "It takes time, little dove. But luckily, with your own mediocre training, it won't take as much. It took me *years* to become what I am today. Usually we start with wooden practice swords but it seems that time isn't in our hands to start with that luxury. You can't expect it to be an overnight change."

"I know what I have to do and I'm willing to do it." I straightened myself up after I grabbed my discarded sword from the dirt, the metal a heavy weight I welcomed in my grip.

He nodded in understanding, "The blade is an extension of your arm, and letting the blade fall away is as bad as getting your own arm dismembered."

Before I had the chance to reply, he unloaded. In three swift movements, he had my sword in the dirt again, with my wrists pinned to the ground in one of his hands and body sprawled out with him on top of me. His other hand had his sword resting against my throat so closely that I swallowed and felt the cold metal graze my throat.

Panic started to override my system as my body trembled from the compromising position the faerie had put me in. The heady scent of florals and teakwood started to fog my mind before my memories took me back to being pinned in a similar fashion by a man who wanted to take something from me that wasn't his.

All I saw from that moment on was *red*.

I would not be weak.

I would not succumb under the strength and power of another.

I would always *fight*.

My mind sharpened as I took in the male hovering his body over mine. The only parts of him touching me was his large hand gripping both of my own and his blade resting against my throat. He kept his thighs far enough apart that they lightly brushed my sides when he shifted his body, angling his face closer to mine.

From the deepest pits of my soul, I knew this male

wouldn't hurt me. If he wanted to, he already would have and he wouldn't be trying to teach me to defend myself against creatures like him. But I couldn't help the way that being at his complete mercy only enraged me further.

His black hair fell to the sides of his face as he peered down at me with those blazing pools of fiery eyes and whispered harshly, "Again."

He released my hands from his grip and backed off to give me room to grab my sword before I unleashed twenty-three years of pent up aggression and anger onto him. Steel on steel, our swords screamed together and I could hear him through the metal crashing, "Use that anger. Hone it. Use it to fuel that fire working through your blood, little monster. The anger and rage you feel isn't bad unless you let it overtake you."

I focused on my breathing as I struck, our swords arcing through the air. My breath was going ragged even as I attempted to pace myself, but I didn't have the same strength behind my blows and my form was no match for his. He swooped his blade down once more, making mine fall from my grip back onto the ground.

The stranger—with surprising patience—waited for me to retrieve my fallen weapon before we continued going through the motions. I started to recognize a pattern through his movements, almost like a dance. Stab, twist, slice, parry, back hand, double grip, repeat.

A smile graced the male's scarred face when he noticed that I had caught on to what he was doing. I followed his movements and at the last second, I double gripped the hilt and dug the blade into the back of his hand with a feral grin of my own.

Sweet, sweet victory at last.

He matched my grin, revealing his fangs but never faltered his hold on his sword while my blade drew blood. He didn't even flinch from the contact of my blade cutting into him. I bet I could cut his arm off and he wouldn't make a single sound.

I dropped my smile, narrowed my eyes and pulled back my blade back before he could snatch it from my hands.

"You're lucky I heal very quickly, dove." He waved his already healed arm with a cunning smile.

"You're lucky I don't skin you and turn you into a nice pair of boots," I countered with another swipe of my blade. Maybe if I cut him deeper, it wouldn't heal as quickly. I wondered if he was like a lizard and could grow his arm back if I chopped it off.

He let out a dark laugh, the sound like smoke on the wind as he dodged my sloppy maneuver. "I'd love to see you try."

I swiped at the faerie again using all my strength, and he simply dodged it with one hand like it was a walk in the fucking park. That only infuriated me further. I twisted and swiped again and again, never faltering while he let out another laugh, "I was raised to view humans as nothing more than cattle to be sold for our convenience, but they forget to mention the tenacity your people hold. The need to fight and fight until death closes in on you." He backhanded his own sword, knocking mine from my grip as he continued, "I was also taught that women, especially human women, are subservient to men. Female fae do have a higher standing than humans but not by much; they're certainly never seen as equals. So you can only imagine what we were taught about *human* females."

I was panting and more angry than I ever had been in my entire life. "What's your fucking point, you Faerie Fuck?"

He smiled at my insult as he grabbed my sword from the dirt. "That they were wrong, so *very* wrong, little monster." He walked over to discard the sword with the others. "That's enough for this evening."

A chill stirred the air, inky shadows forming into another portal for the High Fae male. He stepped through the portal and turned backwards toward me, "You can call me Emrys."

Before I could shout another insult at him, he was gone, along with the shadowy portal he conjured up.

"Faerie Fuck is better than Emrys," I muttered to an empty training yard before I trudged my sore body back up to my rooms to do my nightly exercises.

CHAPTER 14

I dragged myself out of bed the next morning by sheer will, my body aching from the overuse of muscles from the night before.

Muscle aching means muscle building, I reminded myself.

That was a good sign. I needed all the strength my useless human body could muster up.

As I made my way into the bathroom, Minka was already dropping a healing mixture of herbs and dried lavender into the bath. I barely had any cramps this morning, which was unusual because I almost always had them along with the bleeding during the four days.

"If you don't mind me saying, you look like shit," Minka said as my eyes went large at her comment and a trail of laughter fell out of my body as she continued, "You look exhausted, both mentally and physically, so I took the liberty of getting a bath started to soothe your aches. So get in and relax while I go get our breakfast."

I smiled at her words.

Our breakfast.

"Thank you for your honesty. I feel like shit," I remarked as I started undressing. "Thank you, also, for getting it started for me. We can have breakfast wherever you'd like this morning."

Minka beamed at me before leaving the room. Her smile was bright and I could already see the dark circles under her eyes, slowly fading into her pale skin.

I climbed into the tub, the water so hot it turned my skin a light pink. It felt so amazing that I groaned as I sunk myself deeper into the scalding hot heaven. Something caught my eye on my pile of discarded clothes. More like the lack *of* something caught it. There was no more blood in my undergarments, which meant that my monthly bleeding was already over.

Thank the Gods it only lasted a day because the pain was excruciating and I didn't want to become reliant on that tonic. I knew that stress could affect the cycle, so it must've been all the changes and everything that had happened within just a couple days that made it three days shorter than normal.

I scrubbed my skin raw with the washcloth draped over the side of the tub and stayed in the bath until the water went cold and my hands turned into prunes. I put on the silk robe Minka laid out on the counter for me and went out to see a breakfast spread in my bedroom while Minka set out some glasses and plates along it.

"That looks amazing," I said while eyeing the crispy bacon and roasted potatoes.

I loaded up a plate with bacon, potatoes, eggs, toast, fruit, and set the plate down across from me as I gestured to Minka to take a seat. She nodded her head graciously as she sat down and said, "Thank you, Cassandra. You are truly a gem."

I blushed at her words as I loaded my plate up with the same things, and extra bacon, of course.

"It doesn't make much sense that they only feed you one meal a day. Food gives you energy, and with more energy you could get more done so it's a win for you and for them," I explained as I popped a strawberry in my mouth then bit into the crispy bacon.

"They expect a lot out of us. They like to say how weak us humans are but they couldn't get anything done without enslaving us. It's quite frustrating," Minka said in between bites of her eggs.

"I truly hope that I can help implement some changes for your treatment and even your freedom. The Crown Prince is marrying one of those weak humans after all," I pointed my fork at Minka. "It disgusts me how our kind is treated here and all around the continent now."

"Now?" Minka raised her eyebrows in question.

"I found a book about Menodore," I quickly added in between bites of food, "and it was said that they did have humans working, but that's not just it. The humans were *working* for actual wages. They weren't slaves. They had rights, their own homes, and could pick what they wanted to do with their time."

It was Minka's turn for her eyes to go wide at that realization.

I continued on, "Don't you think it's a little suspicious that there was already a kingdom—a very powerful one that functioned properly without the use of slavery—and that very kingdom was the only one that was sieged, enslaving all the humans from Menodore?"

Minka shook her head as if it was too much for her to take in, her blonde curls bobbing about her head.

"We should be implementing those same laws and tactics across this nation. Not having the prince marry a human in *good faith* to the other humans. I still don't understand how our marriage will keep the Rebellion from happening. There are people dying, fae and human alike, *everyday* because of this mess. It just doesn't make any sense."

A knock on the door in the sitting room stopped our conversation, and I looked at Minka with confusion as she flinched from the pounding on the door.

"Let me go check that," I said as I got up abruptly before Minka could even stand. I closed the door to my bedroom to hide the evidence of our little breakfast date and opened the front door to reveal the Crown Prince himself looking rather dashing in black breeches with a ridiculous puffy shirt that looked kind of uncomfortable, but still very handsome on his lithe body.

My cheeks reddened when he gave me an up and down look, realizing I was still in only my silk robe after the bath, the front of it slightly open from rushing to the door. I quickly grabbed the front and crossed my arms over my chest to keep him from seeing too much.

He cleared his throat, his Adam's apple bobbing from the movement as he said, "You look beautiful, Cassandra."

I playfully slapped his shoulder, which made him grin,

flashing those sharp canines. "Don't lie to me. I just got out of the bath and was in the process of getting dressed."

"It's not a lie. You look beautiful with or without clothes, as far as my eyes can see." He wiggled his eyebrows in a suggestive manner, his blue eyes lighting up with humor as I laughed.

"Are we going somewhere or doing something?" I shouldn't have even been questioning him. I was taught to be submissive, never challenging. Do whatever he says. So I quickly added, "I can hurry and get ready if you need me to."

"No need. I simply came to check on you and see how you're feeling. I have some duties to attend to. Prince things." He rolled his eyes at the mention of responsibility.

"I feel much better already. Minka has been a great help in my recovery." I had to mention how wonderful Minka was. Drop another seed to show how valued the humans are in this castle. "Thank you for the books, they were a lovely surprise. Your included notes were excessively detailed and charming."

"Anything to help you feel better," Wesley said as he bowed with a wink. "Anything you wish."

I let out another laugh from his movement, "You're not supposed to bow to me."

"There are plenty of things I'm not *supposed* to do but that just makes it all the better." He leaned in and I held my breath as he pressed a feather light kiss to my cheek. "If I get held up with these meetings and I don't see you later today, we will have breakfast together first thing tomorrow." He promised as he grabbed my head and placed another kiss atop it.

I nodded and smiled as he turned his back and walked

gracefully down the hall.

That male was truly something else.

I fanned my face to cool down my heated cheeks and retreated back into the bedroom where Minka stood waiting, looking almost scared.

"It was just Wesley letting me know he's going to be in meetings throughout the day," I announced and could visibly see the stress leave Minka's body.

"If you have to marry any faerie, he's the best bet. Definitely not my type because he has a dick, but he's always been kind to us," Minka mentioned before plopping back down in her chair. "Everyone else is a pure asshole."

"Not like I have much of a choice in who, but yeah, he seems pretty alright," I agreed with a snort at her open vulgarity. Gods, I loved how easy it was to just talk with her, like we were old friends. "Let's stuff our faces. There are some things I wanted to study in the library today."

I spent my day in the library again, going through books, looking for more that had to do with Menodore and their ability to run a kingdom properly. Or even a book on *Medies* magic, with no such luck unfortunately. It was as if any book, any information, on that kingdom or *Medies* magic was pulled off the shelves, making it impossible to read up on either of those subjects.

They clearly didn't want anybody who had access to the library to learn the truth about Menodore. *Medies* I understood; it was a forbidden magic, making reading about it forbidden as well. But why would the kingdom of Gambriel make it seem like Menodore never existed? Like it had been erased from the map, erased from history?

I needed to go back and return the book that I stole from that chamber, find some more information on Menodore, and maybe even take that book on *Medies* to read more about it and see why it was down there.

It was barely past sundown by the time I made it back to my room. The castle was still bustling with activity, making it impossible to go out and train so my main goal of the evening was to learn what the fuck was going on in this continent.

I attached my belt of knives to my waist, just in case I had another run in with a drunken asshole. They glimmered in the moonlight against my crimson colored gown that, thankfully, had pockets.

Thank you, Minka.

I threw on my black cloak over the dress to conceal the belt and to keep me warm down in that secret passage. I stuffed the bloody handkerchief in some water from the sink to get it wet again and then shoved it in my pocket and stuck to the shadows once more as I made my way back to the concealed chambers.

There were more servants than normal heading back and forth, with trays of drinks and food overflowing. I had to stop a few times and stay close to the wall so they wouldn't notice what I was doing.

When it was clear, I traced the symbols on the wall with the handkerchief and the door opened like magic. Well, not *like* magic, because *it was magic.*

Following the familiar trail into the cold, dark catacombs, I quickly snatched one of the torches off the wall to light my way. I traced my fingers against the stone hallways to feel for any temperature change that may lead to another hidden corridor within the passageway.

Nothing but dust and cobwebs were upon the walls.

Within a few minutes, I made it to my destination. It looked exactly the same as it did the other night. Piles of gold, jewelry, books, and priceless items lined each wall. Candles were still lit by faerie magic that would never let them extinguish. I set the book on Menodore back on the wooden desk, exactly where I found it.

I skimmed the other books around the desk, the bookshelves, and some that were even thrown haphazardly on the floor.

The disrespect. Throwing a book with so much knowledge on the ground like yesterday's trash.

I picked the book up and dusted it off; another book on *Medies*. I stuffed it into the front of my dress and shuffled the pile of papers on the desk with the names and dates listed on them.

"Bullseye," I murmured when a paper with instructions on it grabbed my attention.

Neutralizing Manacles was on top of the page.

The instructions read very clearly; it was a type of *Medies* magic because it dealt in blood. This must be the collars those prisoners were wearing. Magic-stopping manacles, just like Emrys mentioned. No ones power would work when wearing those except for the one whose magic it was infused with. It wasn't enough to keep them in iron cells to stop the magic coursing through their veins, they had to put collars with similar properties to the manacles around their neck to stop the magic all together.

I looked down at my wrist, at the golden bracelet that shared similar properties because it stopped their magic from affecting me as well. I wondered how similar *Medies* magic was to the regular fae magic used to create the protective bracelets some humans were lucky enough to wear. And if the two magics were that similar or one of the same, would Radha's powers still work on me because she was the one who placed it for me?

Too many questions, Cassandra, and not enough answers.

With an irritated huff, I shoved the paper back into the pile where I found it. The dates next to the names must've been when they put the collar on the prisoners or the date they shoved them in the cells. I wish I could have talked to one of them. Even though it was none of my business, I couldn't help the curiosity running through my mind.

I searched throughout the desk but couldn't find another book about Menodore on it. I even got on my hands and knees to look under but there was nothing but a small metal chest under the desk, etched with similar runes to the ones I traced to get into these chambers. I grabbed the damp handkerchief and rubbed the blood onto the symbols along the top of it and with luck, the chest sprung open.

My heart was pattering in my ribcage as I went through the box filled with what looked like letters, unsealed but still in individual envelopes. The wax seal of Gambriel and another that I didn't recognize were on the envelopes but there were no names addressed on them.

Why was Wesley's blood opening everything? Is this all of *his*? It could've been someone he's related to, with similar blood coursing through their veins. That would only leave his mother, Consort to the King, and his father, the King of Gambriel, if it was not Wesley.

I swallowed the bile coming up my throat at the thought of Wesley keeping his people locked down here with their tongues cut out. Was I already so blinded by his charming good looks and dazzling personality to not see the monster lurking beneath the pristine surface he presented?

With shaky hands, I grabbed the letters, shoved them down my dress behind the *Medies* book, and closed the chest.

Before I could regret my decision of stealing more forbidden items from this place, I scurried back up the stairs and ran until I was in the safety of my rooms again and could go through everything that I took this time around.

My whole life was a lie.

The moon drifted in the center of the night sky, illuminating the gardens below as I sat on one of the chairs on my balcony, trying to catch a moment of peace after everything I had just learned.

Everything was a lie. *Is still a lie.* The whole continent had fallen under their lies as well.

I hadn't even gone through the book on *Medies* yet; everything I learned was from those letters. I also found my answer to whose chamber that was. Not Wesley's, but the King of Gambriel himself. Wesley's blood only worked because it was so similar to his fathers.

This marriage wasn't about *saving* our continent and making humans happy. It was about tricking us into thinking they're on our side, making us *trust* the Kingdom so they could continue to use and abuse us until we were nothing but a bloody pulp under their thumbs. Just a way to calm the Rebellion and to stop the chaos, just a way to make it easier for them to control. That's what this all was about.

Control.

Gambriel was aligning with the Western continent and had been for *hundreds* of years.

Fuck.

Durreos Seraphim, High King of Atrium, and Roderick Harrington, King of Gambriel, were allies.

Friends.

They were the reason why Menodore was wiped off the maps, why all the books on my former homeland were no longer in existence, or locked away. The reason my parents were *slaughtered* along with countless others.

For their greed, for power, to rule everyone and everything.

To enslave us all to their every whim.

The magic in the lands of Menodore was tied to the royal family, to Brodyn Choryrth. Passed down through generations when the original Choryrth, Ulric, made his blood oath with our Gods. That tied his magic and his bloodline to the land. For if the magic in the bloodline ended, the land would be inhabitable, and not to mention, the Gods would not be corporeal in this world any longer.

They were attached to the Choryrth line, so when the line died out—was *murdered*—the Gods could no longer be here, sent back to the Divine Realm they came from. With the Gods gone, their magic no longer blessed any of the lands in Ladon or Atrium, causing our dying crops. No one could live in Menodore either; the land cursed with a plight that instantly killed any crops planted there. Cursed to cause earthquakes and unleash vile monsters on any living thing trying to inhabit the land.

This was all the King of Gambriel and the King of Atrium's fault.

I scoffed in anger as I stomped back into my bedroom, slamming the glass door behind me.

The Gods never *abandoned* us. They were sent away, *betrayed* by the very nations they swore to protect. Then their children were hunted down and slaughtered for sport, being deemed a 'threat' when in reality, they were the only thing still able to protect us from the *actual* threat, to protect us from the poor excuse of rulers we had to fall under.

I needed to hit something, to *stab* something. My chest rose and fell but I couldn't breathe. It felt like the walls were closing in around me and there was no escape. This startling realization was too much to handle.

How could I stop this? Who else even knew what was going on?

The knowledge weighed on my shoulders like a leaden cloak.

Still in my dress, I slipped my cloak back on and armed

myself again. I headed out of my room to go find something to stab in the training yard. I needed air and to let this frustration out before it made me explode. Especially after learning about all the bullshit that was happening here, I was not stepping a foot out of this room without some protection.

I stuck close to the shadows in the hallways like normal, creeping lightly on the balls of my feet when I heard a scuffle on the stone beneath my feet. I kept moving forward, acting like I didn't hear it to throw off the stranger following me.

Within a second, I spun and drove my slippered foot into an unprotected dick, taking him by surprise and pinning him against the wall with one of my knives right against his carotid artery. He swallowed, the knife nicking his skin from the movement and I looked up to be met with crystal blue eyes.

Wesley.

"Kinky," he wiggled his eyebrows at the blade against his throat like it was a normal experience.

I retreated from my hold and he keeled over with his hand against his abdomen. I did kick him pretty damn hard. He straightened back up and we both asked in synchronization, "What are you doing?"

I glared at the already healing cut on his throat and said, "You shouldn't sneak up on a lady."

"I was sneaking up on a stranger, not a lady, and also was not expecting a kick to the balls and a dagger at my throat. I went to visit your rooms and you weren't there. So I decided to sneak out of the castle for the night and then I saw you—well, not you, a cloaked figure hidden in the shadows, creeping about the castle—and I wanted to see who you were and where you were going," Wesley explained as he eyed my ensemble.

"So you see a cloaked figure and you think sneaking up on them is a good idea? If it wasn't me or someone you knew, you could've been dead in under five seconds."

"I can defend myself with any means necessary, you just surprised me." He scrunched his eyebrows, looking down at my exposed knife belt, "Why are you carrying a whole belt of knives?"

"Surprise means death," I said as I sheathed my blade back and wrapped the cloak around my midsection.

"Okay, you could've killed me," he admitted with a shrug of his muscled shoulders. "Happy now?"

"Very," I smiled viciously, keeping one hand on the blades.

"Now, what are you doing with a belt full of knives, Cassandra?" He asked again with a curious tone.

"I'd rather be seen as a threat than a target." I pulled the cloak tighter around myself, hoping I could disappear from this conversation.

Having Wesley see me like this left me feeling exposed and embarrassed.

Vulnerable.

I was supposed to be a perfect lady, not a wannabe assassin running around with knives.

But to my surprise he just let out a sultry laugh as he said, "Good point." He then started walking back down the hallway. "I'm still sneaking out. There's a festival happening tonight in town, so it'll be easy to blend in with the crowds.

Do you want to come?"

I wanted to say "No, your father murdered my family and is the reason this is all happening," but bit my lip instead. "Sneaking out? Why would the Crown Prince need to sneak out? You can do whatever you want."

"Ah," he clicked his tongue as I tightened the cloak around myself once more. "That's where you're incorrect. I can't do whatever I want, especially if I were to not sneak out. I would be surrounded by guards to protect me from any threats." He eyed me up and down, at the mention of a threat. "I wouldn't be able to enjoy myself that way and it's nice to escape every once in a while. People may think being a prince gives you all this freedom, but it's just a cage I'm stuck in."

A cage. I knew exactly how that felt.

I stared at the gorgeous faerie prince. We may have been different species but we weren't that different after all. Trapped in a box that we were forced to fit into for others' happiness and for our 'duty.' I only had to do it for the past eighteen years, but Wesley had been molded into what he was supposed to be for over a hundred years, at the hands of a monster.

He held out his slender hand for me to take, "So, do you want to come enjoy the fun or stay in this stuffy castle for the rest of the evening?"

I eyed his hand cautiously. I didn't know if I could trust this male yet. His father was behind everything that was wrong in this world. He was sneaking out, though. Finding an exit to sneak out of, with no guards spotting us, would be nice to know. I grabbed his hand, "Okay, let's do this."

Wesley lifted his own hood up to conceal his face and we walked down the hallway, hand in hand. He cut through a wooden doorway on the left that wafted the smells of fresh bread and spices into the air.

I let my eyes roam over the whole room: it was the servant's kitchen with a few of them still up working. Wesley reached into his pocket and left a large pile of gold coins on the counter near one of the workers, a curvy human woman with sweat beading down her face and her red hair pulled back in a messy bun from working close to a fire all day. She nodded at him in understanding with a smile as he said, "Thank you, Willa."

He opened another door on the other side of the room that led into the cool night, holding it open for me as I made my way through. I clutched his hand tighter when the door slammed shut behind us.

A foul smell hit my nose first, so rancid that I covered it with my free hand. Along the side of the castle were metal bins full of discarded food and trash from the kitchens. Some were still full of fresh produce and untouched food. All rotting now, all going to waste. Those leftovers could have fed the starving families in town or even the slaves in the castle.

Just seeing that wasted resource boiled my blood and kept the fire burning inside me. I was going to find a way to fix this. To stop this.

I couldn't hold back my comment, "Why is all that food being wasted? You could feed so many starving mouths with those leftovers alone. All that wasted food, for what? There's no reason why you should be throwing away untouched food."

He tugged me along as he spoke, "Yes, I brought that to my fathers attention but he didn't seem to care. He said that was the least of his worries at the moment. Willa does sneak some out to families outside of the castle when she can."

I pulled my hand from his grasp and stopped walking as I hissed, "The least of his worries? These are his people, and they're dying from his lack of care and compassion for them."

Wesley walked over and gripped my hand again, a warmth flooding through my body from that simple touch. "I know, Cassandra. There are many things I want to change but cannot because I don't have the power to do so yet. My father has been, and always will be, more concerned with his own self and the power he can gain. He likes to rule with fear, not compassion. He thinks keeping the others weak will stop them from getting stronger and fighting against his rule."

"And he wonders why there's a rebellion? Ruling with fear leads to that. Ruling with kindness is how you create loyalty throughout your kingdom."

"Yeah, it's pretty obvious to most, but not to him. It'll be one of the many changes I plan to make when it's *my* kingdom," he exhaled as he ran his light brown hand through his curls. "I'm a disappointment to him in many ways. I'm not some great warrior like he was; I can defend myself, of course, but I preferred to spend my time learning about our Kingdom in the library and going out into the villages to *see* the people that make up our Kingdom. How to care for them properly, how to rule with love not fear. We have very different ideas of what being a King actually entails."

"You will make a great King if you stick to those ideals,"

I replied, surprised by his words but anxious to see how we could sneak out. "Now let's go see what this Kingdom is made of."

Wesley grinned, his brown hair falling as he dipped his head towards me, "After you, my lady."

"Well, I don't know where I'm going, so after you," I gestured with my hand as I laughed again, just like the first time I met him. His cheeks heated with embarrassment.

He led me along the sides of the castle, stopping every now and then to push us back in the shadows as a patrol of guards went by. When the next patrol walked by, I started to move forward again but his warm hands held me back as he pointed out, "You see that area over there, where the bushes stop? There's a small break in the fence line that's concealed by those bushes that we can squeeze out of one at a time. When we go, we have to run and go through. Got it?"

I nodded my reply in understanding, then realized he probably couldn't see me even with his fae sight. "Got it," I whispered.

He gripped my hand and tugged me forward as we broke off into a sprint to the opening. He was clearly faster than me but holding back so I wouldn't be left alone. We pushed through the thick bushes, their sticks gripping at my cloak as we went through. I slipped through the opening in the fence first with Wesley right on my tail and we popped up onto a cobblestone street right outside the castle.

I adjusted the hood over my face to conceal my features as he did the same and walked forward to blend into the bustling crowds heading towards the town square. I turned back and could see the tall wrought iron gates of the castle with a better view than I had from the carriage. The metal formed into a depiction of the Goddess, Aither. The one that King Roderick played part in banishing from this realm. The Goddess that was sworn to protect Gambriel under all circumstances.

He supposedly worshiped the Goddess but still cast her out back into the Divine and slaughtered her children. I gritted my teeth, trying to hold back from running away from all of this. Running from the problems wouldn't fix anything. I needed to stay and help, needed to stay and put a stop to all of this.

Looking up further, I could make out spherical shapes upon the tops of some of the pointed tips of iron. The light scent of death perfumed the air, strands of something blowing in the wind near the spheres at the top. I stopped walking and stared up at them with my mouth hanging wide open.

Oh my Gods, they were heads.

I snapped my mouth shut and bit back a whimper at the sight but Wesley could feel my hand clenching his. His eyes followed my line of sight as he said with remorse, "Those are human and fae alike, traitors to the crown, supposedly. My father puts them on display after they are executed for treasonous crimes against the crown as a symbol, as a lesson to what will happen if you betray him."

I turned my head back to Wesley as he kept going, "You know the bells that ring at noon everyday?" I nodded. "That's when they get executed, in the center of town square for everyone to see as the henchman lists off their *crimes*." He uttered the last word with disgust.

My heart dropped into the pit of my stomach. *That* was why his expression dropped in the library and he looked so disturbed. The Crown Prince was inside a warm castle, eating delicious food as his people were murdered for made-up bullshit. I squeezed his hand as we walked further into town, away from the rotting heads on the gates. "You don't seem too thrilled to see that. Can't you do anything to stop it? You're the Crown Prince, you should have some form of power."

"Seeing my people dead for crimes they didn't commit, or for reasons that are so folly because he has to instill fear into every being in his Kingdom, isn't too thrilling for me." Wesley clenched his jaw. "All it does is cause more of an uproar, as it should. To agree with the Rebellion and mistreatment of the people on this continent is to speak of treason. But it's not treasonous to me if you're defending the Kingdom, despite the Crown's wishes. I am for the *people* of Gambriel, not the rulers and nobles who say that they are."

Shaking his brown curls, Wesley sighed, "I have no power besides my name and the only power my name possesses is the fear my father has instilled in our people. To see the change, you have to *be* the change and that's exactly what I plan to do. The only good thing my father has brought upon us is the arranged marriage to you."

I could've sworn my heart had stopped beating for a second as his words truly sunk in. This male before me wanted the same change that my soul yearned for. The same change this whole continent *needed*. Remorse flooded my system from thinking that Wesley would've been involved in what his father had done. I still didn't know how much I could trust him but from what I had seen; he was a good person with a big heart who just wanted to help his people.

Wesley turned towards me and grasped both my hands into his large ones, his blue eyes burning through me. "You can help me, you have similar ideals. I can see that after only knowing you for a week. You want to help the people—we can change this place for the better."

Nodding my head, I responded, "I will help *our* people in every way I can."

I already vowed to help this continent when I agreed— well, was *forced*— into this marriage. I would have done whatever it took to set the people of Ladon free once and for all. But when I found out that the male responsible for the downfall of my home, Menodore, was not only King Harrington but the father of my betrothed, I wanted to pick up my skirts and run for the hills, away from that vile faerie king. Except now—with a Crown Prince who wanted to liberate this country by my side—I finally felt like the change we needed could finally come to fruition.

That this plan of freeing our nation would actually *work*.

Wesley smiled so brightly, my heart warmed at the sight, "Then let's go meet these people."

He led me to the town square that was decorated with fresh flowers and vendors with stalls selling fresh produce, meats, jewelry, cloth and all manner of things. Lower fae and human children of every age and size were running around the square. Most had flower crowns adorning their heads as the parents milled about, drinking and chatting with one another. Despite the darkness looming over the kingdom, some of the people were still able to find joy in their lives.

"What exactly are they celebrating?" I asked Wesley as he went towards a drink stall and got us two cups of spiced wine.

"The changing of the seasons. Summer is over, fall is coming. We like to call it the Festival of Torches in honor of lighting up the nights that will now be darker." He handed me the wooden cup, "Don't drink it yet. Give me a moment."

Wondering why I hadn't heard of the Festival of Torches if it was such a popular celebration among the Kingdom of Gambriel, I let the embarrassment of yet another thing I was sheltered from fill my gut. Everyday there was something new that I never learned about and it just made my mind reel in circles because what were Radha and Evia teaching me before? Was every single thing I learned over eighteen years a lie or did they polish over the dark truth in hopes that I could help give them the world they so desperately wanted?

The Crown Prince walked us to another stall filled with an assortment of spices and got us a tiny bag of something in exchange for a few gold coins, which seemed like a bit much for such a small thing. The owner tried to give some back but Wesley insisted and the owner graciously thanked him before Wesley turned back around to me and opened the bag.

It was *salt*.

He sprinkled some in my cup as I swirled the wine around to mix it in. "So you don't black out after one glass." He laughed as he shook the little bag in his hand and then shoved it in the inner pocket of his cloak.

"Thank you," I said before taking a sip of the wine. Flavors of grapes, spices, and elderberry exploded on my tongue instantly, easing the anxiety in my middle. "This is delicious."

"Indeed it is," he agreed as he drank his own cup. His blue eyes were tinged with longing but only for a moment. "I find I always enjoy the wine down here way more than what we get up at the castle."

We sipped our wine as we watched the people enjoying their festivities, humans and faeries dancing together, no hate or divide separating them like normal. There was not a noble or royal in sight, all were up at the castle celebrating the changing season with their own version of celebration. Most likely having a giant orgy that I did not want to witness again.

Some of the people were in simple but lovely attire and others were in tattered clothes but there was no judgment amongst them. For one night, they were free to enjoy life and all it had to offer, surrounded by their loved ones and friends. Hope bloomed inside my chest as I watched them dance in circles with faerie lights in their hands, lighting up the night.

Wesley leaned down and whispered in my ear, "Come on, I know a place where we don't have to keep our hoods up and can just relax."

I looked up at him with curiosity in my eyes, and he held his hand out for me to take again. "You better not be leading me somewhere to murder me," I muttered as I took his hand.

He let out a boisterous laugh. "Wouldn't dream of it. Besides, you would murder me first. I'm confident in your abilities."

I looked down to hide my blush from the compliment.

Yes, being told I look like a potential murderer was a compliment to me, thank you very much.

We walked down the streets, past all the vendors until we came upon a two story red brick building. A sign hung out front with another emblem of the Goddess Aither on it but at our angle I couldn't make out the name of the establishment. He opened the door for me and I was hit by a blast of heat from the warmth radiating inside. I stepped through the door and was met by a big, burly fae male with piercings lining his arched ears and one on his right eyebrow.

I stopped right in the doorway, my senses overtaken with the stench of liquor, smoke, food, vomit, and body odor. The high pitched squeal of a woman's laughter assaulted my ears along with cheery music from a piano and other instruments I couldn't see. I peeked back behind the gigantic fae and could see tables filled with people drinking, smoking, and gambling. More were off to the sides of the room kissing, dancing provocatively, or laughing together in small groups clustered about.

Wesley came in behind me, patted the male on the shoulder and shoved a few gold coins into his hand. He then removed his hood and the intimidating male grinned and grasped Wesley's shoulder in a show of a welcome, his voice a deep guttural sound as he said, "Welcome back, Wes. There's a booth in the corner for you and your friend. I'll have Trisha bring you some drinks."

"Thanks, Gus," Wesley replied before leading us to the empty booth.

I sat down on the leather cushion nervously as I eyed Wesley, "Gus?"

"He's the owner of the only place in town that actually

believes in discretion."

My eyes traveled around the place. It was a bar with many fae females and even humans with generous curves milling about in revealing cut out gowns made of see-through material, and corsets that pushed their boobs up to their chins.

Not a bar. A brothel.

No wonder he believed in discretion. I could feel my cheeks heating to a bright red at the realization. "So you're a, uh, a regular here?" I questioned.

"Yes, but not in the way you think," Wesley laughed as he caught on to what I meant. "It's a nice escape from the palace. I don't need to pay for my pleasure, but there's no shame in those who do, or for the girls who earn their coin here."

"Oh." I looked down at my hands in my lap until one of the girls brought us our drinks with a bright smile framed by long black hair that went exceptionally well with her short dark purple dress. Wesley thanked her before I whispered, "There are humans here."

"Yes, Gus doesn't discriminate. It's a job for all types of people, and they all fall under the protection of Gus. Plus they can live here if need be. It's a good arrangement for females needing that protection or needing coins." He swirled the amber liquid before taking a sip. "Gus treats them all with respect unlike some other brothels in town. This is one of the safest places for them to be."

"So you've never, uh, purchased any of the goods here?" I prodded, not able to stop the pang of jealousy running through me by being surrounded by all these gorgeous women who clearly knew how to use their assets. Strong females who knew how to embody that confidence and use it to their benefit.

Well, more like use it for their survival.

"No, I prefer my women more willing for me, and not just willing for some coin," he grinned at me and winked as he took out the salt and put a pinch in my drink.

I stirred the salt in with a knife on the table and took a sip, the alcohol burning as it went down my throat. "What is this?"

Wesley took a big drink of his before he stated, "Fire whiskey. Made right here. Some of the best in town if I do say so myself."

I looked down at the amber liquid in my glass cup and swirled it again before I brought it up to my lips. The woodsy scent with soft vanilla filled my nose as I welcomed the burn of it. They only served us a small amount in the glass, so I tipped the whole thing back in one gulp as Wesley stared at me wide eyed.

I wiped my mouth with the sleeve of my gown, feeling warm and fuzzy already. "That is seriously delicious. Why don't we have that with our dinners?"

"Because it's much stronger than wine, and after a couple glasses you probably won't know how to walk in a straight line." He laughed before he tipped his own glass back and gestured for another round. "I have a higher tolerance for it because I am *positively ancient*," he quoted my words back at me from the first dinner we shared together.

The beautiful woman with raven hair brought us more drinks, the glasses filled more than the first round. "Thank you," Wesley nodded towards her without taking his eyes off me, "I would pace yourself on this next one, though, unless you want me to have to carry you back."

Wesley sprinkled in more salt before I sipped the whiskey, savoring the woodsy flavor. "If I get too drunk to walk, at least I won't be able to murder you?"

"And hopefully you won't be able to stab me again," he smirked, showing off his deep dimples.

I tossed the cloth napkin on the table at him as I laughed, "That was an accident!" Putting my glass back to my lips, I responded, "Besides, I apologized. So it doesn't count anymore."

"I'll remember that the next time you do decide I need a good stabbing."

My eyes dragged over to the corner where a human woman and a fae male were currently making out, his hand skating up her bare thighs as she moaned into his mouth. It could've been the whiskey or the desire perfuming the air, but heat curled low in my belly.

I put my eyes back on the handsome male in front of me but he looked at me with serious blue eyes, "If you're uncomfortable at all, Cassandra, we can leave." He put his hand over mine, "Just say the word."

"No." I said rather abruptly, not wanting this night to end. "I'm not uncomfortable. It's just a new experience. That's all."

Wesley smiled brightly as he held up his glass, "To new experiences."

I clinked my glass to his, "To new experiences!"

A few hours and glasses of whiskey later, Wesley was on the same side of the booth as me as we people watched and enjoyed our drinks. His presence was a comfortable warmth at my side. All of the troubles that were plaguing my mind earlier faded to the back as I enjoyed the night with my future husband.

My husband.

I laughed out loud at the thought as Wesley turned his head towards me with a question in his eyes, "You're going to be my husband and I still barely know you."

"What do you call this? I thought this was getting to know each other?" He gestured between our closely pressed bodies.

I poked his firm chest, "You know what I mean. I've known you for a week and I'm supposed to spend my forever with you."

He smirked, blue eyes dancing with delight. Blinking innocently, he held his clasped hands in front of his chest. "Forever is a long time but it doesn't sound so bad when I could spend it being stabbed by you, Cassandra."

Throwing my head back, I let out a hearty laugh as he dropped his smirk and his azure eyes blazed into my soul. Blazed with lust hot enough that the laughter quickly died in my throat. A sudden urge of possessiveness hit me.

I wanted him. No, I *needed* him.

My mouth became dry and knees weak when his warm fingers brushed over my cheeks and I could've sworn I stopped breathing. The sounds of laughter mixed with pleasure filled moans around us faded into the background. All I saw and heard was the male before me. Desire filled every fiber of my being as I slid my tongue over my lips to wet them and his lust filled gaze dropped to them.

He was going to kiss me. Gods, this was really happening.

"Are you sure?" He whispered as he lowered his head closer to mine, the fingers on my cheek moved to the back of my head as I nodded. His grip tightened as he breathed, his breath warm against my mouth, "I want you to say the words, Cassandra. Because when I kiss you, I will finally be at the mercy of you. Is that what you want?"

"Yes, Wesley," I whispered against his soft lips, leaning further into his warmth. "That's exactly what I want."

His touch hesitated and I was going to die if he didn't follow through with it. "Fuck it," he murmured before his mouth claimed mine with a demanding kiss. The Crown Prince's hand still grasped onto my hair, kneading it, causing my body to relax in his hold. I yielded to him, opening my mouth as his kiss deepened and I could feel his warm tongue slide over mine. Pushing my tongue back into his mouth, I fought for dominance as he groaned into the kiss. His other hand moved to my thigh over my dress, his thumb working in circles on the fabric and sending a hot pulse of need between my legs. I kept working my tongue in his mouth, the slight touch of his fangs against it had me gasping as he chuckled before pulling away.

Before he could pull away, I gripped his curly brown hair as I demanded, "More."

I was out of my seat and in his lap, straddling him with his hand still fisted in my hair at the nape of my neck. Leaning down, I captured his mouth again with my own, flicking my tongue against the seam of his lips, feeling his smile beneath my own as I rocked my hips over his. "You're going to be the death of me, Cassandra."

I was filled with hunger and something more as I pulled back, looking into his blue eyes. "Then let's go together."

I couldn't even tell you why or how those words came out of my mouth but at that moment, but I couldn't have given less of a damn. Wesley smiled against my lips as he gripped my head tightly with one hand and my ass with the other and whispered, "I could spend forever doing just this."

His words sent a gush of liquid fire through my veins, straight to my core when I felt his hardness underneath me. I clutched onto his shoulders, deepening the kiss further, grinding myself up against him, feeling the warm muscles of his body under my greedy palms. One hand rubbed his knuckles against the back of my neck and the other worked in rhythm with my body, trailing down until it went under my dress and I could feel it on my thigh.

Flesh to flesh.

Gods, I'd never felt anything so good in my life.

He kissed me with everything he had and worked that hand at a torturously slow pace up my thigh until I could feel it brushing against my core. Maybe there were eyes on us and the usual anxiety that followed from being watched faded into nothingness while in his arms. Their judgmental stares fueled the fire within my veins because I wanted to claim him for all to see.

He was *mine*.

I dug my hips in harder, fighting for more of his touch when he let out a breathless moan, "Patience, love. We're not in any rush."

Gripping his shoulders harder, I dug my nails into his skin as I nipped his lower lip between my teeth. Yup, I was definitely going to perish if he didn't keep touching me. He darted his tongue out to trace my lips before going back into my mouth and pulling me closer to him. His hand was still so close to what I wanted, to what I needed.

"Please," I whispered against his lips in a soft demand as I rocked my hips back and forth.

Wesley's hand worked further against me as I ground myself up and down on his hand, pleasure fluttering low in my belly as he slipped a finger inside me. I let out a plea of desire as he worked that single finger in deeper and groaned, "So fucking tight."

Massaging his tongue against mine in sync with his wonderful hand, he moved his thumb right over the bundle of nerves that lit my entire body on fire as he worked that finger in and out of me. I shamelessly ground against it as I panted into his warm and wet mouth.

He smiled against my warm lips, his blue eyes hooded with lust as he watched me. "Fuck my fingers, Cassandra." The way he panted my name was like a prayer to the Gods.

I nodded as I kept moving my hips in rhythm with his hand, moaning to the pleasure as the world around us continued to melt away. He kept kissing me roughly, my pussy clenching his finger as he groaned again, "Be a good girl and come for me, Cassandra."

A sound I didn't recognize left my throat as I fell into an abyss of pleasure. I clenched tighter as the wave of release hit me while he drove his thumb onto those nerves harder. He captured my mouth again to silence my moans of pleasure as I rode out my orgasm. I'd made myself finish before, but it was different being at hands of another. My pleasure, quite literally, in his hands and me, completely at his mercy. It was so different but yet—I loved it even more.

My eyes fluttered open to see the Crown Prince watching me with a hooded expression. In a state of euphoria, Wesley brought his finger to his lips and tasted me with a groan. His blue eyes burned with a bright flame as he stared down at me and that sent another pulse of desire through me.

It was so *filthy*. I moved one hand down to feel his erection, wanting more. I leaned in to taste myself on his soft lips—

The front door slammed open, the cool night air moving through the room and interrupting us. I turned around with Wesley's hand now gripping my thigh to see a group of four fae males stalking into the brothel. One of them gripped a girl by her hair as she screamed and Gus rushed over, knocking the male onto his ass with one single hit and the other three jumped to Gus to fight him off.

Oh shit. A drunken bar fight was about to break into chaos.

Wesley lifted me off his lap, threw my cloak back onto me—hood over my face—and then put his on. "We have to go. We don't want to be involved in this."

"Yup, you got it." I was pulled out of my daze as I followed him to the front door. Before we could get out, one of the males grabbed me by the waist and I threw my elbow up in defense and it met his jaw with a grunt. Wesley turned and punched the faerie asshole right in the face, making him hit the ground with a thump on the wooden floor. I raised an eyebrow at Wesley, "I could've handled that, but thank you."

He grinned, "I know you can handle yourself, but you shouldn't have to."

My eyebrows shot up when I turned to see Gus still fighting off two of the men. The one he knocked out earlier was up again and coming up from behind with a lantern in his hand and the look of vengeance in his eyes. The flame burned harshly in his bruising grip; he meant to throw it on Gus and burn him alive.

Without thinking, I grabbed one of the glasses of whiskey, ran over the male with the lantern, and smashed it onto his face. I flicked the lantern up at him as the whiskey soaked his tunic and the glass cut up face. His face caught on fire from the open flame, his fae healing not working with the active flame. The stupid asshole went down on the floor, screaming while his whole upper body was consumed by the fire. I grabbed another glass and poured it over him to feed the flames and keep him on the ground.

The male rolled and screamed, trying to put out the flames that were searing his flesh. With a smile, I dumped another glass on him and watched the flames engulf his entire body. Satisfaction ran down my spine as I took a moment to admire my work. The beast inside me delighted in control over the situation and wanted *more*. The lethal inferno warmed my skin, *my blood*. Reaching for another container of alcohol, my instincts took over and I could feel the cool glass beneath my fingertips.

Wesley ran to me, gripped my hand, knocking the drink from it and hauled me out of the brothel before anything else could happen to us. The monster despaired from our loss but the adrenaline soon took over and my heart pounded lively with every step we took on the cobblestones. I knew I let that bloodlust take over once more and my heart slowed from the thought of Wesley turning away from me because of it. He kept a tight grip on my hand with a large grin on his beautiful face that I never wanted to see gone. As we were racing back to the palace, he looked me up and down as he laughed, "You're a fucking badass."

The Crown Prince saw me for everything I was and didn't falter, didn't turn his back on me like most would've. He only smiled and accepted every dark part of my soul that I tried to keep chained in and hidden from everyone. I kept running, trying to not stop as the laughter bubbled out of me, "I fucking know, right?"

CHAPTER 15

*A*rms bound to the wooden post in front of me with iron, my wrists burned with each movement. The manacles were enchanted to tighten the more the prisoner fought against them. The prisoners. That's what they were for. Not for our own kind. A guard came up with a grin on his disgusting face at the sight of my beaten and bruised face. A horse's bit with an attached bridle was in his hands. He grabbed my hair to pull my head back but I didn't make any noise from the pain radiating over my scalp.

They wouldn't get that satisfaction from me.

The guard roughly shoved the horse's bit in my mouth while I snapped my teeth at him, which earned me another lash from the other guard at my back, causing me to wince and cease my movements. He then tied up the bridle to the back of my head as if I was some wild horse they were trying to break.

You can't fucking break me. I was broken the day I was born.

That same booming voice that I had heard all my life came from behind me, "You want to protect your precious little animals?

You will be treated like one."

Crack! Another lash from the whip seared through my back, breaking the skin as blood ran down onto the dirt beneath me.

The voice spoke again, "I'm doing this for your own good."

Crack! The whip hit again, and I could feel my blood dripping at a deadly pace from the open wound.

"I'm doing this because I care about you."

Crack!

The same guard who placed the horse's bit approached me from in front of the pole again, but with a hot, salt-covered branding iron in his hand. A large S with a circle around it blazed bright red. The same brand we used to mark our own slaves. My eyes narrowed at the guard in front of me at the realization that I was going to be marked in the same way they were.

I closed my eyes and breathed through my nose to take away from the pain in my back and the agony that was to come. The sound of my flesh sizzling rang in my ears before I registered the scalding burn going through my chest. I couldn't help but try to buck and move away from the pain blooming near my heart. The brand dug in deeper, the smell of my burning flesh tainting my nose.

"Do it over and over to ensure it will not heal. Put some more fucking salt in it to show him what real pain can feel like. And you!" The voice snapped to another guard, "Don't stop whipping until he passes out from the pain and even then, I want a hundred more lashes on his traitorous filth."

The brand was removed just in time for another crack to come from the whip. Before I had time to prepare for another, they kept coming down on me, all over my body.

Crack! Against my arms.

Crack! Against my bare legs.

Crack! Against my face, blood bursting before my eyes.

The brand hit my chest with brute force, searing white hot pain went through me again, teeth cracking against the bit in my mouth as it filled with my own blood, choking me.

I woke up drenched in sweat, a scream bubbling from my throat as I sat up abruptly in bed.

Just a dream. It's not real. Just a nightmare.

I chugged some water from the glass sitting on my nightstand to cool off my skin before walking over to my balcony to see dark clouds rushing overhead, mirroring my own thoughts. My vision blurred from pain as another headache hit me. The sudden burst sucked the air from my lungs.

They were getting worse by the day.

Rubbing my temples, I blamed that delicious whiskey from the night before.

I touched my chest through my nightgown, clutching that same spot where the person from my dream was branded just to remind myself, *it wasn't real.*

A knock on my bedroom door pulled me from my thoughts. "Come in!" I shouted from the balcony and then heard the door open with small footsteps to follow.

I walked back into the bedroom, "How was your night? I had the weirdest dre—"

My words were cut off from the sight before my eyes. It was Minka, but I could barely recognize her. Her usually smooth pale skin was marred with cuts and bruises across her face, leading down her arms with matching ones. When she walked to set up our breakfast on the table, there was a limp to her step.

I rushed over to her, the words bubbling out of my mouth, "What the fuck happened?"

She set the tray down as she said, "I was reminded of my place last night."

"Your *place*?" I asked with anger lacing every word. "What the fuck do you mean?"

She flinched at my harsh words but I couldn't stop the fury from coming through them. I was pissed, not at her of course, but at the person who did this much damage to Minka.

"I am their property, not a person," she said as her puffed up gray eyes met mine.

"Who the fuck did this to you?" I growled, fighting to keep my breathing steady.

"Captain of the Guard. He is the one that dishes out our punishments and deems when it's necessary," she replied simply, like it was another damn day. "I was taking the dishes down after dinner last night with one of the other girls and she made a joke, then the captain heard our laughter."

I just stared at her as I ground my teeth, waiting for a legitimate explanation.

She continued on, "We are not allowed to act like that. Not allowed to have simple joy, such as a laugh here and there. It was quite stupid. Her joke wasn't even that funny." Minka sighed, "We are not to be seen, not to be heard."

Rushing over to my vanity, I grabbed the bottle of the pain relief tonic she brought me days before—there was still some left and I shoved it in her face. "You will drink this."

She shook her head, blonde curls bouncing through the grime and filth of leftover blood from her beating.

"Yes, Minka," I seethed as I pushed the bottle at her again. "That's an order."

She nodded and took the bottle with a shaky hand, uncorking it and drinking the rest of the contents in it. I said, more calmly, trying to ease my anger, "We are going to get you cleaned up. Those cuts can get infected if we don't clean the dirt out of them. Are you allowed to at least see the healer?"

"No, they want us to feel them as a reminder of our bad behavior. This isn't even as bad as the time before, I can at least walk around this time." Minka gave a small but bruised smile.

I rubbed my hands up and down my face, trying to scrub off the anger that was radiating under my skin. I had to fucking *do* something and I had to do it now. Until I could figure out what exactly I *could* even do, first things first. Make sure Minka didn't die from an infection caused by all those markings.

Walking into the bathroom, I started the bath and called over my shoulder, "Minka! Can you please come in here?"

She limped into the bathroom. "Wha... What are you doing, Cassandra?"

"Strip out of those clothes and get into this tub. I'm not letting you walk around, covered in your own blood still. I'll make up some excuse and say I need your help today in my chambers and if anyone has an issue with that, they can take it up with me."

Minka peeled off the dirty garments with a grimace. Fabric stuck to her skin where some of the open wounds still bled. Bruises marred her pale stomach, the size of a large man's boot imprinted into it. She got into the tub, hissing through her teeth from the heat and ache in her muscles.

The rage burning through my chest slowly dissipated at the sight of my friend, practically my *only* friend, in pain and agony at the hands of another. I wanted nothing more than to take that pain away from her and bestow it upon the disgusting King's Guard that deemed it necessary to beat her for laughing.

For fucking laughing.

I would find that bastard and give him everything he deserved and *more*. My pulse roared in my ears as red started to flood my vision from the fury striking beneath my skin. With white knuckles, I gripped the edge of the tub as I ground my teeth.

Images of a High Fae Gambriellian guard dressed in their usual golden armor with dark brown eyes and vibrant white hair flashed through my mind.

A bloody whip with small studs upon it was in his hand along with a sickening grin on his face.

The image changed in a flash to him standing before me, no whip in hand any longer, but now he was covered in blood. My blood. The male curled his upper lip as he looked down at my naked pale body. I shivered with fear against his gaze as he spit on the floor next to me and scoffed, "Mortal scum."

Starting to scoot back on the stone floor away from him, I looked down at my hands and didn't recognize them. My skin wasn't as pale as the hands before me and my limbs were a lot longer too. Sobs built in my chest as thoughts stormed through a mind that wasn't my own.

Please, not again. Please. Please. Please.

The sound of discarded metal pulled me back to the male who was now stalking towards me. Intent on getting what he wants. What he thinks he deserves.

No. No. No. No.

His large boot came down on my chest to seize my movements and I cried out in pain from the pressure as a small blonde curl fell over my face. I screamed out loud enough to shake the walls but my cry for help went ignored as usual. The guard's hot breath crested my face as he towered over me with a look of absolute hatred in his dead brown eyes.

I let my body go slack because no matter how hard I fought, they would always win. They would always chip away another piece of my soul every time they touched me against my will. Mentally curling into myself, I let my mind drift into the heady darkness that would bring me the serenity I needed.

"Cassandra?" Minka's soft voice pulled me from the... dream? A memory?

From whatever *that* was.

I gave Minka a comforting smile to not worry her about yet *another* weird fucking thing going on with me. I needed to take care of her first and then we would worry about that.

"There are too many open wounds for me to put the sore muscle mixture you usually put into mine. I don't want to make the open wounds worse," I explained as I grabbed a small cloth from near the sink. I dipped it into the water that was already turning a light pink from the blood, and started lightly dabbing at the dirty cuts on her arm.

"Thank you, Cassandra. I don't remember the last time I've had a warm bath like this," Minka said with a more relaxed smile on her face. "I remember my mother always adding in her own special oils though. I can still smell the light scent of lavender mixed with bergamot." She sank deeper in the water and groaned, "I dread the day when I no longer recall any of those memories of her."

My heart ached in my chest from understanding that all too well. "Tell me more about your mother," I prodded to distract her as I moved around to clean her other arm.

"She was beautiful and so kind. She had these striking brown eyes, like pools of melted chocolate and curly brown hair to match." A tear slid town Minka's cheek as she went on, "The last time I saw her was before I was taken here, to become a slave at seven years old."

Seven years old. That reminded me of those children working at the docks. Their bodies too thin and tiny, starved with their too big eyes drained of any life. Too big and too hopeless. Nothing to look forward to besides maybe a moment of peace between the destruction they had to endure day in and day out.

"Do you know where she went?" I asked, a ball in my throat from the pain in Minka's voice.

"Yes. She died that night, trying to protect me. Trying to stop them from taking me away." Minka closed her eyes. "The same monsters responsible for taking me away from her were the ones who killed her, but not before they brutally beat her into a pulp and savagely raped her right in front of me. They forced me to watch as she screamed out in pain, but she never stopped fighting them the whole time. I can still hear the snap of them breaking her bones, burning her flesh as they tortured her for hours. All while they held me down to witness every indecent act they did to my mother."

She opened her eyes and I swear I saw flames bursting from her usually kind gray eyes as she met my gaze. "They gouged those beautiful brown eyes out and left her in a pile of bloody pieces when they were finished with her. They told me to behave or I would have the same fate as my mother."

My eyes burned with unfallen tears. "Who were these people that did that to you?"

"The King's Guard. They had the symbol of Gambriel on their chest plates and then I was brought here, to work in this castle, surrounded by the same monsters who tortured and killed my mother. I did exactly what they said and behaved, but I still received similar treatment. I've been broken down, beaten, and raped more times than my brain wants to remember." She shook her small curls, trying to clear the brutal memories that plagued her mind.

I gripped the side of the tub with barely controlled anger as I kept cleaning the wounds. "We were taught that Gambriel and Argyll helped keep Menodore from being taken over by the Western continent. None of this is making sense. I'm not saying I don't believe you," I said as I gripped her arm lightly instead of the tub. "I do believe you, Minka. I will *always* believe you." I reassured her. "But why the hell were they our so-called savior, but also the ones to take you away and hurt your family like that? How does everyone believe their lies?"

"A lot of us have asked those questions, Cassandra. The ones that were heard questioning Gambriel, the Crown itself, were executed for treason. Even as slaves, we are bound to be loyal to this Kingdom, even though this Kingdom is what's killing us."

A loud knocking came from outside of the rooms, interrupting our conversation, and Minka stared at me in wide-eyed fear from the noise as I said, "Wait here. I'm going to see what that is and I'll find a way to keep you in my rooms for the day."

I rushed over to the door, closing the doors to the bathroom and then to my bedroom on the way to create a small barrier between whoever was at the front door and Minka. I opened the wooden door to see Wesley in a loose white linen shirt with black trousers and those same boots from the night before. His blue eyes trailed up and down my attire, widening at the exposed skin and the wet fabric clinging to it.

Fuck.

My nightgown was still covered in wet spots and dried blood from helping bathe Minka. I shifted on my bare feet, not feeling uncomfortable from the Prince's gaze, but anxious to get back to Minka.

He raised a brown eyebrow in question as he asked, "Do you need some time to get ready? I have most of the morning free and wanted to talk to you about some important things." He looked into the hallway both ways before pushing past me into my room with urgency.

"I, uh, yes. I need some time to get ready. I was just starting a bath for myself when I heard you knock. I can get dressed but my room is a disaster from—"

"We have a problem, Cassandra," Wesley interrupted me as he closed the door behind him. "My father is due to come back any day now from his trip, so I only have a little time to explain everything to you, and it may come as a shock."

Walking over to the couch in front of the crackling fireplace, I took a seat and patted the one next to me but he just looked at me and shook his head as he started pacing. "My father is a horrible male. He's a tyrant that rules with corruption that you already witnessed last night. I thought we would have more time together before I could show you everything and explain my plan."

"Your plan?" I questioned with a racing heart as he kept pacing in front of me.

"I'm next in line for the Crown, as you already know. I want to kill my father and take his place. I need to end this war before it begins. The Rebellion is getting stronger, growing their numbers, and with good reason. The slave trade had gone on for centuries until Menodore broke theirs, giving their slaves freedom and the opportunity to work for their wages. I want to implement their strategies in our Kingdom. Give the people what they want, fuck, what they *need*." He ran his hand through his brown curls and stopped his pacing.

My heart was beating slow and I couldn't get a breath out. I stared at the beautiful male before me. He wanted to help, he wanted to fix this fucked up continent, but he still turned a blind eye to everything that was happening *right in front of him.* He knew everything that was going on and spoke of change but yet he did *nothing* to stop it.

My eyes started to burn with unshed tears as Wesley spoke again, "More innocent people are going to die. Fae and humans alike if we don't put a stop to this now."

I stood up and swung my arm into his chest without thinking. "You fucking knew! You knew about Menodore and their ways but still let your father keep his slave trade going, acting as if it was all normal and that was just the way things are!" I hissed as I kept hitting his chest.

"What exactly did you expect me to do? Of course I knew. I witness the abuse of our people everyday. I spend my days having to turn away from it, having to act like it doesn't bother me until I can be in a position of power to stop it. If I step in the middle now, I'll be killed for treason and I'm the *only* royal heir who wants to make the change. If I die, their freedom dies. The ones who question it get slaughtered *immediately*." He ran his hand up and down his face, frustrated. "I don't know who my father was working with to topple Menodore but I know he's not working alone. Whoever it is, they want this whole continent under their rule, to keep the slave trade open and their coffers full."

I stopped my senseless beating as his words sunk in.

I knew who the King of Gambriel was working with. I read everything in those letters and what exactly they were planning for the night of the siege. In a split second, I decided to trust my gut and turned towards my bedroom to retrieve them to show Wesley before I changed my mind.

"Cassandra, wait. I need your help. These are your people

he's hurting too, you have more cause in this fight than I do," Wesley said as he went to follow me. "I need your help ending this before more innocent people die."

"Just give me a second!" I shouted over my shoulder at him.

Going into my bedroom, I grabbed the pile of letters and headed into the bathroom to alert Minka to what was going on.

She was getting out of the bathtub and wrapping a towel around herself as I walked through the door. "I have a solution to our problem. Put that robe on and meet me in the sitting room when you're ready."

Minka nodded as she started drying off and I headed back into the sitting room to find Wesley staring at the fireplace, utterly still.

"Read these and then I have something to show you. I'm going to get dressed real quick," I said as I shoved the papers into his hands. Remorse gripped my heart for a moment from not showing Minka the letters first, but this morning did not go how I expected.

I went into my bedroom, grabbed a blue long sleeve dress from the closet, and slipped it over my head, quickly tying the back myself, followed by matching blue slippers. Gripping my messy hair, I started braiding it and tied it with a leather strap, not caring about how disheveled it looked.

Padding back into the sitting room with the tray of breakfast in hand because my stomach was growling from hunger, I set it on the dining table and turned to see Wesley sitting on the couch, poring over the letters I had handed him.

Minka came in shortly, wrapped in a robe, already looking better than she did when she first came in. She met my gaze with cautious eyes and looked to the Crown Prince and then back to me again as I gave her a nod. She walked over to me, still limping on one foot, and took a seat at the table.

Wesley looked up in confusion at Minka nibbling on a piece of bread as he asked, "Why is Minka covered in bruises and limping like that?"

Minka stopped eating and looked up at me as I explained, "Your King's Guard deemed it necessary to beat her into a bloody pulp the night before for laughing at a *joke*."

His face paled at the explanation as I went on, "Are you done reading those yet?"

He shook his head and stood to pace, "Not yet, give me a few more minutes." His blue eyes popped back over to Minka and I as he spoke with a firm voice I hadn't heard before, "She is going to see a healer after she eats and that's final."

"Agreed." I said as I speared a piece of fruit on my fork before shoving it in my mouth. Minka didn't eat after that exchange with the Crown Prince, still too nervous to move. "Eat, Minka," I said through a mouthful of fruit.

She shoved the whole piece of bread in her mouth and we ate in silence until Wesley walked up, letters clenched in hand, white knuckles showing through his brown skin at the grip on them. "He's a fucking traitor to this Kingdom, to this country. He's been working with that bastard all along," Wesley said with so much vehemence dripping off his tongue, I wanted to hand him a napkin before it burned a hole in the floor.

I stood up from the table, snatched the letters from his grasp, and shoved them into the front of my dress as I said, "Come on, I have something else to show you."

I ran to my closet, slipped on my knife belt, and marched back into the sitting room. "Minka needs to stay in this room until we can get her to a healer. If anyone asks, she's cleaning and organizing my messy rooms at my command."

Wesley nodded in agreement as I stormed out the front doors of my rooms with him on my tail as he asked, "Where are we going?"

I slid my arm through his, like we were taking a morning stroll through the castle and not descending into the dark secrets of it. "I'm going to show you everything I've learned since I've been here."

We walked briskly along the dark corridors until we came upon the spot in the hallway where I traced the runes with a bloody handkerchief. "Give me your hand, Wes," I demanded in a low voice.

He obediently held it out as I took the knife from my belt and sliced a gash across his finger and pushed it against the stone, tracing all the spots where the runes were. They started glowing immediately, forming that same doorway as he asked, "What the fuck is this?"

I met his stare, where anger mixed with curiosity graced his features. Wesley truly didn't know about any of this down here. I was about to show the Crown Prince of Gambriel just how corrupt his own father actually was. My expression of vengeance fell down into sadness at the thought of breaking

Wesley's heart with this information.

But he deserved to know the truth about what was happening around him.

"They're runes that open a doorway with *your* blood. I'm assuming it works with yours because you share the same blood as your father. I used the handkerchief that had your blood on it, from when I accidentally cut you, and traced the runes a few days ago, and it worked." I sheathed the bloody knife back into its holster and tugged his hand, "Now come on."

He followed me quietly as I led him down the dark musty hallways, growing colder the further we descended. Eventually we made it to the glowing chamber and he stopped before entering. "What the hell is all of this, Cassandra?"

As his eyes trailed over the office, the curiosity from earlier left his face and his expression grew enraged by what was before him. Gold and gems surrounded the prince but his gaze narrowed in on the desk stacked high with books and papers.

"I still don't know. But this is where I found the letters." I gripped the box and took the bloody knife out of my belt and ran it along the symbol on the side to open it. It clicked open in an instant. I put the letters back in the box and placed it back into its original spot under the desk.

Wesley marched over to the desk, looking down at the box on the ground. "That works with my blood too?" He asked with his eyebrows drawn together in question.

"Yes, it seems like a type of blood magic that works on it; *Medies* magic, I think. I haven't gotten to go through the book

I found down here yet. I just read the letters last night before I ran into you. I also found these," I held up the ledger of names and dates from the fae in the iron cells next door.

He grabbed the paper and read through them, his eyes going wide, "I recognize some of these names." He put the papers down as he ran his now healed hand through his hair. I saw now that it was a habit he exhibited when he was nervous or working through something in his head.

"Where do you recognize them from?" I inquired as I looked through the list of names once more.

He shook his head in disbelief, "Some of these names are from the noble families, some of the *most powerful* noble families. I mean power in magic *and* in money. They wouldn't be on this sheet with intake dates like a prisoner."

"They *are* prisoners though." I jerked my chin towards the three doors, "If we go through that door, you'll see them with iron-bound hands and feet. They even have iron around their necks, suppressing their magic, and their tongues are cut out."

He scoffed, "That's awfully convenient for their tongues to be cut out, so we can't even get some answers as to why they're down there, chained up."

"I found a paper about *Medies* magic. One taken right out of the book that might answer that. Hold on."

I shuffled through the papers until I got to the one from the night before about power exchange. I handed it over to him as I explained, "I think he's made the blood-oath with them. The same one our Gods made to King Choryrth, to exchange power and blood between each other. The ledger has dates from when they were taken in and you say that some of those fae are powerful, so it makes sense for him to want them and their power for himself."

Wesley's blue eyes skimmed through the paper and then met mine with rage, "My father is not only enslaving humans, but his own kind as well? All for more power. Can you show me the ones in the iron cells please, Cassandra?" His voice softened when he said my name. The anger that was radiating off of him was directed at the one behind all of this, not at me.

His father.

The King of Gambriel.

I got up from the desk and went over to the wooden door leading down to the cells and gestured with my hand for him to follow. I opened the door, but Wesley went in first and I followed right behind him. Nervous sweat ran down my spine as the clanking of metal against metal and groans of pain came from the cells littered with people.

"Do you see any of the names you recognized?" I asked as he searched through the cells; there had to be hundreds of fae crammed into those small areas.

Wesley stopped in front of the second cell and let out a breath, "Yes, that's Edward Norbury. We grew up together. He has very powerful fire magic coursing through his veins," He pointed at the one with fiery red hair to match his power, the same one I saw first, huddled in the corner of the cell, shivering. "He was always so lively and vivacious. Always had a smile on his face. I barely recognize the male before me, but I know it's him. His parents are very wealthy nobles, loyal to the Kingdom, and Edward has been gone for over fifty years. We all thought he might've just left on an adventure or to go be with a nice female—he was always a ladies man—but now I know... My father must've taken him."

The fae male, Edward, looked up at us. His green eyes pierced our souls, and he opened his mouth to talk, but only gurgles of would-be words came out. Wesley went to the iron bars and gripped them, hissed from the pain, and let go. "The iron is enchanted to cause pain to any magic carrier who touches it. Their shackles must do the same. That's why they don't move. To move would cause more pain. Magic like this has been outlawed from this continent for decades. It's dark and can consume the one wielding it, sucking the life force from the wielder day by day."

"Just like the blood magic used for the runes and the magic in the power exchange," I said in agreement. "Your father's soul is tainted by now from all the dark magic he's been using."

"Just another reason why he needs to die." Wesley turned to look back at me, fire blazing through his usually calm eyes. "We need to stop this."

"Yeah, but how? If your father is connected to all of these people's magic, then how hasn't he gone insane from the darkness? And how are we supposed to kill him when he has this much power?"

How were we supposed to save our continent from someone with that amount of power? And not just him, but the King of Atrium too. My head started to pound, matching my unsteady heartbeat, as everything flooded my mind. I was overwhelmed with all we needed to do because I didn't even know where we would start. My breathing became erratic as

I looked at the cells surrounding me.

Everything was a cage for us to be locked up in, and I still couldn't find the damn key.

Wesley grabbed my hand, his so warm against my cold, clammy one. "I don't know yet, Cassandra. I'm going to figure it out, though. I can easily get close to him because he's my father, but overtaking him and being able to murder him is a lot easier said than done. I'm going to look into *Medies* magic and see if there's a way to overpower someone wielding this magnitude of it."

He then led me back to the doorway into the chamber filled with gold. "I have meetings with the Crown's Advisors in an hour but I don't know if I can trust them with this information because they might be a part of it all as well. They're all power hungry, just as much as my father."

Wesley started pacing again, running his fingers through his brown curls. Stress and rage were pouring off his body with every step he took. His magic started swirling around him, making some of the papers twirl into a tornado from the betrayal he was facing.

I stepped towards the prince and grabbed his arm to stop his movements. He stared down at my hand and moved his to cover my own before squeezing it with hope. Wesley's magic settled as his breathing calmed and I squeezed his hand right back.

"Then let's keep this just between us for the time being. Until we can figure out a way to stop all of this. One thing's for certain though," I stared at him with rage burning through me, "Your father needs to die."

He locked his blue eyes with mine, the same rage mirroring mine. "He *is* going to die. For all of this."

After taking Minka to the healer, I spent the rest of the day in my rooms with her, telling her everything that I learned within the past week. She ended up having to leave and bring us up some dinner, where I once again made her sit and eat half of the meal with me. She was already looking better by the end of the day but was still limping with every step she took. After eating dinner together and talking for hours, she left to go back to her chambers for the night.

I couldn't count how many times I offered for her to stay in my rooms with me. The anxiety of her being back down there, facing similar treatment as the night before had my hands shaking in a palsy of rage. But Minka refused over and over, wanting to go check on Edith, the girl who made the joke, to make sure she was okay. I sent her down with the leftover pain relieving tonic hidden in her servant's dress and some food for Edith as well.

I hadn't seen or heard from Wesley since this morning when I revealed to him everything that was corrupt in this Kingdom. The thing that still didn't make sense was why I was even *here*. Yes, they wanted to use the arranged marriage to bridge two kingdoms together and to convince humans they care and respect us. Surely they could've waited for Aunt Radha to produce an heir to bridge the kingdoms together. They could even sign a fucking treaty, or I don't know, stop treating the humans like shit. That would make the Rebellion stop.

None of this made sense and it was beyond frustrating.

They already had so much power over us, they already took most humans against our will and made us their slaves, so why couldn't they just keep doing that? Why would they need some grand gesture? It wasn't going to stop a Rebellion from continuing to rise because a damn human and a fae prince got married, if they didn't stop treating us like shit.

Fae and humans had been married before, after all. Not in the royal sense but married nonetheless. There were thousands of half-fae half-humans on this continent, but it was frowned upon and they were considered half-breeds by some of the fae who were just as prejudiced as King Harrington in that sense. But still, it existed and had for years.

It wasn't as groundbreaking as my aunt made it seem. I wondered if my aunt even knew what terrible things King Harrington was doing. Surely not, otherwise we wouldn't even be trying to combine our kingdoms.

Well, maybe she did? My heart dropped to the bottom of my chest from the notion.

In Argyll, there was still a slave trade that was predominately made up of humans. I didn't know how their treatment was, considering I had been locked up in a tower for practically my whole life and was only surrounded by the fae. But I just couldn't fathom my sweet Uncle Arron letting anybody who resided in his Kingdom be treated that way.

Walking back into the bedroom to change into my training clothes, the light from the full moon poured in through the open doors of my balcony. I went over and shut them but not before I caught a glimpse at the night sky looking like a velvet blanket littered with bright stars twinkling in the distance.

The number of beautiful and cruel things those gorgeous lights had seen throughout their million years of life was unfathomable. I was not going to waste my time gazing at the stars anymore, looking again for answers to all the problems plaguing this land. They might hold all the answers I was looking for, but there was no way for them to give me those answers, or help me in any way, like I kept waiting for.

Turning back and slamming the doors to the balcony, I shucked off my blue dress and put on the black clothes, my knives, boots, and cloak.

Instead of asking for answers, I was going to *take* them.

I wasn't strong enough yet, but with that Faerie Fuck, Emrys', help I just might be someday.

Throwing my hood up, I snuck through the hallways once more and found myself back in the training yard.

The Faerie Fuck wasn't there yet.

Typical.

He seemed like the type to always need a big entrance to announce his presence.

As if on cue, clouds of shadowy smoke created a circle a few feet away from me and out stepped the Drama King himself, dressed in all black training clothes, similar to my own again.

"How do you always know to come right after I arrive?" I asked while I walked to pick up a sword.

His voice was like a smoky caress, the shadows reaching out to me to engulf my hand but I shook them off like usual.

"I have my ways."

"Can you keep your little friends to yourself already?" I demanded, pointing my sword at him.

"They do what they please, princess," he snickered.

I curled my upper lip as I snapped, "I'm not a princess! Call me something condescending again and I'll rip out your tongue with my bare hands."

He raised his midnight eyebrows, amber eyes glittering with humor, "You most certainly are *not* a princess," he looked me up and down with judgment.

"Are we going to train or not, *princess*?" My voice remained sweet but laced with venom.

Emrys looked up at the stars, his golden eyes as bright as them. "I want to show you something first." He turned and walked down towards the forest in the distance.

Should I follow the Faerie Fuck into the dark scary woods, or trust my intuition to not?

Fuck it.

That seemed to be my motto lately.

I ran after him, following him into the darkness where the light of the moon and stars no longer touched the forest floor.

"In my homeland, there are an abundance of these throughout the land, but here there are only a few blessing us with their presence," Emrys explained as he walked and pointed down to a white flower with delicately thin petals that opened up in a circle, with a pink center surrounded by little pollen ducts dusted with yellow. It had a fragrance that was sweet, calming, and familiar. I wished I could bottle it up and dab it onto my wrists daily.

"It's a Datura, also called a moon flower. It only blooms at night and hides from the sunlight, but basks under the moonlight, making it's fragrance strong and unforgettable. The scent is absolutely delicious but if ingested, it can kill you within minutes. Sometimes the most beautiful and delicate thing can have the most deadly bite." He looked back to me with a softness behind his amber eyes as he said, "To my people, it's a symbol that not all things hidden in darkness are horrible, if you can look for the beauty in them."

"It is beautiful," I leaned down and stroked the delicate petals with my fingertips, "and the scent is amazing."

"So is your darkness. You can't see the stars that bless our sky without the darkness around them. The darkness is beautiful and it's necessary," Emrys expressed as I looked up at him, his eyes molten amber pools of honey. "You cannot know the depth of your light without knowing the depth of your darkness."

"This was another lesson?" I questioned as I stood back up and wiped my hands on my black pants.

"Everything is always a lesson," he retorted with a chuckle, "Now let's go and work on your shitty fighting."

"You're my teacher now, so the only person to blame for my shitty fighting is you."

He walked back into the training area and withdrew his blade as he leaned his head to the side with an annoyed look on his scarred but handsome face, "I guess it is true then."

"What?" I snapped as I reached for a sword.

"You can't teach stupid," he laughed, his voice like dark

velvet.

"Fuck you!" I shouted as I swiped my blade at him, messily, not helping my argument whatsoever.

"Maybe later," he smirked, scarred face lighting up in a grin as his blade met mine. "Anyways, listen here." He pointed the sword at my legs, "Your knees should never be locked. Be on the ready, always. Bend your knees slightly, keep a strong foot forward and never lock your elbows either."

I immediately changed my stance, not even realizing how I was standing, too blinded by my own rage to stab the Faerie Fuck in his heart.

Then he struck. I arced to the left, quicker on my feet than I was before, and his sword breezed past my ribs, "Good. Keep those knees bent and stay on the balls of your feet." His next move was swifter than the first, aiming right at my neck and I ducked low to dodge the blade. I could hear it slicing through the air where my head was just a second ago.

I popped up and swung my blade at him, only for his own to knock mine with a jarring clang of the clashing metal. I held steady on the blade, not letting my grip falter, as I let another swipe loose from a different angle.

He dodged it.

He always fucking did.

I snarled and lunged at him again. He placed one arm behind his back with a smile on his face as he thrust his sword to meet my own with more power behind his one-armed attack than both of my own.

That only served to add more fire to the rage that was bubbling inside me.

Everything faded to the sides of my vision, my full concentration on the male in front of me.

Taunting me.

We carried on for what felt like hours, but I knew it had only been minutes.

He parried my next blow, knocking the blade from my hand to fall onto the dirt. Before I could pick it up to retrieve it, he placed his boot over it, "We're going to try something else."

I stepped back and put both my hands at my side, waiting for further instruction.

He ripped a piece of his long sleeve tunic off his arm and moved towards me.

"What the fuck are you doing?" I asked, slowly backing away.

"You need to sharpen your other senses. Stop relying only on your vision." He tied the piece of fabric over my eyes, his scent of teakwood and something else overwhelming me.

He placed the blade back into my hand. I double gripped the hilt, waiting for his attack. I could hear the crunch of dirt under his boots, as if he were circling me like a shark getting ready to attack his prey. The hair on the back of my neck stood up as the air shifted to my right and I shoved my blade up to meet his blow before it connected with my skin.

"Good girl," He murmured as he started circling again. Heat rose up my spine from his praise and butterflies filled my chest but I ignored his senseless words. Taking another step, I spun as I could feel the air shifting from behind me again. The sound of the blade whooshed through it to meet mine with a resounding clank of metal.

We continued this dance, Emrys changing his pattern so I couldn't keep track of any rhythm he was trying to create like when we normally spared. He finally knocked the sword from my hand once again.

Irritated, I ripped the blindfold off, "Can you stop doing that every time?"

"Can you stop letting the sword fall when I hit it with more force?" He rebutted as he raised his right eyebrow, scar flexing in the night. "Your enemy isn't going to go easy on you just because it's more convenient for you."

I picked up the sword with an exasperated sigh that he was right. "Fine. Let's keep going then."

He shook his head, long black hair dusting his shoulders from the movement. "No, we're done with swords for the night. I brought you something a little more powerful than those tiny knives you like to decorate your pretty little waist with."

Looking down at my waist, I gripped my knife belt defensively as I said, "I happen to love these tiny knives." I repeated the words I'd heard the warriors in Bellator Fortress say, probably not even talking about their weapons, "It's not about the size, it's about how you use it."

Emrys stifled a laugh with a shake of his head as he sheathed his sword onto his back strap and withdrew a smaller blade from the compartment next to it. "This is a Shadowblade." He handed it to me, the smaller pommel glimmering in the moonlight with a black stone embedded into it, small writing in another language upon the handle.

"It is not to be used lightly. The longer the blade is inside a person, the more the blade absorbs that person's life essence."

I took the dagger carefully, finding it was more of a short sword than a dagger. It had a blade that was as long as my forearm and a darker metal than the other swords. I could feel the power and magic pulsing off of it. "So it not only stabs someone, but sucks the life out of them as well?" I looked up, my green eyes wide in horror as he nodded his head.

"I also have this strap for you to sheath it in. You can keep it easily concealed under dresses by strapping it to your thigh, much easier to hide than that knife belt you love so much." His mouth twitched into another smile. I was going to get that broody face to give me a grin that could rival the stars.

He held out the black leather strap and before I took it, I gripped his forearm with my hand as I looked into his golden eyes. "Thank you, Emrys. You're kind of an asshole, but also very thoughtful." That smile of his turned into a feral grin, razor sharp canines glinting.

Okay, not what I had in mind for a smile.

"Rather be an asshole than a weakling like you." He arched a midnight eyebrow my way as he smirked.

"And there goes the nice moment," I laughed with a roll of my eyes as I fastened the strap to my thigh and went to sheath the blade into it.

His hand stopped me with a tsk, tsk sound from his teeth, "You need to learn how to properly use it, little dove." He grabbed one of the knives from my belt and curled his large fingers in a *bring it on* motion.

I swiped with the small blade; like I would a sword and

he grabbed me, spinning me around. My back molded to his front and my own blade pressed against my neck as his breath tickled my ear, "In close combat, it's all about looking for openings. Just like when that man attacked you. What did you do?"

I let out a breath of my own, his smoky scent invading my senses again, "I found my opening."

"Right in his neck, one of the most vulnerable spots." He moved the blade from my neck and spun me back around. "You cannot hesitate. You have to strike. If they're armored, find the gaps in that armor and use them to your advantage."

He swiped the small blade at me and I parried it with the longer one as he continued, "Like the armpit, neck, or even the lower abdomen. Almost all armor will leave those spots in an in defensive position while battling."

We swiped and dodged each other in a circle. I kept my knees bent, feet on the ready always, just like he said. He switched his hold on the dagger and used the butt of it to hit my inner wrist at the pressure point, and my new blade went flying from the force. The Faerie Fuck caught it within an instant.

I was glaring daggers into him as he smiled and sheathed both of them, one on my thigh and the other on my waist. I tried not to shiver against his slight touch and the way it made my body pulse. His eyes danced with flecks of gold and bored into mine, "One of the most important things to remember is the difference between battle and butchery."

A portal of shadows opened up behind him, as he spoke again, "You kill because you have to, not because you know you can. That is where honor comes in." He turned and walked through the portal once again, the shadows following him as the portal winked out of existence.

I looked down at the Shadowblade on my thigh and smiled as I thought, *I'm never going to take this badass thing off.*

CHAPTER 16

I woke up just before dawn, surprisingly not that tired from the night before. My body was still sore from the use of my muscles and my head still pounded like it usually did. But it wouldn't kill me to do another workout before the sun was completely up along with the rest of the castle.

Going through the motions of more sit ups, push ups, and hell, even some squats, left my body sweating and aching for a hot bath to soothe it. I padded over to the bathroom and stripped out of my sweat drenched nightgown while the bath filled up with a steaming bliss that was calling for my body.

I submerged myself in the water and immediately felt my muscles unwind from their overexertion. Laying my head back on the warm tub, I let my eyes drift closed to catch a moment of relaxation.

Only that moment didn't last long because the spiraling thoughts of everything that had been going on outside of this peaceful bath came rushing back in.

Minka was still hurt, her body beaten down for no damn reason other than a useless King's Guard who got off on pulverizing women.

King Roderick Harrington, my soon to be father in law—I curled my lip at thought—was trying to put the entire continent under his thumb and enslave any lesser being, all while forming a sickening alliance with the dreadful Western continent.

I dunked my head under the water and kept it under until all I could think of was the burn in my lungs, begging for a breath of air. I didn't even know where to start to find a solution for these problems.

By the time I got out of the bath, the water had gone cold and the sun was up, birds singing in harmony in the distant forest.

What I wouldn't give to be a bird right now, as free as can be, soaring through the sky with the ability to fly far away from this place. With the ability to be free and never have to return to this place.

Until someone captures that bird once more and throws it back into a cage.

Skull pounding once more from the stress—they seemed to be getting worse the longer I was here—I dried myself off and threw my robe on. I headed back into my bedroom where Minka was already setting up breakfast on the small table, a bright cheery smile on her no longer bruised face.

"Good morning, Minka. How do you feel today?" I prodded as I walked over to the spread of delectable fruits and warm bread on the table.

"Much, much better, Cassandra. The bruises and cuts will fade over time, I won't let them break me. Won't let them break who I am," Minka said defiantly with a lift of her small chin.

I nodded in agreement, "Very wise words." I picked up a warm biscuit. "Let's stuff our faces to feel even better then, okay?"

She laughed, the sound a twinkle in my dark thoughts and I smiled before shoving the entire biscuit in my mouth. No need to act like the perfect lady when it was just us and everything was bullshit anyways.

After breakfast, Minka helped me into a lilac lace gown with a halter neckline that framed my chest in an almost seductive manner. The back dipped to the small of my back and I felt utterly feminine in this gown, like a seductress waiting for a man to fall into my trap. She styled my hair in a half up, half down style with pearl tipped pins pulling it back from my face, the long brown hair tickling my exposed back with every movement I made. I slid on white slippers for comfort and for the final touch, I attached my new dagger to my thigh with the black leather strap.

I gave myself a look in the body length mirror and the woman looking back at me was someone I didn't wholly recognize from just a week ago. She was the embodiment of power, beauty, and strength. Who knew that a killer dress could bring me almost as much confidence as the dagger strapped to my thigh?

I was only venturing to the library after all. A dress of this magnitude was not needed for that but I personally needed the confidence boost that came with it since all the ominous thoughts flowed through my brain endlessly today.

Heading on towards the library to try to dig up any information that could help Wesley with his plans, my thoughts continued to spiral to the dark depth of my mind.

I was going to have to meet that evil dick of a King.

Fuck.

How was I supposed to look that bastard in the face, the bastard that murdered my parents and ruined my home, and not reach for the dagger on my thigh and slam it into his eye?

I did have some semblance of self control, but I would need the Gods on my side to help me with that one.

Stepping through the doors and entering the library would never stop being a sight that took my breath away. The endless amount of books among the shelves, with the sweet smell of paper and ink wafting through the air, brought my anxious thoughts down to a lulling calm. Almost like a warm embrace, if only books could actually physically embrace me in the same manner they embraced my mind.

After a full morning and afternoon poring over any and every book I could get my hands on that could possibly help, I came up with nothing.

The only thing I found that could relate to *Medies* magic close enough would be that of a Sibyl, a knower of past, present, and future that worked through one's blood to determine their fate. They used the blood in their magic, making it a dark art. The same kind of magic that could ruin a person's mind with too much use, slowly deteriorating them until the person you once knew was nothing but a creature filled with that dark magic.

Just like the Gods' children, the Sibyls had been hunted down to near extinction due to the use of that magic and the threat they posed on our society by knowing, well, practically everything. The Sibyls started out as humans who harnessed elemental magic, just like a witch, but then moved into the dark arts for more power. They opened their hearts to similar magic, like *Medies*, allowing them to see everything within this world, and it even elongated their mortal lifespan.

Unlike *Medies*, the magic that the Sibyls used didn't pull from another's life force. Just like witches and mages, they used the elements or the blood you *willingly* offered them to use a stronger form of that magic. From what I had read, they used the blood that was offered in their rituals and read that blood to tell the past, present, and future.

If I could find a Sibyl and give them the offering they wanted, they could possibly tell me what the hell was going on and how I could help Wesley put a stop to it. Since they worked in blood magic, I could use my blood as an offering to call upon one, but it was an unlikely chance one would answer my call. If they were almost extinct, it would be a shot in the dark to get one to come to me with my shitty mortal blood.

I would just have to borrow more of Wesley's blood for the offering—they would surely answer to the blood of a Faerie Crown Prince. Well, not borrow, because I wouldn't be giving the blood back. Maybe I could even convince him to perform the offering with me and we could both get the answers we needed.

I perked up at the thought—maybe we could finally get

the answers we needed and kill King Harrington.

As if my thoughts conjured the male himself, Wesley strode into the library and over to the table that I had piled with all my books from various aspects of differing magic and the history of it.

"Hell—" I started to say but was quickly interrupted by Wesley pulling me out of my seat with eagerness. "What are you doing?" I asked as he started to pull me with him into a fast walk.

"My father's here." I faltered a step at that. "I sensed him through our blood and tracked it up to his rooms. I think something is happening in his chambers because he didn't announce his return to the castle. He likes to make grand entrances usually, and he didn't notify anyone on his staff or even my mother. I want to see what's going on and what the fuck he's doing now. There's the King's Guard outside of his room, like they're guarding something too," he said quickly and quietly as he dragged me alongside him. "I know a secret passageway where we can see into his chambers. It was used as a servants passage years ago but not anymore. It's been blocked out so you can't get into the room, but you can still see and hear what's going on in his bedroom and the sitting room. I found it when I was child because I used to eavesdrop on him—horrible, I know, but I couldn't help but be a nosy child."

"How do you know he's doing something? What if he just doesn't want to be disturbed after a long journey?" I pondered while keeping up with his hasty steps.

"Because the wards on this castle are down, Cassandra."

He stopped walking as he ran a hand through his brown curls. "My blood is a part of those wards because I share his. I can sense when they're down and when they're back up. They block anyone that's unwanted from being able to step foot in this castle, and it stops anyone from creating portals in and out of here. With them down, that means anyone unwanted can walk or portal in anywhere in this castle. The wards are never down, they were made by him and can only be taken down by him. He's expecting someone or something, and I want to know who it is."

"I understand." I gripped his hand, "Let's go."

"There's also something else." His blue eyes were two pools of pure regret.

"What?" I bristled, moving my other hand over my dress in nervousness.

"I just got a report back from a legion of the Gambriellian army. They were out scouting for rebels near the border of Jindera and came across a whole group of them. Over eight hundred of them." Wesley shook his head and looked down at the ground as he continued, "They captured them all." He looked back up, his blue eyes blazing with anger. "They were to be taken to a camp in Alryne, which is just south of here, as prisoners of war. Some of them tried to escape because they knew what was waiting for them in Alryne."

Death, abuse, and destruction was what would be waiting for them in Alryne. I had seen the small encampment on our maps. When you weren't taken as a slave into one of the larger areas or if you continued to rebel, you were either slaughtered or taken to Alryne, to the coal mines as their workers. Those children on the docks in Rimont probably came from there, with how much coal they were covered in. They were most likely bringing in a shipment for the vessels to take out along the coastline.

Wesley gripped my hand tighter, my breathing coming in ragged gasps at the thought of all those people heading to that nightmare of a place. "The soldiers that were escorting them, killed them all as punishment for the ones trying to escape. They butchered all eight hundred of them and burned their bodies right outside of Jindera. There were men, women, and children. Some were fae and some were humans, but they killed them all for trying to escape to take what they deserve." His voice was thick with conviction, "*Freedom.*"

Tears burned my eyes and bile rose in my throat. All those people. Killed for trying to reach for a chance at a better life, killed for not wanting to spend the rest of their days being abused and starved at the hands of these monsters.

I pushed the tears back, my eyes blazing with rage as I looked upon the fae male in front of me, "Let's go see what your father is up to. And then I'm going to butcher him like he did to all those people."

Wesley nodded quickly and pulled me along the castle corridors in a fast walk.

We went through multiple passageways within minutes, so many that I lost track of where we were even at in the castle. Wesley held up his hand for me to stop walking when we were in a dark passageway similar to the one I opened with the ancient runes, but we made it this way by going through the human's quarters.

He grabbed my hand and put a finger to his lips in a 'stay quiet' gesture, as he pulled me along into further darkness. I could see some light shining through the cracks in the stones from up in the distance and we passed through quickly. More light was shining through further up, larger breaks in the stone, big enough for us to see through and Wesley stopped us right in front of it. He nodded his head, brown curls falling in front of his face before he swept them back and looked through one of the cracks.

Mimicking him, I peered through the small crack and could make out the royal chambers with a gaudy amount of Gambriellian yellow across the room. You would think after being surrounded by it for all his life that King Harrington would be sick of it but nope, everything was still draped in the bright color as if to mask the darkness that he embodied daily.

The King was there, pacing in front of his bed, his dark blonde hair bound back by a piece of leather, skin pale like he hadn't seen the sun in days, and from my view, it seemed like his eyes were the darkest shade of black, matching his soul. He was of course dressed in Gambriellian finery, gaudy yellow silk to match his room and dripping with jewels and gold that adorned his fingers and neck.

My attention was quickly drawn away from the King and to the sound of crackling fire across the room. A portal opened up where the sound was coming from, outlined with bright fire and darkness. A tall, broad faerie male with cropped black hair, equally pale skin and matching black eyes to King Harrington stepped out of the portal, but didn't close it. His boots rang hollow on the smooth marble floors as he walked over to the King of Gambriel. To which the King dropped into a bow as he welcomed his guest, "It is my greatest pleasure, King Seraphim."

I had to hold back the gasp I wanted to let out. I curled my fists against my sides at the sight before me, itching to reach for my new Shadowblade.

King Durreos Seraphim of Atrium.

The most powerful male within these two continents, the deadliest male who wanted nothing more than to enslave over half of humanity to be his pets, his *livestock*.

My lips curled to match my fists, but a slight touch from Wesley's warm hand loosened my grip as his hand fell into mine with a touch of solidarity.

King Seraphim's voice boomed through the room, "The pleasure is mine, King Harrington." His black eyes traveled throughout the room, studying it. "Very lovely room. Though also a very odd place to call a meeting."

"I couldn't break the wards in Inverness, without stopping the process of our new additions. This is the safest place for us for the time being," King Harrington matched the booming tone of King Seraphim's voice.

"How goes the newest additions to our army?" The King of Atrium's voice was thick and smoky, almost familiar.

"They are getting stronger by the day," Gambriel's King said with a prideful voice. "Though I am in need of more numbers, but with due time, it will all fall into place."

A shrill voice cut through their conversation, "Numbers you shall have by next week!"

I moved my gaze to where that voice came from to see

a woman stepping through the portal; no wonder he left it open. But not just any woman stepped through, though.

My Aunt Radha. The reason I was even involved in any of this.

Wesley squeezed my hand as I let out a loose breath and squeezed his back tightly, trying to hold back the tears that were burning behind my gaze. I didn't know how much more betrayal my heart could take.

Radha was *here,* with the same people who were attempting to enslave the entire world.

There had to be some other reason for her to be with them right now.

She couldn't *be* like them.

My Uncle Arron's right hand to the King, Falkur—the snake himself—stepped out of the portal after my aunt. He was dressed in Argyll's regalia, dripping in more silver and jewels behind his slender High Fae body and pale complexion.

"How are you going to do that, Consort Radha?" King Harrington asked as he brushed off a piece of invisible lint from his shoulder.

Radha's black eyes fused with fire before she went on, "You, King Harrington, are going to throw a ball to introduce your son and the human girl's matrimony in a week's time. We will consider it the couple's official introduction to the people. Everyone from Gambriel to Argyll will be invited to it. Faeries and *humans.*" She seethed the last word with venom-filled hate.

Pushing back down the bile, I fought to keep my breakfast from making an appearance and I flinched at the way she spoke about my kind. She always made it seem like she loved humans, despite our differences. Radha wanted a world of peace and harmony, not the bullshit slavery those two filthy Kings wanted. Clenching my fists, I ground my teeth as I listened to another deception from someone I loved and trusted.

King Seraphim walked over to Radha with a genuine smile gracing his lips and put his pale hand under her chin to lift it as he said, "You are a very smart female indeed."

Radha gave him a seductive smile that made Falkur stand straight in discomfort. "After the ball, we will round up the humans in attendance and change them into Raken to increase the numbers. Those vermin breed like rabbits, so it is easier to take them and use them rather than our own kind. We need to keep our numbers aligned with our bloodlines, not sacrifice them. That's what humans are for, after all." The King of Atrium released her chin and strode over to King Harrington's chaise and took a seat lazily, like enslaving humans was just another casual day.

Well, duh, Cassandra. That *was* his every day.

It was King Harrington's turn to speak, "I will transport the vermin to Inverness and help him turn them to Raken like we've discussed, and they will no longer be useless. They will be the warriors we need for this, completely loyal to their creators."

Radha turned towards Falkur and nodded at him. Falkur clapped his ring-covered hands together twice. A human man fell through the still-open portal, bruised and scarred from the brutality he must have been facing. Radha's voice chirps in, "I have been practicing my skills at producing Raken as to not leave all the creating up to you, for I know how exhausting it must be." She batted her eyelashes at the two Kings, feigning innocence that I so easily fell for.

The human man looked around with alarmed eyes, hands and feet bound in rope to inhibit his movements from the floor. Radha sauntered over to him, her hips swinging seductively in her black skin tight gown as she moved and placed her hand on his face. She whispered an incantation I couldn't make out but I could see the dark magic pulsing through her fingertips and into the man. He started to pant, his body shaking, and he cried out from the pain before he went slack on the marble floor. His blue veins were prominent against his skin, snaking through and turning into black lines across his body.

His body laid there for a moment before he started to twitch, a gurgling noise coming from deep in his throat. His hair started falling out in stringy black strands around him as he flopped and twitched on the floor. The black veins formed and pulsed beneath skin that was turning a gray matted color, like it was flaking off with every movement. The bindings of rope around his wrists and feet snapped with inhuman strength as he sprung up from the floor with a screech, revealing razor-sharp teeth to match the new long talons protruding from his fingertips. He was like a walking human corpse with how his skin was dark and desiccated, little bits falling to the floor with every movement.

My body started to shake uncontrollably as I put a hand over my mouth to hold back the whimper building in my chest. I recognized the monster that was howling in pain from his transformation.

The jagged yellow teeth, clawed hands and hollow eyes that burned through my soul.

He was what haunted all my nightmares.

The creature reeked of dead and rotting flesh as he fell down on all fours while screeching out in pain. Radha snapped her fingers and the screeching ceased immediately. The once-human man stood at attention on two legs, waiting for her command.

King Seraphim clapped his hands. "Marvelous, Radha. He is a true beauty," he boasted from his seat at the bloodthirsty creature.

King Harrington just glared at Radha and her creation, "Yes, very marvelous." He looked at Radha up and down in disgust, "But Consort Radha, why must my son be seen with the human vermin? It's a disgrace to our name and my Kingdom. We clearly don't need to keep up this façade with your ability to create Raken."

Wesley grabbed the hand that was covering my mouth and brought it up to his own to press a feather light kiss to it. The shaking in my muscles ceased from the warmth of his kiss as it calmed my anxiety.

Radha bristled again, clearly annoyed. "Because we need this Rebellion to calm down. We can't make Raken while being fought every step of the way. We need their trust so they can fall into our hands. The disgusting vermin need to be reminded of their place once they do."

The King of Gambriel kept going, his voice filled with

anger. "I will not have my son involved in this nonsense with that human girl, let alone be *seen* with her." He scoffed, "I won't allow him the chance to think with his cock before his brain and breed with that filth."

Fire burned through my middle but I bit my tongue before I accidentally revealed us. Wesley squeezed my hand tightly again, and I returned his squeeze immediately. That small gesture anchored me back to him, even with everything going on in front of us.

Radha's laughter filled the air, "I would never let it get that far. I will take care of the girl before it gets to that, before it even gets to a wedding. This is all a part of the greater plan and everyone has to make sacrifices, *even* your son's image." She patted the King's shoulder, "Those puny little humans out number us with their fast breeding by a hundred to one. If they figure that out, we're screwed out of our way of life and then *we* will be at the bottom. We need to round them up and turn the numbers to our favor. We need a way to keep them in line and if we earn their trust, rather than their hate, it makes the job that much easier."

"Which brings me to another form of business," King Seraphim added in, "Jindera's borders are still closed to everyone. We need to sway their opinion to our favor before we can complete the takeover of this continent. I have sent my son to see what he can get out of them. It would be a lot harder to win a fight happening on two fronts. We need Jindera to fall in line with us rather than defending the humans like they have in the past."

"I didn't know the Prince of Bloodshed had resulted

in using persuasion tactics that don't have need for a blade. Wouldn't it have been better to send someone better suited for the job?" King Harrington questioned.

I balked at the mention of that name. I'd heard some of the warriors at Bellator Fortress telling stories of him. He had many names that they whispered around campfires. The Prince of Bloodshed, the Shadow of Death, the Destroyer of Realms, the Lord of Nightmares, and most importantly, Prince Durreos Seraphim, the Second. He was known for his absolute slaughter on the battlefields, no mercy given. Ever. The only mercy he would ever give you was a swift death.

"My son is trained in all areas of war," he smirked, his black eyes sparkling with defiance. "He also swore his warrior oath to me when he was a child, so everything I need done, he will do with the utmost regard. If he breaks any of the rules that I set in place, he will die. So I'm not worried about his usual tactics ruining our needed alliance with the bloodshed that he's been accustomed to."

King Harrington nodded in understanding as the King of Atrium stood up and walked back to the shimmering portal, "With that being said, I will see you in a week's time with our newest recruits and will update you with any news from my son in Jindera."

Radha clapped her hands again and the creature followed her as she walked behind King Seraphim towards the portal. She turned back to King Harrington, "I have some more loose ends to tie up and will be back in a few days. Please get everything in order for the ball, so we can round up the vermin."

Falkur followed behind the creature and turned around to bow at King Harrington before departing. The King folded his arms across his chest and dipped his chin in acknowledgement before they all stepped through the portal and disappeared.

I turned with tears in my eyes towards Wesley, who was watching everything through the small crack with rage marring his beautiful features. How my Aunt Radha referred to humans twisted my insides and caused my heart to fill with ice. The Consort of Argyll who raised me and turned me into the woman I was now, turned out to be someone I didn't even know.

I already knew that my life was a lie when I read those letters, but I didn't realize how deep these betrayals would go.

Or how much pain they would cause.

My heart cracked as the thought that I always pushed back to save myself from the heartache came roaring to the front of my mind.

I was just another pawn to her.

Wesley met my tear filled gaze with his bright blue eyes as I pressed my fingernails into my palms, creating small crescents. All that anger and rage directed towards his father fell from his expression at the sight of the hurt flooding my body.

I wasn't the only pawn they were using though.

All of us, human and fae alike, have been nothing but livestock to these corrupt rulers. They've kept us busy and turned against each other, so we wouldn't rise up and turn against them.

But just like the moon when night time falls; we would always rise to lighten that never-ending darkness.

The Crown Prince of Gambriel softly wiped away my fallen tears as I once again held back the sob building in my chest. Through the dim light, I could see his pools of blue reflecting that same hurt and heartbreak back at me. He gave me a single nod that voiced those unspoken words, *you are not alone*, before gripping my hand and leading me away from those cursed walls.

CHAPTER 17

L ifting a small tea cup to my lips, I plastered on a serene smile to the Consort of Gambriel sitting right in front of me, before taking a sip. It had only been two days since Wesley and I found out what my Aunt Radha and King Harrington planned to do. Having no idea who to trust, we kept the information to ourselves and went about our days as we normally would've, trying to act like the world we grew up in wasn't filled with deceit and lies made by our own families.

I guessed it was very common for last minute balls to occur because everyone had a seamstress on standby, waiting to make their next creation. While I didn't have one, I was fortunate enough to have mine made for me by the modiste that designed Keva Harrington's dresses. Since she was Consort to the King of Gambriel and mother of the Crown Prince, she already had a vast closet filled with gowns, but this occasion called for something new.

After being pricked and prodded by the pretentious seamstress, who showed a clear dislike towards my kind, the Consort invited me for some tea. Keva was dressed in a yellow satin floor length gown with her dark braided hair pulled up into a low bun resting on the nape of her neck. The golden bangles adorning her rich brown skin chimed together as she lifted her wrist to pour herself another cup of tea.

I gave her another soft smile before speaking, "Thank you again for having your talented seamstress make my dress. I really appreciate it."

The Consort returned the smile that reminded me of Wesley's, flashing an elongated canine as she replied, "You're going to be my daughter-in-law." My heart started pounding as she went on, "It's the least I could do to get you ready for this marriage."

I blinked at her easy words. She held no disdain for my kind like her husband, the King of Gambriel, did. She also expected this marriage to come to fruition, so maybe she didn't know about her husband's plans to entrap all the humans that would be in attendance. Wesley had told me that his mother was kind but depressed from the loss of her daughter only eighteen years ago. Her children and her court were her life, so with one of her beloved no longer around, she had fallen into a state of hopelessness.

The Crown Prince had also said that she spent most of her time in the gardens or helping the farmers crops, resurrecting the dead plant life and hosting parties almost every evening to distract herself from the overwhelming feeling of loss.

Each time I looked at Keva's dazzling face with a smile upon it, I could see the desolation whirling within her soft blue eyes. My heart started to ache for the Consort. No mother should have to lose a child like that. I felt a small sort of kinship towards her because we both lost those we loved during the Siege of Menodore.

I shifted in my seat, uncomfortable in the gaudy red gown Minka chose for this occasion. The corset was digging into my rib cage with every move I made as I set down my teacup. "I always hated those things." I halted at the Consort's words and sat ramrod straight as her gaze burned into my chest. Hoping I didn't say or do the wrong thing, I gave her a soft smile. Although I was sure she would have a far softer reaction than my traitor of an Aunt would've, I still couldn't help but feel scared of disappointing another person.

"Corsets," the Consort chuckled while gesturing at my confined chest.

Running a hand down the caged bodice, I nodded while thanking the stars that it wasn't something I had done to garner that reaction. "They are truly dreadful, but beautiful contraptions."

She sipped her tea again as she leaned back in her embroidered chair, "They're very confining, like being trapped in a cage with no way to breathe." A servant came into the room and placed a tray of warm biscuits on the table. The Consort looked up with kindness in her eyes as she thanked the human girl. As I studied their interaction, I noticed that Keva treated the servants with the same affection that she treated the nobles with.

Always courteous and compassionate to others despite the pain she felt everyday. I couldn't help but notice the differences between her and my Aunt Radha. They were both Consorts from noble bloodlines that married royalty, but the way Radha held herself was with this strong demeanor that was intimidating. Whereas the Consort of Gambriel radiated this tenderness that was inviting and comfortable to be around.

Keva Harrington was what I imagined a true Queen would be like, if Ladon followed that tradition. She turned her blue gaze back to me before biting into a biscuit, "Over my years here, I found that there are different ways to find relief from the restrictions they bring you."

I arched an eyebrow her way; I didn't think we were talking about corsets anymore.

The Consort chewed thoughtfully before continuing, her voice barely above a whisper. "You know, my marriage was an arranged one as well."

"I didn't know that." I eyed the biscuits in front of me, wanting so badly to sink my teeth into one but my corset was drawn too tight after the seamstress put it back on rather aggressively.

"*Corsets*," she said louder, like it was a slur, "can be very controlling and demand you bend and break until you can fit your entire self into one."

In the corner of the sitting room, the same servant with long blonde hair stood off to the side with her hands behind her back. At the Consort's words I could've sworn I saw the girls lips tip up into a slight smile. The girl looked healthier and more filled out than Minka did when I first arrived.

I dragged my gaze back to beauty in Gambriellian yellow as she went on, "You don't want to break yourself to fit into a mar—I mean, a *corset*, do you?"

Okay, we definitely weren't talking about clothing anymore.

I shook my head at her question, too nervous to speak. If the Consort of Gambriel couldn't even speak freely and had to resort to using some sort of code for a conversation, then I didn't want to screw it up by saying the wrong thing.

"There are a lot of limitations when it comes to wearing corsets, as I'm sure you already know. That list of things you can't do will only grow over time. It's important that no matter what corset you are *forced into*, that you remain who *you* are and you don't break for the God's forsaken invention." Keva sipped her tea as she studied me beneath her long lashes.

The human girl couldn't help but smile at her words. She seemed at ease in front of the Consort and that made my heart feel lighter. The thought that not every human forced to serve here was treated with so much hatred and disdain brought the same smile to my lips as I asked, "Are all corsets bad?"

"Oh no," she stated immediately. "Definitely not. Some just have more restrictions than others and some are just as beautiful as the day you put them on until the end of time. From what I've seen, the corset that was chosen for you seems to be a very good match and wouldn't require that same *bend* that most do."

Keva still thought her son and I were going to get married, or we wouldn't be having this conversation. And not just that, she thought that we were a good match. My heart fluttered at the thought. Our engagement may have been fake, but my feelings for Wesley were as real as the air we breathed.

Keva didn't seem too happy in her marriage and that made

me wonder how much she really knew about her husband. King Harrington was behind our Gods leaving us and the Siege of Menodore. If that siege never occurred, then Carina Harrington, Princess of Gambriel, would still be alive today. From what I had seen, Keva had no idea about what was going on around her, or she just turned a blind eye towards it, like her son had. There was no way that she would sleep in the same bed as the male who played a part in her daughter's death.

My appetite quickly ceased at the memories of Menodore burning all around me and the screams of people dying. Dying at the hands of the *monsters* that promised them protection and safety. Bile immediately rose up my throat; because the memories were becoming clearer everyday, I could practically taste the ashes of the deceased on my tongue.

Her soft voice pulled me from my thoughts, "But some aren't so lucky. My father forced me into a corset at a very young age, just like you, and I had no other choice but to bend and change myself until I could fit into it properly. I lost parts of myself that I will never get back, but if you ever feel like that's happening to you, please come to me and I will help in whatever way I can." The Consort reached across the small table and gripped my hand gently.

Gulping back the ball in my throat, my eyes started to water from her generosity and the kindness she was showing me. I squeezed her hand as I batted away a tear with my forearm. "Thank you, Your Grace."

Keva picked up a cloth napkin and dabbed at the tears building in my green eyes. "As females, we don't always get to pick our destiny, it's usually outlined for us by other people in our lives. But you can control how you react to it and where to go from there." She gripped my hand tightly once more, "We do what we must to survive."

And for the first time in what felt like a long time, my muscles relaxed as I enjoyed the comfort of a mother. Not mine, but still a mother nonetheless and a damned good one at that.

After the heartfelt conversation with the Consort, I spent the rest of the week going through the library with Wesley in any free moment he had. We tried to find more about *Medies* and if there was any way to stop that magic in case the Sibyl didn't answer our call. Every night, I would still go train with Emrys; I was getting better at the hand-to-hand combat and even got a couple jabs in at the Faerie Fuck, and the rest of my time was spent with Minka in my room.

The castle was buzzing with activity between Wesley's mother and the staff getting everything ready for the giant ball that would host two kingdoms. Horses with carriages were lined up outside of the castle, waiting to make their entrance and attend the ball that had been the only thing the people had talked about for the past week.

The King of Gambriel didn't announce his arrival and wouldn't until tonight, the night of the ball. From Wesley's guess, he was busy preparing for a way to trap all the humans that were going to be in attendance tonight, to turn them into those foul creatures that haunted my dreams.

The Raken, as Radha was calling them.

I was going to be officially meeting King Harrington tonight, would have to curtsy and play nice with the person who set Menodore up to be attacked, who murdered countless people, including my parents. I had been trained my whole life to play the perfect, docile little human wife, so I was confident in my ability to keep playing that part—but not confident in holding back from gouging that monster's black eyes out of his head.

Staring into the reflection of the mirror on the vanity, my green eyes flashed like twin daggers from the thought of killing that vile faerie. If I tried tonight, then everything would go to absolute, utter shit. It wasn't like I could actually kill someone with that amount of power when I had none of my own. He could slaughter me with half a thought, even with my bracelet stopping his magic from affecting me. We needed the perfect timing to take him on and it couldn't only be Wesley and myself. I would play my part as if my life depended on it. Well, scratch that, it *did* depend on it, and so many others as well.

In the past week Wesley had gone around the kingdom, looking for any trace of the Rebellion to bring to his side and help us. None would come forward and I didn't blame them. Why would they out their only source of power; because the Crown Prince wanted to help? For as much as they knew and trusted, Wesley was on his father's side and wanted to gather them up like cattle heading to slaughter. The best thing anyone in that Rebellion, and any human, could do was heed Wesley's quiet warnings to not attend the ball tonight, no matter the invitations and good-natured attempts that the Kingdoms of Gambriel and Argyll were putting off.

I looked back up at Minka's pale hands, fast at work in the mirror, pinning my long brown hair out of my face and having it cascade in a pile of loose waves down my open back. The pins she was using tonight were shaped like golden dragon wings, to honor our Gods. One on each side of my head to form the perfect wingspan when looking at my hair from behind. The cool metal against my scalp kept the fire burning within me. A constant reminder of how the King of Gambriel and Consort of Argyll sent our Gods, *our protectors*, out of this realm.

The royal seamstress was not happy with my choice of color for my gown, she thought I should wear Gambriellian yellow to honor my marriage to Wesley, but I decided upon deep emerald green to honor my own country; the only place I would ever actually consider my home even though it had been long forgotten: the Kingdom of Menodore.

The satin gown brought out the green in my eyes, matching the dress almost to perfection. It had a halter neck style similar to the lilac lace gown I wore last week, but instead of just dipping low on my back, the emerald satin dropped down to a deep vee in the center of my chest and stopped just along my ribs to expose quite a bit of cleavage. The halter created a collar of green around my neck that accentuated it perfectly. My back was fully open and exposed besides my hair cascading down it in soft waves. There was also a slit on the left side of the dress that went all the way up to my upper thigh. The fae were sensual beings and this dress wouldn't be anything on the risqué side but my human heart still felt a pang of rebellion within myself for wearing such a thing.

I stood from the vanity once Minka was finished with the final touches of my hair and she started to drape the long, golden necklace that was covered in crystals on my neck. The brisk metal and gems trailed town my exposed back in similar fashion to the ones on the front that were shimmering in the candle light, sending small rainbows across the room.

I was still able to keep my dagger from Emrys sheathed in my thigh strap on my right side, the satin long and flowy, keeping it concealed even against such thin fabric. Minka added some more golden glitter to my face, some falling in the valley between my breasts, accentuating them in the light. She helped me slip on the strappy golden heels that would make running a real bitch. If all went well with our plan to call upon the Sibyl tonight, with so many other distractions, hopefully I wouldn't need to run anyway.

If it came down to that, I'd just toss them aside no matter how gorgeous they truly were.

Rapping on the door told me my date and fake future husband had arrived just in time to head down to the ballroom together. We didn't know if the marriage would even happen after overhearing the meeting in the King's chambers. We still played the part to keep up the façade and also because I had started to really enjoy his company and he enjoyed mine. Even if this marriage was a farce all along, I couldn't help but wish we could still be together in some way when it was all done with.

Fool's hope, I supposed.

My heels clacked against the stone floors as I went to open the door to a stunning Wesley dressed in the finest clothing I had ever seen. He wore a pewter tunic, embroidered with the bright Gambriellian yellow that almost looked gold, and matching gray pants, with his brown curls pushed back to reveal his light brown handsome, courtesan-like face. His blue eyes glistened in the firelight and his gaze swept over my dress as he cleared his throat and held his arm out for me to take.

My tawny beige fingers glided out to his outstretched arm as I smiled at him. "Now you look absolutely delicious," I said, repeating the words he said to me when I first arrived.

Wesley chuckled deep in his throat. "That dress is something else. I don't think myself or anyone else will be able to take their eyes off you."

"That's the plan, isn't it?"

Seriousness flashed in his ocean-like eyes as he nodded, his voice dropping into a whisper, "I walked through the ballroom as the servants bustled about getting everything ready, and could taste the dark magic on my tongue. I'm guessing that he set up more wards, the kind to trap people in rather than keep them out." Wesley started walking towards the ballroom as he continued, "I'm going to need to break the ward otherwise any human that comes into the ballroom will be trapped in there."

I stiffened against him, "How am I supposed to go and summon the Sibyl if I get trapped in the ballroom with everyone else?"

"I thought of that on my way here; The ward won't hold

me in with my High Fae blood but you're going to take this vial," he reached into his pocket to retrieve it and handed it over to me, "And keep it on you and that should offset the ward from keeping you trapped in. We're going to test it right when we get there to make sure our plan doesn't fall to shit."

I nodded and grabbed the vial of blood; I was also going to use it to call upon the Sibyl in case it didn't answer to my human blood. I slipped the vial next to the dagger sheathed on my thigh as Wesley watched me before we continued on and he cleared his throat again.

Wesley's eyes smoldered with lust at the exposure of my thigh with each step and a blush crept up to my already-rosy cheeks from the creamy rouge that Minka brushed on. As we got closer to the ballroom, my grip on his arm grew tighter and he patted my hand in reassurance as he spoke, his voice low and sure, "You can do this." He stopped and gripped my arm as his blue eyes blazed into mine. "You are not their prey, Cassandra. You are a *wolf*. A predator trapped in a cage of their making. Even draped in silk and jewels and finery. You are a wolf—a predator that is not to be messed with unless they want to see how deep your bite can go."

Fire replaced the unease that was filling my gut. I held my head high as I repeated his words. "I am a wolf, a *predator*. Trapped in a cage of their making. Even draped in silk and jewels and finery."

They raised me to be a sheep but they got a predator instead. I took one more deep breath to steel myself, "I am a wolf."

"That's my girl." Wesley spoke barely above a whisper

as I leaned into his touch, loving the way he called me *his*. Those azure eyes softened as he gave me a dimple filled smile. I returned it with one of my own before we walked into the ballroom.

Wesley smiled at the guards and quickly backtracked his steps as if he dropped something in the hallway before entering with my hand still wrapped around his arm, testing the ward with me. I let out a breath of relief when I was still able to leave the ballroom.

The guards decked in golden armor lined the doors of the ballroom and stirred in their armor, ready to make the announcement of our arrival. One of them banged a long staff on the marble floor, getting everyone's attention. The music stopped abruptly and so did the dancing and all movement from the crowd as they turned towards the loud noise.

"Announcing the arrival of The Crown Prince of Gambriel, Wesley Harrington and soon-to-be Consort to the Crown Prince, Cassandra of Argyll!" He bellowed out, his magic enhancing the announcement to everyone in the ballroom.

Wesley started moving forward and I held back, so he could make his grand entrance but he gripped my arm and whispered, "I want you by my side, Cassandra. Not behind me." My heart panged in my chest from his caring words. He always had a way to make me feel like his equal in whatever we were doing. As a human, I was always treated with low regard and like my opinions didn't matter. I've had to hide myself away, put on a mask for the world to see and never make myself vulnerable or appear weak. But with Wesley at my side, I finally felt seen, felt *cared for*, for the first time in my mortal life.

I nodded as I stared into his blue eyes and stepped up, matching his strides as we made our way to the throne on the other side of the room.

The crowd erupted with cheers and booming applause including whistles and hoots for their Crown Prince. Some fae sent scoffs my way or muttered obscenities as I walked past but I didn't let that falter my movement. Mingling between it all, I could make out the small applause from the any humans, from the people who had lived in fear their whole lives. People who believed this marriage would be the answer to their endless prayers and the end of the nightmares they saw regularly.

Glittering chandeliers lit with faerie light hung from the golden ceiling and flames danced in sconces throughout the walls and flared with bright light. Banners hung down from the ceiling, every one of them a different color with a separate depiction of each of the Gods fluttering through the warm air as we walked under them. It disgusted me that they would dare put them up in honor of the Gods, when no honor flowed through the King's blood, when he was the reason that we could no longer call upon our Gods.

There were various tables set up along the sides of the room filled with all types of foods and beverages. The amount of food seemed endless and yet the people on the outside of the castle were still starving to death because of this King's selfishness. I kept my expression composed and neutral, even though there was a fire of rage burning through my veins, begging to be let out.

The fae males were clad in tailored suits and tunics, looking every part the rich nobles with differing fabric adorning their skin. Suede, silk, and even velvet around them. Whereas the fae females milled about in gorgeous but outrageous gowns covered in crystals, gems, and metallic colors. You could see the difference between the humans and the fae just by their attire. The humans weren't dressed in as much finery as the fae but still were in lovely but more simple gowns and two-piece suits.

I could feel everyone's stares blazing through down to my soul, their unanswered questions going through their minds.

Why her?

Why this human for his wife?

Why did this pathetic human survive the Siege of Menodore and get to become practical royalty while we scrounge for basic necessities?

Keeping my eyes on the marble floor as I walked, their questions raced through my mind as well. I had asked myself the same thing every day I woke up in a new Kingdom, locked in a tower to become the person we supposedly needed to stop the death and destruction.

Wesley squeezed my hand with his own, the warmth pulling me from my spiraling thoughts.

Looking up before me, I could see the floor was slightly raised to create a large dais that the King of Gambriel sat on. His throne consisted of jewel-encrusted gold, and he was draped in more golden finery to match the crown atop his dark blonde hair. He looked so gaudy in his ridiculous outfit;

he reeked of power and it was not the good kind.

My eyes trailed over to my Aunt Radha standing on his side, in a deep blue gown with a poofy bottom covered in glitter. She smiled with blood red lips at me and I returned it with a sweet smile of my own, turning hers into more of a sneer when she looked up and down at my dress. Those black eyes filled with disappointment but instead of flinching away, I held her gaze, loving the way I got under her skin. But I wanted *more*.

I created small crescent indents from pressing my nails into my palms despite the smile upon my face. I wanted to scream and shout and rage at Radha for her deception. She not only betrayed my trust, but her entire Kingdom's too. Yet, here she sat with the male who helped her deceive the nation, with a treacherous smile on her face to match the knife in my back.

Metaphorically of course.

Wesley's mother, Consort to the King, stood on his other side in a crimson silk gown with golden embellishments throughout it. I couldn't help but smirk while I noticed she again wore no corset. A small golden circlet sat atop her head, and her ringlet black curls framed her dark, stunning face. She was beauty incarnate. Cutting cheekbones, full pink lips and soft blue eyes to match Wesley's. It made me wonder if Wesley's sister took after her or their father. Hopefully their mother because I doubted someone who was actually trying to help during the siege would take after that horrid fae in any way. She gave me a soft smile as she looked between her son and I, love filling her eyes.

I released Wesley's arm and dropped into a curtsy before them while peeking up as the King nodded in slight approval at my curtsy, not at the fake marriage between his son and I. I found my legs weak and palms sweaty from being in his presence. I wanted nothing more than to reach for my dagger and drive it straight through his skull but instead I stood from my curtsy and gave him a soft but fake smile. He revealed no emotion on his face, just stared at me with his cold, black eyes.

The King's voice roared above the crowd, but he never took his eyes off of me. "We are gathered here today to celebrate the soon-to-be alliance between two nations and two peoples. This will be the first royal marriage between fae and humankind, and the first alliance between Gambriel and Argyll. Let us celebrate our alliances and the strong Continent of Ladon until dawn approaches!" He clapped his hands and the band continued their music as Wesley grabbed my arm and dragged me to the dance floor, away from his father's harsh gaze blazing into my soul.

Wesley spun me on the marble floor, his hand warm in my own, waltzing as smoothly as I had ever seen. I kept my steps up with his but was clearly no match for his experience in dancing, among other things. Other couples joined the floor not long after, faeries with other faeries and humans with themselves. Tiny pixies fluttered about as forest nymphs moved their limbs like branches in the summer breeze. I trailed my eyes across the ballroom, not seeing any other mixed couples with a faerie and human like Wesley and I. I guessed the alliance and prejudices could only go for so long in the presence of the royals and nobles. Maybe throughout the night, more faeries and humans would mingle, become more comfortable, and dance with one another.

Or hopefully, they would listen to Wesley's warnings and try to get the fuck out of here before all hell broke loose.

We danced in circles, slowly moving farther away from the dais and back towards the entrance for a few songs until the revelry took over, the music's tempo picked up, and everyone started to dance with more freedom in their steps. Gone was the slow waltz that we began with, and the seductive dance I was used to seeing the fae perform was taking over the entire ballroom. More drinks were passed around as the humans and fae celebrated together, the humans clearly drinking the wine without the salt added and growing more wild by the minute.

Wesley's warm hand tightened on my waist as he leaned in, stopping my wandering eyes and I was solely focused on the High Fae Crown Prince before me. "Let's sneak out the back and then you can go call upon the Sibyl and I'll try breaking the wards," Wesley whispered against my ear, breath tickling my skin.

We continued the dance, moving through the rambunctious crowd until we were back at the entrance of the ballroom, out of sight from the King's hateful gaze. I could feel something, no, some*one* watching me. I turned around and my eyes locked with deep golden ones in the center of the dance floor.

Emrys.

No partner in his arms swaying to the music. Just him,

alone, with his eyes on me. I trailed my eyes down his figure to see him dressed in all black. Go figure. I wondered if he had one smattering of color in his closet. A smile tugged at my lips at the thought of it filled with black upon black clothing. He narrowed his warm, amber eyes at my hand on Wesley's arm and I looked down at it myself to follow his gaze and looked back up to see he was already gone.

"Cass?" Wesley asked with a worried look filling his eyes.

I shook my head to clear my thoughts of Emrys before we stepped through the barrier, successfully again but I could feel the invisible pull of it on my skin. I grabbed Wesley, "Did you feel that?"

He nodded, "Yes, it was like something trying to grip on to me, drag me back in. I'm glad the vial is working against it."

We strolled towards the large wooden doors that led out to the garden. No guard adorned them this time, most were near the ballroom keeping everything and everyone in order there. That meant that none would be out around the grounds of the garden.

Thank the Gods.

Wesley led me out to the gardens where stars crowded the sky but the moon was bright and full, lighting up the greenery surrounding us. I stole a quick look at Wesley, looking every part the Prince in the moonlight. He caught me staring and gazed down at me, flashing his elongated canines in a smile.

He stopped right in his tracks with that same look of wild lust in his eyes, "You are the topic of conversation in all parts of me, Cassandra." I tilted my head to the side in confusion as he went on, "My hands can't shut up about you, always telling me to reach out and touch you, to assure myself you're real and you're here. My chest is eager to feel yours pressed up against mine again. Shoulders whispering to have your head rest on them as I feel you breathe me in." He leaned down, his hand trailed up towards my face, cupping my chin. "I know that this marriage is a sham and this alliance is nothing but a tactic to hurt others, but I am thankful for it.'"

My heart dropped in my chest.

Thankful?

For the destruction of others? I moved to bat his hand away from my face but he caught it, "I'm only thankful for the opportunity to have met you, to get to know you. Whether they say that this is real or fake, it doesn't matter. What I feel for you isn't fake."

Relaxing his grip, I reached my own hand up to his smooth cheekbone, tracing it with my fingertips, memorizing every line of his face. "I am thankful to have met you too," I whispered.

Wesley's other hand gripped my waist with a strong grasp as his mouth met my own. Both my hands flew to his chest, pulling him closer, trying to inhale every part of him. The kiss was tender and sweet, not crazy and erratic like the one in the brothel. His mouth was soft and warm, his chest amazingly solid against my hands as I trailed one of them up to his silken hair to deepen the kiss. His mouth opened against my own and his tongue brushed lightly against me with a teasing flick. I groaned into it and grabbed onto him as I stood on my tip toes to selfishly ravish him.

I wanted more.

I wanted everything he could give me.

He pulled me tighter against him, our bodies flush against one another. Everything stood still in that moment as he kissed me under the stars, the moon our only witness. I was utterly lost and so was he, but it was the type of lost that didn't require finding.

Wesley ended the kiss but didn't pull away, my mouth tingling still from the pressure of it as he whispered against them, "I would wait a million lifetimes to have met you. I would give up all of them to just spend one moment with you."

I giggled at that obscene declaration and I could feel his smile against my mouth as he nipped at my lips, his voice filled with desire. "Of everywhere I've been, of all the things I've seen, your happiness has been my favorite sight and sound. No matter what happens when this is all through, I will find you." He caressed the column of my neck with his warm hand, "Always. I will wait for as long as I need. Time doesn't matter as long as I end up back with you."

I kissed him ferociously back, putting all my strength into the kiss before I repeated his words back, "Whatever happens, I will always find you." Kissing him again, I whispered the words against his now swollen lips, "Always, Wesley. Always."

CHAPTER 18

The cool wind whipping in the night bit at my heels as I ran farther into the forest to make my offering. My heels sank into the soft dirt with every step I took but I kept moving, away from the others enjoying the impending disastrous ball, away from the light and further into the darkness.

My steps slowed as I passed by the closed up moon flowers Emrys showed me a few nights ago, their scent still a heady aroma perfuming the night air. The forest was a flurry of activity from the small critters running around on the dense forest floor, birds matching each other's harmonies within the tall evergreens.

I came upon a small clearing between the large evergreen trees and thorn bushes, the moonlight highlighting the bright green grass with a smattering of small flowers throughout the clearing. Taking a deep breath, I centered myself and cleared my mind of all the other thoughts racing through it. I came here for one reason and that reason was answers.

And I wouldn't be leaving without them.

Well, maybe I would because Sibyls could have been extinct by now.

Gods, I didn't even know if this was going to work, but it was our last shot at figuring out a way to finally kill the corrupt rulers using *Medies* magic and to put an end to the oppression of humankind.

Please, please, please let this work.

My hands started to sweat as I grabbed the vial of Wesley's blood and dropped some of it onto the forest floor—making sure to leave some for me to get back out of the ballroom when I returned—as I spoke the incantation, "Hear my words, hear my cry, Sibyl on the other side. Come to me, I summon thee, I now lay down my pride."

Dark clouds started to move overhead, a flash of lightning striking down an evergreen tree to my right, the wood bursting into flames while a manic cackling filled the air. Thunder rolled throughout the night sky and more lightning struck the ground in a complete circle around the clearing. The tree that was struck down became a roaring inferno of angry flames that reached up to touch the sky.

The hair on the back of my neck started to stand up along with the goosebumps that graced my exposed skin. I held my ground regardless of the Sibyl's call bursting the forest into flames around me. My heart started pounding harder and faster as the clouds moved in a circle overhead, matching the earlier lightning strikes. I started to sweat despite the chill moving through the air.

What did I just do?

Who did I just summon?

Did I just call upon a demon by accident?

The clouds and thunder came to a complete stop but that manic cackling kept coming from a distance. I stood completely still, not even daring to move an inch while the cackling came closer, closer, and then a small humanoid figure dressed in a shabby black cloak appeared, the hood concealing its features.

That laughter ended as it tilted its head up, studying me. The Sibyl threw back the hood to reveal a woman gnarled with old age, gray hair falling in stringy strands around her face and eyes a milky white besides the black pupils that dilated as she looked at me with curiosity. Her voice cracked, "You are not of the blood that summons me, my child."

I audibly gulped, held my shoulders back to feign confidence, and responded, "I did not think my blood had the power to summon you, Sibyl."

She let out another laugh, throwing her gray strands back as she did, revealing a row of sharp yellow teeth, "The blood coursing through your veins has more power than you know."

I found my head tilting to the side with curiosity, wanting the Sibyl to explain what that meant, but I didn't have that luxury of time on my side. So I snapped out of it, ignored her remark and got straight down to business, "I wish to know how to kill the King that is drenched in *Medies* magic."

"Ah yes. There is more than one King drenched in that dark magic. But you can kill them all the same," the Sibyl replied, clicking her long fingernails together in front of her chest.

I waited for her to continue, but she just stared at me with those milky eyes. "And how is that?" I whispered, trying to not show my impatience.

She gave me a dark smile full of rotting teeth and spoke in a low, hollow voice as I held back the grimace. "You cannot seek answers and expect them without proper payment."

"What is your price?"

"*Your* blood," she said quickly, then eyed me up and down. "And that pretty little necklace you wear."

I gripped the necklace and pulled it over my head, handing it to her immediately. "I will pay in blood once you answer my question."

She snatched the necklace from my hands, admiring the way it glimmered in the moonlight, "Smart child, very smart indeed." She placed the gemstone necklace upon her neck and continued, "The King wears a gold necklace filled with black obsidian, as protection against the dark magic that would consume him. If it were to be destroyed or if he were to remove it, the magic would slowly start to consume his soul. Take the necklace and destroy it, and he will have no protection. Then kill him like you would any mortal and the King shall perish."

I nodded in thanks and understanding. My memory reeled back to the beautiful necklace I had always seen on Radha's neck, the golden locket with symbols swirling on it and the large glittering black stone in the center. She wore it to protect herself from the dark magic that would consume her, *that* was why she was always so protective of it. The King of Atrium, Durreos Seraphim, wore it as well. Destroy the necklaces and kill them all. It sounded almost *too* easy, but nothing in this life ever was.

I reached for a sharp rock on the ground to give her my offering but her wrinkled hand reached out and grabbed mine. "No, my child. Not that way. Follow me." She turned and walked rather quickly for her old bones over to the tree still on fire from the lightning strike. I followed behind her, and the warmth of the fire warmed my cold body from the chilled night air.

The Sibyl turned towards me and grabbed my hand with a strong grip. She took her long fingernail and slashed my palm open, the blood gushing as she held it over the fire. Hissing against the pain, I watched my blood drip into the flames with confusion written across my face. I turned to look at the Sibyl who was gazing at the dancing flames as she spoke in a low voice, "Watch the fire. It will reveal all that needs to be uncovered."

My gaze flitted back to the fire as she released my bloody hand. The flames started to dance, forming figures I could barely make out. Involuntarily, my body started leaning towards the fire. The picture became clearer the closer I watched and the harder I concentrated on it.

A male and female High Fae walked through knee deep rolling grass hand in hand, the female's long brown hair flowing in the wind, kissing her tan skin as it whipped around. The vision moved in close enough for me to make out her chocolate brown eyes that gazed in adoration at the male with cropped blonde hair, light skin, and deep green eyes with gold around the iris. He gazed back at her with love twinkling in his eyes. I couldn't help but notice how his body moved in sync with her own, a constant pull between them like the Divine Moons themselves. They stopped walking as he pulled her into an embrace, kissing her with all the passion in the universe. He pulled back from the kiss and snaked his hand down to her flat stomach, caressing it. She beamed up at the male, love bright in her warm eyes and she said something that I couldn't make out through the crackling flames. They moved back into their embrace, kissing with undying love as the soft grass moved like an ocean of green around them.

I recognized them both.

Brodyn Choryrth, the last King of Menodore and his Consort, Dalinda Choryrth, from the paintings.

The image quickly changed, the female now in a lavish bedroom, her stomach largely round and full with a child as she laid on a bed covered in emerald green blankets. Her beautiful face glistened with sweat and contorted up in pain; she let out a fierce cry and the male was next to her in a heartbeat, pushing her hair from her face, stroking her arm, speaking words in a whisper to her arched ear. The female screamed again and a healer was at the foot of the bed, hands pulling out the baby as the female flopped back in exhaustion. The male kept one hand caressing his wife and held the other out for the baby to be brought over. The healer quickly cleaned the small baby with a cloth and swaddled her in a larger one before handing it over to the King. The female sat back up, fae healing helping her recover quickly as he put the baby between them. The female let out a tear from utter happiness at the sight of the perfect baby, wailing for her mother's warmth. The King handed the baby over with a soft kiss to her sweaty forehead as she whispered something to him, a look of worry on her face. He nodded in stern agreement before the vision changed again.

I thought the last King of Menodore never had any children? It wasn't in any of the books or in our history. They were killed before they were able to reproduce, supposedly.

The flames started to crackle louder; the shouts and cries of pain flitted through the crackling as I refocused back on the dancing flames. An eagle eyed view swept through the Kingdom of Menodore, of the great Dragon King Haco with his black glittering scales flying through the winds and burning through crowds of the Raken wreaking havoc on the people trying to make their way into the castle's safety.

The view changed quickly back to inside the castle, to the fae warriors of Menodore fighting the Raken. The King of Menodore, Brodyn, in his emerald dragon form burned through them just like Haco, the King of Gods, carefully making sure to not hit any of his warriors with the deadly fire he was blessed with. He changed back into human form, picked up a blade, and started hacking through the Raken, pushing them into the already burning bodies to kill them.

A portal of fire opened up before him and the King of Atrium, Durreos Seraphim, stepped through, and with him poured in more Raken from his realm. The King of Menodore stopped fighting and let out a fierce battle cry as he rushed the King of Atrium. They fought fire with fire, their elemental magic pushing against one another, neither burning the other because they were both built to withstand the flames. The King of Menodore was so overcome with his battle against the other King that Radha, dressed in battle leathers with a vicious smile curving her crimson lips, stepped up to King Choryrth and sliced his head off his shoulders with no resistance. My heart dropped as I let out a scream from the horror before me. The history had already played itself out years before, but the pain of loss was still fresh.

The King of Atrium lifted his arms in victory as the remaining Raken stormed the castle, killing everything and everyone in sight.

Until all that was left was ashes, rubble, and blood.

The image changed to the Consort of Menodore, Dalinda, carrying a small child with matching brown hair to a small compartment underneath the floorboards of the castle. My heart panged in recognition from the memory. She held the child close with one arm as they went into their hiding spot. Dalinda, *my mother*, spoke the familiar words I heard in my nightmares over and over, "Baby, keep your eyes closed."

Child me closed her eyes against the safety of her mother. A Raken came up and grabbed my mother, ripping her away from me as a group of them unleashed their fury on her, ripping her body to shreds, their claws and teeth gnashing against her flesh as she let out a scream of terror and agony. The creatures looked down at my face, covered in tears, shaking from fear as I screamed for my mother to come back. Their yellow fangs dripped with the blood of my mother as they smiled cruelly at my small, shaking body. Radha stepped up to the hiding spot and the creatures stepped aside, letting her through to me as she stepped in and I grabbed at her with familiarity. Child me *knew* her and *trusted* her but adult me couldn't remember where I knew her from before. She grabbed me from the spot and hauled me up into her arms, cooing at me with soft words and sweet caresses against my small back as I wailed in her arms and reached for my mother's torn apart body on the floor.

The image dissipated to only the flames crackling against the fallen tree.

Tears were streaming down my face from the horror that played out before my eyes. The Sibyl put her hand on my shaking shoulder as she said, "You are Selene Kaida Choryrth, Heir to Menodore, Dragonborn and marked by the Gods. You were born with magic in your blood, fire at your fingertips, and the light of the Divine Moons in your eyes. Born on the night of the Moons of the Divine, at the exact second the double moons interlocked."

I let out the sob that was building in my throat from everything that had been exposed. I didn't know who I was. I didn't even know *what* I was. Not only was everything I was raised to believe untrue, but my whole family lineage was a lie. Those people in that small picture I kept on my nightstand were nothing but strangers to me.

I didn't know if my memories were even real anymore. They had always been fuzzy, but was it because they never happened, or did Radha distort them like she did my entire life?

Shock crystallized like ice beneath my skin.

My breathing became erratic as everything flooded my mind at once. I wasn't even twenty two years old because that math didn't add up. I wasn't five years old when I was taken,

I was seven years old and that would make me twenty-five right now, turning twenty-six this winter. My powers should already be fully developed at this point, and the cause of those constant headaches that had gotten worse by the day. That was just caused by my magic not getting the release it needed as I grew into its power. My body always seemed to heal faster than should've been possible for a human. I had blamed the adrenaline and the excitement but it was because my magic was battling against the manacles, fighting to heal the damage that was done to me. Gods, even my freaking period was screwed up. Just so many things piling up that shouldn't happen to a human's body, but it did anyways.

Because I *wasn't* human.

I was High Fae.

"Your parents knew you were to be blessed with great power and chose to keep you a secret from the outside world, knowing that others would thirst for the power flowing through your veins. You possess the power from *all* Gods, you are built from *all* parts of this universe. You contain the power of fire, wind, earth, water, ice, thunder, sound, sight, darkness and light. You are marked by all of the Gods, your power contained by your supposed savior. You are Selene, Goddess of the Moons, bringer of the light to the darkness."

Tears kept streaming down my face; *everything* in my life was a lie. I looked down at the golden bracelet, the manacle locking in my power and pushing it down, trying to remove it.

The Sibyl continued, her voice a soft caress against my anger and sadness, "Once your magic is restored, nothing can kill you except one with the power of a God themselves. You *are* a God, an immortal, and the last of the Ten Divines. Once that magic is restored and flowing through your veins, the Gods can return to our world, no longer cast out by the dark magic concealing your bloodline."

"How… How do I restore it?" I asked with a shaky voice, my tears stopping as the determination to release our Gods settled in.

"Only death can pay for life in *Medies* magic. You have the power to kill the one concealing you and it shall set you free. From then, you and the other Gods can kill the Raken that are about to plague this continent, just like they did on the night they made their blood oath with King Ulric Choryrth, your great ancestor. The Raken do not breathe, do not eat or sleep. They are the undead of man, demons given form to serve the master harnessing their bodies."

My thoughts reeled on and on from this new information; I finally had the power to stop everything that had happened. I turned away from the Sibyl, ready to go release my new found power and end this mess before it repeated history again. I stopped in my tracks and turned to see the woman still standing by the fire, "Do I owe you another payment? The blood went to the fire, not to you."

"No, my child. The Fates have already decided that stopping those creatures will be payment enough. My people were once plentiful on this continent, until the corrupt people in power thought of us seers-of-all as too dangerous unless controlled under their thumb. They hunted us down, just like the Gods' children. Only you have the power to stop this catastrophe and bring peace back to our nations, back to my people, and then we can come out from hiding." Those milky white eyes glimmered in the moonlight, with something like hope swimming within them. "Your payment will be my freedom and that's more than we could ever ask for."

I ran back over to the Sibyl and embraced her. She stiffened against me as I held her, "Thank you. I will do whatever I can to stop this. Your people will be welcome again, without fear, once this is over. I promise you this."

The Sibyl relaxed in my embrace and patted my back with her small, wrinkled hand, "Go, my child. There is still more for you to learn and to know. Things that are not a part of my Fate to show you."

CHAPTER 19

Walking back into the castle, my hands shook from the new found truth I had just discovered. I stopped abruptly when I heard voices coming from near the garden entrance into the castle. Something nagged at the edge of my consciousness to stop and listen. So, I moved quietly into the shadows at the base of the castle and pressed my body against the cold stone wall.

"The wards are in place, any with human blood will be trapped in the ballroom and then transported into the mountains of Inverness. King Harrington is already on his way up to await his new arrivals. We placed the sedative into the wine that'll make their transportation easier. The idiotic human filth won't know what hit them. They deserve it for thinking they could ever be like us," a deep male voice ranted, almost familiar but I couldn't name who it belonged to.

I clenched and unclenched my fists in rage, I needed to get this damned bracelet off so I could put an end to all of this. So I could put an end to these malevolent people ruling our continent. I wasn't born to be the soft and meek, docile little human Radha raised. I was born to make this world tremble at my fingertips, to *shatter it*. I was made to destroy the very people and their creatures that enslaved us all.

"Very good. Go get the wagons ready and we will begin taking them out," another voice replied, a dark caress that was so familiar. My body froze at that voice and ice filled my veins once more.

Emrys.

"Yes, My Lord. If you don't mind me asking, how are the negotiations in Jindera going?" The other faerie pondered.

"I *do* mind," Emrys snapped, his voice filled with rage. "Now get the wagons ready."

A set of footsteps walked away back into the castle as a tear fell down my cheek. I batted it away with a swift hand, feeling my heart break from yet another set of lies that I had believed. The pain went deeper, like my very soul was lashing out against the notion that another person I trusted was using me as a pawn for power once more.

Fury took over the hurt that was coursing through my veins. I didn't want to stand there and cry over another person breaking my trust. I wanted to scream and kick and shout at him for his betrayal. I wanted to take out all of my anger that stayed locked away in the darkest parts of my soul.

I wanted to *hurt* him.

I stomped out of the shadows and saw Emrys standing by himself, hands in pockets, as if he were waiting for me to reveal myself.

His amber eyes locked onto mine, pure animal instinct blazing through them as he sniffed the air. He spoke low, his voice too soft, "Why are you bleeding?"

I ignored his question and hissed with venom, "The Prince of Bloodshed!" Poking a finger into his chiseled chest. "The Prince of fucking Bloodshed is *you*."

Emrys nodded, his midnight hair falling in front of a scarred face, "There's a lot you don't understand. I can explain." He gripped my hand within his scarred one as his shadows caressed my bare skin. "Why are you bleeding? Who hurt you?" His voice was soft and serene, my heart slowing from the sound of it.

I snapped out of the trance quickly, remembering what was going on around me. My golden manacle wouldn't let his magic affect me, but my emotions had a completely different plan when it came to him.

When it came to this *murderer*.

This… This… *This liar.*

"No, enough!" I screamed as I shoved at his chest again and ripped my hand from his grasp. "You've done *enough*! You're his child! My enemy's child and you've been, what? *Using* me this entire time?" I rubbed my hand up and down my face in frustration, "It's all been so easy, I've been too trusting."

I didn't mean to say that last part out loud, but in my fit of anger I couldn't control my words anymore. All I heard and saw was *him*. All I knew was this male before me had hurt me, *used me,* for his own advantage. He was just like everyone else. My heart was splintering into a million tiny shards that were all filled with affliction and regret. Mostly regret from taking the time to become his friend and building that trust with him, only to be let down once more.

"Sel—" Emrys' voice cracked when he was about to say my true name. His usual molten amber eyes were turned down in sadness and heartbreak as he reached one of his scarred arms out towards me.

"Don't fucking call me that," I seethed with hatred as I took a step back. "You knew what I was? What I *am*? The entire fucking time, and didn't think to tell me? I trusted you! We were friends," I wiped my hand down my face again, clearing the angry tears. "No, not anymore. We were friends, but friends don't betray each other or withhold information that is *beyond* important."

He flinched at my words, "The King of Atrium, *my father*," he practically spit the words out, "Has been planning to take over this continent for hundreds of years. It started with the different courts in Atrium, but that wasn't enough. He wanted more, *needed* more."

A hundred years was a blink of an eye compared to an immortal, so I was not surprised to hear he had been planning this for hundreds of them. But I was surprised to know that someone I trusted helped that crazed High King become the ultimate powerhouse he was known as. Emrys—or should I say Durreos the Second—was his son and the epitome of the darkness that High King Seraphim loved so much.

Emrys ran his hands through his black hair, exposing his angelic face, "That's the thing about power. Nothing will ever be enough and it comes at a high cost." His golden eyes filled with pain and sorrow, the scarred one crinkling with unshed tears. "He enslaved all lower fae *and* humans in Atrium and now he wants to do the same here."

I crossed my arms in defiance, not letting the surprise of the lower fae being enslaved show on my face. I wouldn't let this asshole see another ounce of the hurt that he had caused me. "And you're, what? Helping him enslave this nation just like he did your own?"

"No, I'm not. I'm actually trying to help you. But I am sworn under a Warrior's Oath I made at eighteen, over four hundred years ago. I can't kill him because of that oath and I have to do everything that he commands me to. The magic is bound with my life force and if I disobey, I die."

"I'd rather die a thousand deaths than help enslave an innocent nation in the name of power," I scoffed as I studied his face. He was over four hundred years old, and he only looked to be in his mid-twenties. Evil didn't age, I guessed. "So what now? You're going to try to kill me or use me for one of your ulterior motives?"

A portal of fire and shadow opened up behind Emrys— he turned as he muttered under his breath, "Not fucking now." The shadows surrounding him began siphoning into the portal, their soft tendrils fighting against the pull as he turned back towards me, "Everyone has ulterior motives. There's so much more going on in this and not everyone is against you, Selene. You need to trust me."

"That trust has been broken."

And would never be formed again. I would never be so foolish and trusting again if this was the agony it caused me. Over and over again, I had it proven to me that there were very few people in this world worth that amount of heartache.

Emrys was not one of them.

"Never again," I whispered those last words as I watched his golden gaze fill with torment and longing. Those same cold and calculating eyes were no longer the mask of strength he always put off, but something deeper I couldn't name. Like sorrow mixed with the same ache I felt in my chest. Those eyes searched mine, looking for the answer of forgiveness he would *never* get.

"Sel—" He tried to say something else, his voice straining once more. He was pulled through the portal of shadowy fire before he could finish it, leaving nothing but his heady teakwood and floral scent behind, caressing my body, trying to calm the ragged gasps coming in and out.

I shook my head to clear my thoughts of him and his overwhelming scent; I had more important shit to deal with than that asshole lying to me.

My list of people I trusted was down to two, Wesley and Minka, and I didn't know how much more betrayal my heart could take.

Gods, this night just kept getting worse and worse.

I threw back my shoulders, braced myself, and headed off in my search for Wesley so we could stop those faerie assholes from enslaving this entire continent.

CHAPTER 20

My heart was pounding so hard as I came back up to the ballroom. Screams and shouts broke out, drowning out the noise of my heart beating in my ears. I started running to see if their plan of locking everyone in was a success but before I made it, I saw humans and fae alike sprinting from the ballroom to the open front doors of the castle in a frenzy.

Thank the Gods.

Wesley must have broken the wards containing them.

He fucking *did it*.

Covered in sweat and tears, I pushed my way through the crazed mass of people flooding out of the ballroom. There were so many people still here. They were all screaming and shouting, moving in a disorderly fashion to make it to the exit and away from the chaos. Some of the King's Guard were yelling at people to calm down but nobody would obey their demands. The crowd was too scared for their own lives to listen to anybody but their natural instincts to flee.

I rushed and shoved my way through, trying to find my

way to Wesley. He should have been closer to the entrance, where the wards were originally placed. When I finally came upon the giant double doors to the ballroom, what I saw took the breath from my lungs.

It was Wesley, on the floor surrounded by the King's Guard, his eyes closed and surrounded by dark circles from exhaustion. His brown hair flopped lifelessly onto the marble floor and his once pewter attire was now stained in his own blood. People were running around him, leaving the palace but not trampling him due to the guards surrounding him. Most were already all cleared out and I tried to push my way through the guards to get to him but they stood tall and unmoving so I couldn't go through.

"Move, you bastards!" I shouted while clawing at the guards with all my might.

I needed to get to Wesley, needed to make sure he was alive. I couldn't see his chest moving up and down with breath. I needed to see him, to see his laughter light up those ocean blue eyes. The pain in my heart only increased the longer his body laid limp on the floor.

I couldn't hold in the tears that started streaming down my face. A loud guttural sob left my body and my vision tunneled to the male I had come to love, laying lifelessly on the cold ground. I hadn't even told him how I felt. Dark blood dripped from his nose and formed a pool of red beneath him. The world swayed beneath my feet as my words came out, barely above a whisper, "No, no, no, no no."

Wesley's lips turned a blue-ish gray color as his chest stayed unmoving. The circles beneath his usually vibrant eyes seemed to get deeper and darker the longer I watched his body perish.

I started clawing and hitting the guards around him in a fit of rage and tears. One of the guards looked down at me with hazel eyes and shook his head, which only enraged me more.

"Let me throu—" My words were quickly cut off by someone else's commands.

"Grab the girl now! Take her to her new quarters and bring the boy with her!" Falkur stated as he stalked towards us with anger buzzing off of him.

My gaze stayed on Wesley's body as the disgusting snake, Falkur, let out more commands to the King's Guard. They were *not* allowed to touch him. Dead or alive, Wesley was *mine* and I wouldn't let these monsters desecrate his memory any further.

Two of the guards stepped away from him and gripped my arms tightly. I kicked and clawed at them, reaching for my dagger on my thigh. I elbowed one in the face, causing him to loosen his grip as his head shot up from the pain and I reached down, gripped my dagger with my right hand and swung it to meet the other guard on my left. I stabbed him right in the stomach and he made a gurgling sound from the blood rising up his throat as the blade sucked the life essence from him; it didn't transfer to me because of the Gods damned manacle on my wrist.

Falkur let out a dark chuckle, "Well, well, well, what do we have here?" I withdrew the blade from the dead guard as more came at me. I sliced at them with it but it was too much, too many. Nine guards to one and I only managed to hit two of them while the others adapted to overtake me. I was restrained by my hands and feet, still kicking and fighting every moment as Falkur took the blade and studied it, his eyes lighting up with intrigue. "I'll be taking this to *my Queen*." He said the last words with love and adoration.

His Queen? There *were* no Queens in Ladon.

I gnashed my teeth at him in anger, pulling against the remaining four guards holding me. His eyes flicked up to my face, and a cruel smile broke through his cold demeanor, "I'm going to have so much fun breaking you."

"I'm going to kill you before you d—" I couldn't finish my threat, my words stopped right in my throat. I kept moving my lips but no sound would come out. The only sound in the room was the rustling of the guards picking Wesley's body up off the floor and the click of heels on the marble floor.

I tried to scream at them to put him down and never touch him again but the words never made it past my throat.

I peered over Falkur's shoulder and saw Radha walking towards us, heels clicking, her blood red lips in a feral grin and her pale hand raised towards me. "That's enough out of you, little flower." She purred as she brought her other hand to caress Falkur's face. "Well done, love."

He got onto his knees before her in submission and held my dagger up in offering, "For you, my Queen. The Blade of Vita. The Shadowblade."

Radha's black eyes sparkled in the chandelier candle light as she gazed down at the dagger and plucked it from his outstretched hands. "Well done indeed." She flicked her head at guards restraining me, "Take her to her new chambers and bring the boy along too. I have plans for the both of them."

She gripped Falkur by his shoulder and brought him up to his feet, following behind us.

Falkur's cruel chuckle reverberated through my spine as I tried to shout at the guards again but it was no use. Radha possessed the magic blessed by our Goddess Reombarth, and could block me from making any noises from now on. I fought against their bruising grips, kicking and trying to claw them again, flailing around like a fish out of water, but nothing would break their grasp. Growling vibrations moved through my chest but it was never released through the magical hold. The beast within me was screeching to get out and destroy these monsters before us. Angry tears filled my eyes at the constant betrayal—because monsters were *real*. And they looked just like us.

A different set of guards were holding Wesley's broken body, moving his still form away from me and that only pushed me further into the bloodlust.

May the Gods have mercy on their souls, because I never would.

I would never stop fighting them.

Never stop until their blood ran like a river of chaos they created.

My flailing around loosened a guard's grip and I saw my opening. I swung my left leg out with a harsh kick and it almost hit its mark but the guard that loosened his grip only took the pommel of his sword and bashed it against my skull, and the world faded to black around me.

The last lingering thought I had was that Wesley was *dead*.

CHAPTER 21

I woke up with my limbs sore, head pounding, and my mouth dry from thirst. My nose wrinkled at the smell of rusty iron and old decay. Heart pounding against my ribs, I sat up to study my surroundings but didn't get very far. My wrists and ankles were restrained with rusted iron against a cold stone floor, keeping me from making any movement. I gulped back the dryness in my mouth, throat moving against the iron pushing against it too.

Oh Gods. I was restrained the same way those faeries were in that passage.

And Wesley was *gone*.

I blinked against the darkness, letting my eyes adjust against it, and tried to see past the incessant pounding in my skull. I could barely make out that I was in an iron cell, alone. I pulled against the restraints for any give, only for them to burn my skin with every movement I made. I was still in my green gown from the ball, the chill of the bitter cold biting against my exposed skin. I pulled against the restraints again, fighting past the pain to see how far I could get.

A dark chuckle came from the air in front of the cell, and Falkur's head peeked in. "I wouldn't do that if I were you. They're enchanted to cause pain the more you move them. That little bracelet can't stop their magic." His sick grin flashed against the darkness and made my stomach turn.

I bit back my retort, not giving him the satisfaction of it. He snapped his fingers and I could hear footsteps coming towards us. A flickering torch illuminated more guards coming towards me, their steps loud and sure against the cool stones beneath them. The iron cell door opened with a creak as four of them stepped into the too small cell.

I moved against the restraints again, biting back the whimper building in my throat from the pain as one of them reached down to undo my feet and another pushed both my legs harshly against the floor to limit me from kicking them in their faces. I never let my eyes drift away from Falkur's disgusting face as the guards unchained me from the floor. The Right Hand to the King of Argyll stood in the light, with a cold-blooded smile upon his face.

Slippery fucking snake.

My legs felt like jelly and buckled underneath my weight, only the guards keeping me up right as they pulled me up. They dragged me along the cell and out the door, feet rubbing against the ground and bleeding on the rough stones along the way. Bright candlelight lit up a room at the end of the hallway and burned my eyes. I squinted against it until my eyes adjusted to my new surroundings.

White marble floors sloped slightly to a drain right in the center of the room, streaks of blood left behind near it with the thick stench of pain in the air. A long wooden table was off to the side of the room with a large throne-like chair at the head, where Radha perched atop it. Draped in a silky blood-red gown to match her lips and my dagger in her hand, she picked dirt out of her fingernails with it. Her black eyes popped up, shooting daggers at me as she said with hatred, "Nice of you to finally join us, my little flower."

Glaring at her, I said nothing. I kept my face composed, not showing any emotion as I met her stare. My heart was thundering in my chest as bile rose in my throat. I wanted to wrap the iron chain around her pale neck and snap it for all that she had done to me.

For all that she had *taken* from me.

The uncertainty of not knowing what was going to happen to me next was shedding away the strong exterior I put on. I kept my limbs completely still despite the war raging inside me. Kept that same mask in place regardless of the monster sitting in front of me, taunting me.

My hands were itching to snatch the Shadowblade from her hand and drive it straight through her black heart. She slowly stood from her throne and walked down the small dais towards me, thrusting the dagger under my chin and angling my head up towards the ceiling.

Radha clicked her tongue, "I'm willing to make you a deal, Selene."

From the corner of my eye, I saw Falkur bow and leave the room, back towards the iron cells.

I blinked back a set of tears at her use of my real name. I swallowed against the blade pressed to my throat as she went on, "It's quite simple. Submit to me. Make the oath and give me access to your powers and no one else needs to get hurt. The magic only works with intent, so I need you to mean the oath in order for it to work. Full submission to me, and this will all be over."

I wanted to scoff in her face. I wouldn't believe her lies for a second longer. Holding my body still, she moved the dagger towards my stomach and I dropped my gaze to meet hers, "Never."

Radha plunged the blade into my stomach and I screamed out, a hoarse sound coming from deep within me, the flash of white hot pain seared my skin and started to suck the life essence from me. She withdrew the blade and brought it to her lips, licking my blood from it and groaning with pleasure, "Such power within you. It's too bad your parents didn't have that. It was all too easy to kill them. The mighty King of Menodore, killed by a lowly half breed in one swipe of a sword."

Breathing through the pain, my blood gushed from the wound onto the marble floor beneath my feet. The guards were still holding me, keeping me from buckling under the pain. I coughed, blood coming along with it, "I know you killed them. You betrayed them."

I didn't know how *exactly* she betrayed them, except by killing them in the end. I didn't even know how she gained the trust of my parents or that she was only half High Fae. Keeping my face as cold as the floor beneath me, I didn't let the surprise change my expression.

Her black eyes flashed with anger, "They killed themselves

out of stupidity. Hiding behind their walls, keeping you and your power a secret from the rest of the world. They should have reveled in that power, honed it, made it into something great. Not hide it away." She sneered in disgust, "I took my opportunity because I was born without power. With nothing. Just a lowly half human half fae, a *half breed* with nothing to my name. My mother was a weak human, and died giving birth to me. *Weak.* Just like your parents were. I vowed to never be weak like them, never have to fall under another's power. There is no such thing as peace in a world like this, only blood and *power.*"

My mind raced with the revelations; she wanted to enslave all humans because she *was* one? What in the backwards fuck was she talking about? My warm blood dripped beneath me, fae healing not helping because iron still bound me and my powers. Radha started pacing in front of me, red dress flowing behind her to match my puddle of misery.

"I *needed* that power for myself. King Seraphim sensed my weakness and brought me into the light, showed me the way to take what I want. To obtain all the power I thirsted for, I betrayed my father and your parents—my own aunt, your mother—and I helped besiege Menodore."

I couldn't help the way my eyes widened at that declaration. Radha wasn't my aunt. She was actually *my cousin.* In that book on Menodore I read that my mother, Dalinda Choryrth, had a younger brother named Cal Aeson. Aeson was my mother's maiden name before she married the King of Menodore, Brodyn Choryrth. The book's lineage stopped after their names and didn't indicate if the younger brother,

Cal, got married or had any children. But from what Radha was saying, her father married and had a child with a human woman who died while giving birth. That made her the niece of Consort Dalinda Choryrth, and my *cousin*.

Radha betrayed her own family, *my family*, all so she could have more power over those she deemed lesser than her.

"Power always comes at a great cost. I had to sacrifice my one true love to obtain that power." Her black eyes had a slight flicker of pain beneath them, "But I would do it all over again to get what I want. That's just the cost that not everyone is willing to pay." She tapped my cheek with her long nails, "You should be thanking me. King Seraphim could've found out about you but I kept that secret to myself, kept you to myself. Just another ruse to get you where I wanted you, where I needed you—"

I held back the shiver building in my spine from the thought of what King Seraphim would do to me if he found me. His son, Emrys, already knew who and what I was, but yet the High King still hadn't come after me.

"—At the prime of your power, ready to release it and submit to me. All while appeasing the lowly humans who fight for their nothingness." She let out a dark laugh, pulling me from the thoughts of another betrayal. "Those idiots truly think that our Gods have abandoned us. *We* cast them out by killing your father and containing the magic in your blood. It was all too easy with that simple incantation and a small glamour to your appearance."

That was why every time I looked in a mirror, I didn't recognize myself. Like there was something, no, *someone* looking back at me that I didn't even know. A whole other person with the power of the Gods inside of me, waiting to be released.

No. That power was *clawing* at the surface to be free.

"You," she flicked the blade against my chin again, "An actual fucking God, believed you were a weak human. Evia gave you a tonic every month to keep up the charade, to keep you thinking you were nothing but a means to an end of this war. But you, my little flower," her black eyes darkened once more, "are just the beginning of it all. Because of you, Evia is dead now. Just a sacrifice she had to make for the greater good of this continent. To bring Ladon to the true greatness it deserves."

I stared in horror. *That* was why she was wiping her hands when we left the fortress. Wiping her hands from Evia's blood after she slaughtered her. Because she knew too much. My own nursemaid, the one person I considered my mother, was *using* me all along too. Poisoning me to alter my body and make me believe their lies.

Radha's words hurt despite the detachment I already felt for her, but I drew a wall of ice around my heart to stop the pain from sinking too deep.

Everything and everyone I had ever cared about was lying to me.

Using me.

"We made this world believe that their protectors left them behind and burned their villages in a fit of rage that killed more innocents. Those people didn't die in the siege, we still have most of them. Well, they're not quite the same people anymore really. The winners get to rewrite history, Selene. You'll learn that soon enough." Dragging footsteps interrupted her rant, and I twisted my head to the side to see as Radha clapped her hands, "Ah, now the fun can actually begin." She stabbed the dagger back into my stomach, right next to the initial wound and I cried out again. "*You* killed your parents, Selene. *You* were their weakness. If you submit to me, no one else needs to die. No one else needs to get hurt."

Taking the blade back out of my stomach, my red blood pooled beneath my feet and my head dropped from the amount of pain my body was enduring. I lifted it up with all the strength I could muster and saw Wesley in the same restraints as me, his brown skin slicked with sweat and blood, blue eyes ablaze with fire as he fought against the guards pulling him forward.

Wesley was *alive.*

I wanted to get down on my knees and cry and pray and thank the Gods for giving him back to me but I couldn't let my gaze leave him. I fought against my own restraints but couldn't move an inch as the guards kept me steady and more blood poured out of my middle. The tears started falling from my eyes, but not of happiness because he was *here* and *alive.* They were tears of concern because I wanted him to be somewhere safe and not in the hands of these *monsters.*

Letting the sob out as the guards moved his body closer, I breathed, "Wesley."

Those azure eyes flashed to me covered in my own blood and instantly portrayed everything he was feeling. A mixture of anguish and betrayal, pain and loss at the sight of me.

His voice came out hoarse from the disuse, "Cassandra! I did it! I broke the—" One of the guards silenced his words by punching Wesley square in the face to which the Crown Prince spit the blood out on the guard's face.

My heart careened at the strength Wesley still had. The strength to rebel endlessly and never yield to those who wanted nothing more than to break us.

Radha glided over to the table on the side to set the dagger down and picked up what looked like a pair of pliers. She stepped over to Wesley with a cold smile as I shouted, "Stop!"

Wesley's eyes shot to me, hurt in them as he took in all the blood around me, his voice scratchy as he croaked out, "Whatever she wants, Cass. Don't give it to her! I can take it, don't give i—"

The words fell flat in his throat as Radha gripped his hand in hers and plucked one of fingernails off with the pliers. He bit back the howl of pain as I pushed against the ones holding me. "Stop!" I shouted again and Radha ceased her movements.

Looking over her shoulder at me, she smiled sweetly, "Are we at an agreement?"

I spit at her, but it didn't go very far, just falling onto the floor below me. I definitely had a different desired effect in mind. Radha let out a laugh and turned back to Wesley, gripped another finger and tore another nail off as she snapped the bone in it at the same time. He clenched his teeth and breathed heavily through his nose as he sneered, "My father will gut you for this. He may not like me but I'm still his only child now."

She tilted her head at his words and cackled, "Speaking of weak. King Harrington is just another weak little Kingling hiding behind his walls and magic for the past century. He already sacrificed one child for his power. What's another? When this is all over with and he comes back, he will be thanking me." She tapped the pliers to Wesley's chin, "You, my boy, are just collateral damage. Power always comes with a cost."

Wesley fought harder at the realization. Carina, his sister, didn't die in the siege trying to save people. She was sacrificed by her own father so he could steal her power. He growled with hate, "I will fucking end you and gut him for touching Carina. For killing his only daughter."

Flickering her head to the side in a quick gesture, she shouted, "Chain him to the wall!" The guards moved quickly and attached Wesley's body to the wall with the shackles around his wrists and left him dangling up there, feet not touching the ground as he kept shouting obscenities to her about how he would end her. No amount of threats would bring back Carina but he would never stop. They killed his only sister to bring more suffering to this continent, to have more power that they didn't need.

Radha walked back to the table and picked up a whip with small iron studs embedded in the leather as she put the pliers back. She sauntered back over to where Wesley was dangling by his arms, blood dripping from his broken fingers and missing nails. The guards ripped his shirt off of him and exposed his muscled chest.

I started screaming again but no actual words would

come out. Just my voice shrieking from the pain that Wesley was experiencing as I had to sit there and watch the male I came to love being broken by someone I used to trust. Radha had a twisted smile on her face, clearly getting off on forcing misery onto others. Pushing and pulling against the iron on my wrists, ignoring the burning pain, I roared for Wesley to be let go but to no avail.

The whip whooshed through air and connected to Wesley's now exposed chest with a large crack. He couldn't hold back the scream as the pain registered throughout his body. Before that scream was even finished another *Crack!* sounded against his skin, blood oozing from the lashes and exposed flesh, no healing magic working through his body with the iron around his wrists and throat.

Crack!

Crack!

Crack!

Until his head slumped over and he passed out from the pain, blood making a pool of suffering beneath him. Radha turned back to me, barely breaking a sweat from the endless whipping. "Now, my fragile little flower. Have a change of heart yet?"

"*Fuck,*" I took a deep breath against the pain radiating from my stomach and my heart, "*You.*"

"I'm going to pluck every little petal off of you, flower. We both know how this ends, my dear." She gestured to the guards and they pushed me down to my knees; they landed with a loud crack against the cold floor. "I may not be able to kill you, but I can hurt you."

I didn't register the zing of the whip through the air until it sliced into my back and I keeled over from the pain. The guards pushed me back up and held me steady as she struck again. It just kept coming, cutting through new flesh with every strike.

I screamed from the pain, my voice going hoarse and cracking from it all.

Radha stopped whipping and stood before me, grabbing my chin with anger, her fingers bruising down the bone. "Had enough? Ready to submit?"

I gave her a deadly glare through the pain pulsing from my exposed back and smiled with the blood between my teeth, "Never. Against tyranny, against slavery. It'll never be enough no matter whose freedom I'm defending."

Swishing the saliva and blood in my mouth, I spit the mixture right into Radha's face, level with my own. Fire lit up behind her black eyes as she dragged her hand through the blood and wiped it from her face. I kept my bloody smile, feeling proud that I actually got a shot in at the bitch.

She returned the smile, her crimson red lips sparkling in the candle light, "Get the iron and the salt." Releasing my chin, she stood up and put the whip back on the table and waited for the guards to return with her requested items.

I looked at Wesley still slumped and hanging from the wall. I let out a single tear from his pain and mine. If I could endure this pain, I could endure anything.

I would never stop fighting.

I will find a way to get both of us out of here, I vowed in my own head as I burned my gaze into his broken body. This was all my fault and he wouldn't have been here if it wasn't for me.

I was the reason why he was here and I would be the one to get him out.

The guards returned with a bucket and what looked like a branding iron, similar to the one from my dream. A large S with a circle around it. The mark of slaves. I always thought that the royalty should be the ones with the brands on them, to remind them they should be slaves to their people and not the other way around.

I breathed deeply through the pain all over my bloody body, already knowing what was to come.

"We don't brand our slaves anymore, that practice was outlawed across the continent by your own father. I think it's only fitting that we bring it back and start with you, slave lover." Radha laughed as she picked up the large iron and placed it into the crackling fireplace near the table.

Once the iron was heated and glowing, she took it out and placed it into the bucket of salt. My mind scrambled from the familiarity of it in my dream. Bringing the salt coated iron over, still blazing hot and bright red, one of the guards gripped me by my hair roughly and bared my throat to Radha. A vicious smile broke out across her face as she pressed the iron against my throat and I let out a wailing scream as my flesh sizzled against it.

My last thought was that I would end them all, and then I blacked out from the pain.

CHAPTER 22

I missed the night sky with the stars dancing along in the shadows, and the moon kissing my skin as I soaked up everything it had to offer. I had always loved the moon because just like myself, it shined brightest in the darkness, when no one was around to witness it. But here in the shadows of corruption, I felt like the little flower she had always called me. Like the petals of my soul were dying, dripping away, wilting into nothingness.

It could've been days, weeks, or even months. I lost track of all my time down there with Radha. Nothing for company but mine and Wesley's screams as we endured the torture. Nothing to eat or drink, but that wouldn't kill me. That was the bad part about being an immortal God, nothing they could do to me would kill me, only make the suffering worse. But Wesley, he needed food and water to survive. Without it, he was getting weaker by the day and withering away with every second that passed. There was less fight in him, his bloody and now scarred body nothing but skin and bones. He was deteriorating right before my eyes and there was nothing

I could do to help him but watch him die.

I had grown numb to most of my emotions over the countless hours of torture by Radha's hand. All I felt now was despair and regret. Regret for ever getting Wesley involved in any of this. Despair because nobody was coming to save us.

Every time I saw Wesley, he looked more broken than the day before. He was no longer the male that would make crude jokes just to see me blush. In his place was a shell of the person he used to be. The only thing recognizable was that brilliant blue color of his eyes and the fire in them that never dimmed. I wanted to give in to Radha's demands, just to see Wesley free and whole again. But I knew that if I submitted to her, she wouldn't let us go and live our lives.

I would become Radha's slave for all of eternity if I gave in to her.

The only thing I could do would cost us countless lives. So no matter what pain Radha caused us, I would not submit to her demands.

I would never stop fighting her.

I would not break.

I would not tire, would not falter, and I would not submit to her.

Ever.

I couldn't help the disgust that I felt for actually believing someone like her would care for me, would come to help and save me from the carnage that she caused.

Everyone had ulterior motives, just like Emrys said. But the poets also said that when you weren't fed love on a silver spoon, you learned to lick it off knives, and that's exactly what

I did with Radha. Any ounce of kindness that was sent my way as a child, I absorbed with ferocity and now look where I was.

In a dark, cold place with the only man I had come to care for, dying right before me.

All because of *me*.

A harsh breath punched out of me when I came back to where I was, no longer lost in the pit of despair considered my thoughts. I barely registered the sounds over the roaring in my head. Snapping pain streaked across my back again, sudden and intense. The whistle of the whip going through the air was the only warning I got and I let my body slump, no longer tense. That would only make the pain worse. Fiery pain erupted no matter what I did and it would never end.

I could handle this.

I would take a thousand years of this torture if it meant not giving in, and saving the lives of innocents outside of this place. Sweat and blood beaded down my exposed back despite the cool and moist air as I clenched my teeth to stop my whimper from escaping. My green dress had been taken after my first night and replaced with scraps of fabric that barely concealed my skin, making it easier for her to try to break me.

Radha had already gone through various methods of hurting us: plucking every fingernail; breaking every bone in my body only for her to heal it with her magic and break it again; burning my skin off to create new soft tissue for her to scar in whatever way she deemed fit.

The days had mixed into weeks, with no ability to count

them or even measure how much torture I had endured. She would heal me quickly only to break me again, and I eventually lost the ability to tell what was real or a nightmare.

Everyday the guards would clean our blood and fluid off the floor, only for it to get dirty again within a few hours. As if they could wash away all the torment that was inflicted upon us. I watched the blood flowing from the open wound on my back stream towards the drain in the center of the room.

On the still clean spots on the marble floor, I could make out my reflection and I wanted nothing more than to close my eyes.

To act like what I was seeing wasn't real.

I was covered with welts, slashes, and a brand on the side of my neck of a large S with a circle around it to signify slave. Any skin that wasn't marred with cuts was black and blue from bruising.

The incessant whipping ceased as the guards brought Wesley back into the room again, having to drag him. My chest caved in every time I saw he was no longer the fiery male I met before, but a ghost of what he once was.

This was *my fault*.

His head slumped between his shoulders, bones creaking and dragging blood behind him everywhere he went. My heart cracked as they dragged him into the center, right next to me, and held his body up as Radha went to get her next torture device.

Her voice flowed throughout the room, "This is taking far too long, don't you think?" I ignored her useless questions and kept my eyes on Wesley. He lifted his head in defiance against Radha and I could see the slight sparkle in them; he would fight until his very last breath. "Let's speed things up!"

Before I even noticed what she was doing, she held a long sword to his throat, "Submit or he dies." Wesley's blue eyes pleaded with me to not give in to her. I knew I couldn't do it but I also couldn't lose him. Couldn't lose the only person I came to love and actually trust.

Without him, I had no one.

I shook my head as hot tears fell down my bloody cheeks.

"I said, *submit*!" Radha roared at me again, pushing the blade further into Wesley's neck until blood beaded onto the cool metal.

I couldn't get the word out. I couldn't say no, but not saying anything was the same.

I couldn't lose him and I couldn't give him up.

Tears burned my eyes with every second that passed and he shook his head slightly, saying no.

Don't give in.

He realized what was going to happen. I couldn't stop the sob from building in my throat because he knew it too. Couldn't stop my body from shaking and the tears from flooding my eyes as I stared at the broken male before me. Radha clicked her tongue but I kept my tear filled eyes trained on Wesley as she careened, "Poor little flower." Those black eyes filled with hatred, "Still waiting for her happy ending."

Wesley's voice croaked next, and more blood trickled down the blade from his throat. His azure eyes, filled with love, searched my own, "I will always find you, Cassan—" His words were cut off from the slice of the blade and his head fell to the floor.

My heart was breaking, shattering into a million tiny pieces as I looked at his decapitated head in horror. I was yelling and scrabbling through the blood as the guards released me. I couldn't make out the words that Radha said. Something throbbed deep inside me, painful and sharp, like my heart had burst open from the inside out.

I couldn't do anything but scream from the pain roaring through me.

The world slowed around me.

This wasn't real. It was a dream. It had to be.

No.

It was a nightmare.

There was no way that I could exist in a world that was this cold and cruel.

It wasn't real.

I curled up on the floor next to his headless body, I put my hands on his unmoving chest, desperate for his laughter, his voice, his anything. Just one more look, just one more laugh. One more wiggle of his eyebrows when he would tease me. His still hot, dark blood spilled over and covered my hands until that was all I saw. I gripped the bloody scraps of fabric as I sobbed on his remains, "Please. Please. Please. Please." The words were barely audible between the ragged gasps.

I clung to Wesley's headless corpse as I rocked back and forth on the ground. Begging, crying and pleading with the Gods for him to come back to me. Desperate to keep us connected, I tried to tangle my fingers with his cold, dead ones one last time.

But to no avail; Two guards hauled me up, away from his lifeless remains. His decapitated head lay off to the side with his blue eyes stuck open, staring through me on the floor. The fire in them was fully extinguished and never to be seen again. I kicked and clawed at the guards holding me, the rage building like hot lava in my veins.

They took him from me.

She'd taken everything from me.

Everything.

I would *never* give her what she wanted.

No matter what she did, no matter what pain she caused me.

Nothing would be worse than this.

That was the thing about threats; they no longer worked when you had nothing left to lose.

CHAPTER 23

When the single most beautiful thing in your life was turned into the thing that caused you the most pain…

That was all you would feel. That was all you would *ever* feel again.

Pain.

Never ending, all consuming pain.

And that was all I could feel on every inch of my body.

I let myself shed the final tears I would for Wesley, swiping away at them with my bruised shoulder, hands restrained above my head as I dangled from the ceiling of my iron cell.

I took a deep, shaky breath as I let my storm of thoughts turn into soft waves crashing against the shore. I wouldn't give into the sorrow, otherwise it might overtake me, overtake the goal of this all.

Crying in a cold, dark cell wouldn't bring him back.

Nothing would.

His death became the birth of a new me, a new me that would be the death of everyone.

Breaking someone's spirit hurt a hell of a lot worse than breaking someone's bones. They could break every bone in my body, burn every inch of skin off me, gouge my own damn eyeballs out, but she would not break me in the way she wanted.

I would survive. I would rise.

Then they would all fear me and run from my wrath. And when there was no heart left to break, I would find him again.

Always.

His words circled in and out of my mind.

I will always find you.

I will always find you.

I will always find you.

I had to forget who he was and who I was when I was with him.

I was taught from the moment Radha took me in to always be the quiet, docile little flower, but the monster inside me, hiding in the deepest shadows of my own darkness, wouldn't break over a few bruised petals.

I was taught to bend for the world, to bend whichever way they needed me to. To be compliant and never question.

But now?

The world would bend for me.

The monster inside me was no longer able to hide in the shadows. She wanted to come to the surface and destroy *any* who got in her way. She was clawing and screaming from inside of my skin, begging to be let out. To seize her vengeance.

I would not deny her any longer.

Rule Number One that I had always known: no one was

coming to save you. You had to be your own hero and save yourself.

But in this case, I wouldn't become the hero. I would become the very monster they wanted, the one they wanted to control. I would not be afraid, and would not give her the satisfaction. Fear gave more power to the wielder and I was not letting that bitch have another ounce of it.

Anger was better than fear, better than remembering I was stuck in a mortal body surrounded by the demons that haunted me in my dreams and my reality. I wouldn't let them be the ones who haunted my nightmares anymore.

I would *become* the nightmare.

Instead of asking how *could* they? I would forever demand *how dare they*.

I would take that anger, that pain and darkness. I would take it and do exactly what that traitorous Faerie Fuck Emrys had told me to do.

I would take the fury, the anguish and torment, and turn it into power.

He had said to not let it overtake you. To not give in fully to that darkness.

But was the dark really so bad, after all? We were supposed to be afraid of it, run from it and turn to the light, but death made the dark seem so welcoming in comparison.

I let the fiery rage burn through me, consuming every part of me. It struck a cold fire in my bones. Those who had hurt me and the ones I loved would pay. They would all pay in blood and I would bathe in its beautiful glory.

I let my body slump against the chains that bound me,

reserving my strength. I still didn't know the strength of the power that coursed through my veins. I had no access to it but they would feel its wrath.

A crazed grin broke out across my face.

They would come for me, like they always do.

And when they came, I would no longer be the girl that they bruised and beat down.

I would be the monster they created.

A monster of vengeance.

A Goddess of Death.

CHAPTER 24

One of the guards came to retrieve me for my next torture session with the wannabe bitch queen, Radha. The beautiful thing about looking so broken, was that they started to underestimate you. Started to think you were weak and wouldn't fight back anymore. Sending only one guard to drag me back was the last mistake those fuckers would *ever* make.

That could also be said about power; the more you had, the more it would make you a sloppy and cocky asshole.

It would be the downfall of them all.

I kept my shoulders slumped in towards myself, like I had already been defeated. The guard got closer, readying to lift me up from where I dangled but I didn't think I was done hanging around just yet.

Rule Number Two that I had learned: *everything* was a weapon.

The guard stepped right in front of me, hands moving to my waist to lift me. My emerald eyes opened with a flash and I swung my legs out around his head and gripped it with all my strength. He was too busy fighting against my hold to reach for a weapon of his own. I gripped him harder, cutting off his air supply and twisted my hips hard to the left until I heard the *crack* of his neck.

The vicious crack gave me the chills, the thrill of it sang to my blood. The rage burning through me was almost a tangible thing. That wasn't enough violence, though.

It would never be enough.

He slumped down beneath me and before he hit the floor, I used his body as leverage to lift myself from the hook I was hanging from. I dropped down on the balls of my feet, adrenaline pouring through my veins. I cracked my bones from lack of use and patted the guard's dead body like the good little errand dog he was for Radha.

I walked silently to the entrance of the torture room. Three guards started to rush towards me, no doubt sensing their lost dog was now dead. I smiled as they pulled their blades out, hands still restrained between two iron cuffs with a line of chain between to limit movement.

Perfection.

When the first one reached me, I let him grab me by the throat with his free hand. I took my arm and jammed it into the inside of his elbow and kicked up towards his other so he released his sword. I wrapped my arm around until I got a better grip on the one that was now loosened around my throat and kicked his knees out from under him. He landed with a thud to the floor, pinned underneath me as I wrapped the iron chain around his neck. He let out a scream from the iron burning into his skin as he suffocated.

Sadly, I didn't have all night to wait for that with two others coming towards me. I pushed through the skin on his neck with the iron chain between the cuffs. Blood pooled underneath him as it sliced straight through the bone and snapped his neck.

I was still in a crouch on the floor when the next one reached down for me. I jumped up high in the air and landed messily on his shoulders with my hands on either side, the iron cutting through his neck next. I pushed back against him with enough force that he was taken off guard by the pain sizzling through his exposed neck that he hit the ground with a loud crack against his skull, more blood pooling beneath him. I then took the cuff around my wrist and drove it into his face and up the nose, lodging it into his brain and killing him on impact.

His fallen ax still on the ground, I flipped it over so the sharp side was up and drove the chain against it until it snapped and my hands were free for more movement. The last guard was staring at me with wide eyes in shock, surely knowing his demise was coming swiftly. He faltered but quickly recovered and charged at me with a spear in hand. I gripped the discarded sword, ducked under his spear, and sliced his wrist with the blade. He released the weapon with a grunt of pain and I drove the pommel of the sword into his temple, causing him to fall back from the pain disturbing his vision. The guard's voice came out broken, just like I was. "Please, I have a family," he begged for his pathetic life.

"So did I," I replied with hate before I backhanded the blade through the base of the neck, down to his back. A swift and quick kill; he should be thanking me for that mercy.

Heart pounding against my chest from the adrenaline still flowing through my veins, I walked out of the dark chamber and into the large room covered in blood. Radha was sitting on her throne, dagger in her pale hand drawn against Minka's bruised throat. "That was quite a show, Selene. Who knew that a frail mortal body could do so much."

Instincts flared to kill and devour Radha, but I didn't want Minka to get caught in the crossfire of my rage. I would not let her die because of me. I put the sword down and slowly walked over to the throne, limping from exhaustion.

Radha smiled at my obedience.

I fell to my knees in front of her makeshift throne, offering my hands with my palms up in a sign of submission. Radha clicked her tongue, confident in my reverence. "If only it were that easy before. Your little lover boy wouldn't have had to die." She released Minka as she stood up in front of me. Minka ran to the side of the room, near the table of weapons and grabbed a short sword for herself.

Smart girl.

Radha ignored her and looked down at me with her cold, lifeless black eyes, "Do you know the oath you need to speak?"

Nodding my head as she leaned down further, I could feel the anticipation buzzing off of her from finally getting what she wanted. Keeping my shoulders rolled like I'd been defeated, I lifted my palms and gripped the black obsidian necklace. I snapped it off her neck at the same time I reached for my shadow blade in her hand. Before Radha could attack me with any of her magic, I drove the dagger into the black stone and it exploded with black shadow-like figures dispersing everywhere, their screams filling the air.

Radha keeled over and howled in pain, her body went a bitter white, black veins snaking through her skin. She shriveled up into a hag with wrinkly skin, her hair losing all the luster it usually embodied as the dark magic started to consume her soul. She looked up at me with hate in her black eyes, leaking tears of blood. "You stupid bitch! I will fucking own you."

Behind me Minka stuttered, fear laced in her words from the sight before us, "Oh my Gods."

Radha's head snapped over to her as she shouted, "The Gods are gone. Dead! They are no more!"

I was feral with bloodlust that I would never cage again. I was a *God* with the heart of a human and I would submit to *no one.*

Keeping the dagger in hand, I let out a mocking laugh, "Not all of them." I slit Radha's throat before her head shot back over to me, her words not coming out over the gurgle of blood filling her airway. No one talked about the power you felt when you held someone's life in your hands and how you can take it away within a second.

That *power* felt invigorating. Marvelous. Absolutely *Divine.*

Goosebumps rose on my exposed skin as I shoved the

dagger into her stomach for good measure, feeling it suck the life essence from her callous body. I smiled as her lifeless body dropped to the marble floor before my knees gave out and hit the unforgiving ground with a loud crack. Excruciating pain worked its way up my spine next as I screamed and the room exploded in a cold, black shadow of fire.

CHAPTER 25

Minka's screams matched my own as my body caught on fire—no, it wasn't *on* fire. My body *was* the fire and it was everywhere all at once. Agony blazed over every inch of my skin, feeling like I was stuck under fiery water, fighting to get to the surface. I was encased in a shroud of flames licking at all of my nerve endings, flowing through my veins and trying to find a way to get out.

I could hear thunder booming throughout the room as lightning struck down around us. Rain started to fall from the ceiling above, and quickly turned to ice as the shards cut through my exposed skin. The marble floor started to shake and split open, right where the drain used to be. Despite the water and ice hailing down on us, my fire still blazed throughout the room. Burning away Radha's body, the blood that had fallen, and any evidence of mine and Wesley's pain. Shadows mixed with light danced across the broken floor as the power of a thousand winds created a tornado of all the God's powers combined.

My golden manacle fell to the floor in a melted heap as my body reformed. The power of our Divine Gods rushed through me, I could feel it filling my veins with every second that passed. My blood dripped from my nose and onto the floor, no longer a bright red but a mixture of red and pure gold.

Gods' blood.

The magic surrounding me lessened enough for me to see into the now clean marble floor below. The person staring back was not the same as earlier. My long dark brown hair flowed with the fire as if it was a part of it, the cuts and bruises across my skin healing into a darker tawny color than before. Once rounded ears formed into a slight arch exactly like the fae, and my emerald eyes were now more almond shaped and ringed with gold around the iris that glowed with power emanating from every ounce of me. Like two full moons were staring back at me in the reflection. My pupils switched back and forth between a mortals and that of a dragons, with a slit down the middle.

The pressure behind my skull exploded in blinding white hot pain as I screamed against it. Pressure in my ears, eyes, head, teeth, in my entire body, fought for a way out as multiple voices started to scream inside of my head all at once.

"Can you hear us!"

"They will pay for what they did to us!"

"Where are you!"

"Death upon them all!"

"Selene!"

"Answer me!"

My voice cracked against the agony radiating from every inch of my body as I let out another howl of pain. The voices were still shouting at me to hold on and that they would come for me.

But no one ever came to save me before and I wasn't going to wait for the next disappointment.

I felt a figure step before me and I peered up through the torment and saw Emrys, fiery rage in his eyes to match the shadowy fire that was unleashed upon the entire room. Black and silver flames danced along his fingertips, and he was dressed in head to toe solid black leather that clung to every part of his body, his sword sheathed along his back and his black hair pulled from his face by a leather band.

The shadow fire was *his*.

His father's elemental magic of fire mixed with his mother's element of shadow created something that nightmares were made of. It wasn't warm like a normal flame but as ice cold as the blood running through his veins. That bitter fire could burn through practically anything, leaving nothing in its wake but the emptiness of what was before.

He was the Destroyer of Realms.

The Prince of Bloodshed.

The Shadow of Death looming over you, waiting for you to take your last unforgiving breath.

Emrys was the Lord of Nightmares.

And most importantly, the *King* of all of mine.

Tears streamed down my face from the searing ache and pressure behind my eyes. There was no escaping him or this darkness he held over me. His midnight voice broke out over those chilled flames as he held his hand out for me to take, "You need to breathe through this change, Selene. You're stronger than this."

Between the howls of pain, I managed to spit out, "Fuck you!"

I didn't want Emrys near me, consoling me. He betrayed me, just like everyone else had. I wanted to see his head on a platter with his blood on my hands as payment. I swiped at his outstretched arm through the rage with a clawed hand but he held it steady and didn't show an ounce of pain when it shred into his already scarred arm.

Those golden eyes blazed into my soul as I fought against the lure they held over me. His shadows swirled around him, reaching out to me with dark tenderness that I snarled and snapped razor sharp teeth at.

He was nothing to me.

Those *shadows* were nothing to me and they would forever remain that.

Nothing.

Another kernel of power swept through me, bones cracked, and dragon fire burst through my skin towards him but didn't burn a single inch of him, like it was skirting around him, not wanting to hurt him. His own fire burned and blazed and devoured as I screamed from the rage and pain as my powers morphed together, forming one.

"I've got you now, little dove," Emrys whispered as he picked me up. It was the last thing I heard before the intoxicating darkness overtook me.

EPILOGUE
HACO—KING OF GODS

My memories fueled my need for vengeance. Vengeance against those who imprisoned me and my kind. I wanted to drink their red blood, wear it against my scales, and let it rain down on this world.

Our lives were destroyed. Our sanity, *destroyed*. Our children, *destroyed*.

It was all their fault.

Letting out a stream of deadly fire from my lungs, I pumped my wings higher into the sky with the other Gods by my side.

Their shouts worked down our bond, and Bomris spoke first, "I will devour them whole. They all deserve to pay in blood."

Reombarth said next, "I will drain every last one of them dry!"

The continent shook from Ragnar's power and anger, "Death is coming."

Oceans stormed and waves crashed with Kano's fury.

Lightning struck down on all who had entrapped us, with Evander's wrath. Deadly winds howled through the air, increasing our speed with Aither's power and the snowy alps fell into avalanches with Eirwen's might.

The wolves let out howls, horses stampeded with us, wild cats let out ferocious roars as we soared overhead. All animals, big or small, joined us. True to their nature of being protectors. Our golden blood pulsed beneath the realm within the ground, pulsed within the trees pumping our energy through the soil and rocks. Crops sprouted once more, leaves that were once old and withered turned green as the Divine storm raged on.

The Gods had returned with vengeance for all.

I let out another stream of fire as I shouted through the chaos, "I am the King of Darkness! The King of Death! I will haunt your nightmares and will lay waste to your kind!"

My reptilian eyes adjusted to the top of a tower over the Inverness mountains, a small figure shouting, "Master! Master! Something is wrong!"

Gnashing my fangs against their helpless cries, I smiled.

Something is indeed very wrong. Isn't it wonderful?

The end is just the beginning.
Preorder book two of the Moons of the Divine
Trilogy: Queen of the Broken on Amazon today!

https://www.amazon.com/dp/B0BHDRTXPC

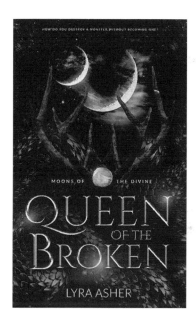

ACKNOWLEDGEMENTS

First, a gigantic thank you to my favorite part of baggy sweatpants, may you always keep my butt comfy and warm while I stare at a blank computer screen. Thank you to my one true love—my Keurig #2. May you never break and always bless me with your bountiful glory! A huge thank you to Peter Mark Roget, for creating the first thesaurus. You, Peter, deserve all the chocolate and french fries the world has to offer.

To my partner in everything, thank you for being my biggest supporter. Thank you for all you do for me and our precious fur baby. I love you more than the stars.

To my brilliant editor, Emily, thank you for believing in Cassandra from day one and working with me day and night to bring her story to life. You are a freaking gem to work with and an amazing individual with a brilliant mind. I cannot thank you enough for everything!

To my cover designer and formatter, Books and Moods, thank you for gorgeous designs and for taking the time to bring my cover and this book to *perfection*!

To all of my readers, all of this is possible because of *you*. Thank you for taking the chance and picking up my first novel. I hope you enjoyed reading it as much as I did writing it!

RIP
Keurig #1
You are missed everyday.

ABOUT THE AUTHOR

Lyra Asher is an indie author with a love for all things romance and fantasy. She has thousands of ideas for stories running through her head that she attempts to write out as quickly as humanly possible. When she's not creating compelling worlds filled with smut and dragons, she spends her days with her fur-baby, sipping tea or coffee while reading through her never ending 'to be read' pile, or watching Lord of the Rings for the millionth time.

You can find out more about her, her upcoming novels, what she's currently binge reading, and fanart on her socials.

Instragram: @author.lyra.asher

TikTok: @author.lyra.asher

Printed in Great Britain
by Amazon

15260013R00201